Seeking
PERSEPHONE

OTHER BOOK AND AUDIOBOOKS BY
SARAH M. EDEN

Seeking PERSEPHONE

a novel by

SARAH M. EDEN

Covenant Communications, Inc.

Cover image: *Old Scottish Manor* © KjellBrynildsen, courtesy iStockphoto.com. Cover photography by McKenzie Deakins, photographybymckenzie.com.

Cover design copyright © 2011 by Covenant Communications, Inc.

Published by Covenant Communications, Inc.
American Fork, Utah

Printed in the United States of America
First Printing: September 2011

10 9 8 7 6 5 4 3 2

ISBN-13: 978-1-60861-281-9

To Barbara, who taught me to cheat at solitaire
And Larry, who took me for my one-and-only "Coney Island"
You lived far away but were always close
With love and gratitude

CHAPTER ONE

Northumberland, England
Late August 1805

"*THAT* IS THE FUTURE DUKE of Kielder?" Adam Boyce, the current Duke of Kielder, watched the retreating conveyance of a cousin not nearly distant enough for his tastes.

"The heir *presumptive*," his man of business, Mr. Josiah Jones, replied.

"The man's an idiot," Adam said.

"Yes, Your Grace." Jones's agreement came immediately, the way everyone's did.

"I assume there is no way for me to have him disinherited."

"None, Your Grace," Jones said. Though a man of few words much of the time, Jones grew unbearably talkative when matters of law arose. "The succession is quite specific. The letters patent allow the title to pass to a male heir through a female line when no further heirs exist on a male line, as is the case now."

"Well, then, before I die I intend to burn Falstone Castle to the ground," Adam declared. "And, with any luck, Falstone Forest will go up in flames along with it, and Mr. Gordon Hewitt, he of the blasted female line, will inherit precisely what he is capable of managing: a pile of ashes."

Adam noticed Jones pale. The man didn't doubt he would make good on his threat. He would, too. Adam had no intention of handing over the castle and lands that had been in the

Boyce family for well over six hundred years to a sniveling slug like Gordon Hewitt, no matter what his feeble claim on some distant line of Boyces. It seemed, however, that he had no choice.

"And I plan to travel to Town and wager half a million pounds on the turn of a card," Adam further added. "Several times. Hewitt will be bankrupted."

"Best not do so until you are closer to the end of your own existence," Jones suggested.

Adam narrowed his eyes in disapproval.

"Not that I mean to advise you, Your Grace," Jones hastily amended.

Adam turned his gaze from the quickly disappearing carriage to the incomparable view from the first-floor windows of Falstone Castle. A forest, unsurpassed in its breathtaking beauty, stretched out before him. Adam's ancestors had planted the woods, forever changing what had once been a vast track of moorland, and he, their progeny, perpetuated the effort. Just over the western rise sat a crystal-clear lake. The lane leading away from Falstone Castle disappeared quickly among the trees, leaving behind the feeling of peaceful isolation. His family had lived in this precise location for more than twenty generations.

He, himself, was the fifteenth Duke of Kielder, seventeenth Earl of Falstone. Henry, the third Earl of Falstone, had found favor with King Edward III after fighting rather valiantly in the Hundred Years' War and was elevated to Marquess of Kielder as a result. Less than a decade later, he was made Duke of Kielder. The Boyce line had gone unbroken since that time some 450 years earlier.

"Boil and blast!" Adam slammed his fist on the stone wall beside the window, rattling the ancient stained glass and making Jones jump beside him. "I would sooner run Hewitt through than leave a single inch of Falstone land to him."

"I am not sure murder is the best solution to your difficulties, Your Grace."

"I could make it look like an accident." Adam moved away from the window and walked in long, quick strides down the corridor, past tapestries and suits of armor he'd seen his entire life.

He'd have known if anything in Falstone Castle were moved as little as an inch—so familiar was it to him.

"Next in line would be George Hewitt." Jones had obviously followed him. "Mr. Hewitt's younger brother."

"Probably not much of an improvement," Adam grumbled as he strode to his book room, a sanctuary even Jones was not always permitted to breach. Adam threw the door open and made his way directly to his desk. Jones remained at the door. "Quit hovering and come inside," Adam snapped impatiently.

Jones tiptoed inside and sat gingerly on the edge of the chair on the opposite side of Adam's large-scaled desk.

"How many backup heirs have the Hewitts provided?" Adam asked.

"Four sons, Your Grace." Jones looked understandably miserable, quite accurately anticipating Adam's displeasure with the news. "Gordon, who just left. George, who is next."

"And also an idiot, no doubt," Adam added under his breath.

"Gary is the third. Lastly is Gerald."

"Mr. and Mrs. Hewitt, apparently, were not aware of the existence of any letter other than G," Adam observed dryly. "Grasp of the alphabet ought to be a prerequisite to becoming a duke."

"Yes, Your Grace."

"Mr. Hewitt made little pretense of calculating the value of everything in sight." Adam clenched his fist at the memory. "I wonder how valuable he determined my dueling pistols to be."

"Did he see your dueling pistols, Your Grace?" Jones sounded nervous.

"Hard to miss them."

"You didn't happen to be pointing one or both of them at him, did you?" Jones had grown pale. He had reason to worry, Adam silently acknowledged with a well-hidden smile. Adam had been known to pull his pistols without warning. It added nicely to the fear he'd taken great pains to engender in those for whom he did not care.

"Of course not," Adam said. "I was simply cleaning them in his presence. Several times a day for the entire week he was here."

"No wonder he ran off."

"An idiot *and* a coward," Adam amended.

"Not what one would wish for in an heir," Jones said.

"So what am I to do?"

"I would not presume to advise you, Your Grace."

"Presume," Adam ordered. "Or I shall not presume to pay your wages."

Jones cleared his throat. "There, really, is only one way to prevent Mr. Hewitt from inheriting the title and lands."

"Yes, but I cannot possibly live forever, Jones," Adam drawled. "I am surprised you believe the rumors about my having sold my soul to the devil."

"I believe the rumors are that you *are* the devil." Jones produced a rare smile.

Adam ignored the moment of wit. "I suppose I will have to torch the old pile of stones, after all."

"There is another option, Your Grace."

"Spit it out. I haven't the patience to listen to you blather."

"No, Your Grace. I mean, yes, Your Grace. That is—"

"Jones."

Adam's beanpole of a solicitor cleared his throat nervously. "You could marry, Your Grace," Jones said on a strangled whisper.

"Have you lost your blasted, bloody mind!"

Jones made some kind of whimpering noise. If the man weren't a genius with numbers and matters of law, Adam would have dismissed him ten years earlier. He was tempted to at that moment.

"What makes you think I would ever—*ever*—entertain the idea of a wife?"

"For an heir, Your Grace," Jones choked out. "To cut Mr. Hewitt out of the succession."

"It seems you are as much of an idiot as Mr. Hewitt. What lady would want to tie herself to me?"

"It could mean a great deal of money for her family," Jones suggested, his tone tentative.

"Buy her, you mean?" Adam's chillingly calm voice set Jones to trembling once more.

A muffled "mm-hmm" sounded from Jones's throat.

"Quit shaking," Adam snapped. "I'm not going to shoot you this time."

"I am relieved to hear that." But not, apparently, relieved enough to prevent the quaver in his voice.

"So," Adam said, a hint of sarcasm in his otherwise neutral tone, "I am to offer some impoverished gentleman a small fortune in exchange for his obviously desperate daughter. How long would it take, Jones, do you think, for her to change her mind? Within an hour of arriving, or is thirty minutes a better guess?"

Jones's eyes crept to the right side of Adam's face, though he quickly pulled them back. The movement was not lost on Adam. He knew precisely what Jones was seeing—he'd seen it often enough himself . . . seen the repulsion on faces for years.

Adam had been born with a stub of flesh where his right ear ought to have been. A long line of sap-skulled surgeons had, in a vain attempt to locate the ear they were convinced was somehow just beneath the surface, spent most of his early years butchering him until he was left scarred from the place his ear—which was never located—ought to have been, out across his cheekbone, with smaller scars running up along his temple and out along his jaw.

The stub of an ear was long since gone, but he wasn't much improved in looks. Quite the opposite, in fact. His mother had watched him pityingly for the first six years of his life, whimpering over her "poor boy." Eventually she'd moved to Town. Adam only ever saw her when he wandered down to take his seat in Lords—something he did only out of a sense of duty, not for the pleasure of the company. The *ton* he had discovered was not much different from Harrow, very little toleration for deformities.

No one mentioned the scarring any longer. Adam had seen to that. He'd gained a reputation that bred fear into the chicken-hearted, which he decided was just about every person on the face of the earth. He was generally left alone, but he was never ignored.

Not once had even the most ambitious of parents attempted to convince him to so much as dance with their daughters.

"No one is that desperate," Adam answered his own question, his footsteps echoing through the room as he walked to the glass-inlaid doors installed by his grandfather, cut directly into the outer wall of the castle. The door overlooked the back gardens, a formal hedge garden which would be the envy of all England if Adam ever permitted tours. Tucked up as near to Scotland as one could get without actually leaving Britain, Falstone Castle was not precisely a destination for travelers.

"If I knew of a family of good lineage but very limited means with more children than could possibly be provided for," Jones said, his voice apprehensive, "and possessing a daughter of marriageable age, would you consider the possibility?"

"Blast your eyes, Jones!" Adam spun around to face the quivering mass of jelly. "If you have had the audacity to act without my permission—"

"No, Your Grace! Of course not, Your Grace!" Jones's face turned as white as Irish linen. "I merely thought—"

"I do not pay you to think."

"No, Your Grace!"

"Have you been so bacon-brained as to contact this family?"

"Not yet, Your Grace."

"Yet?" Adam thundered. "Had you planned to?"

"Only if you wished me to," Jones insisted, beads of perspiration appearing on his forehead.

"I think you had better take some air, Jones," Adam said, narrowing his eyes. "Take a refreshing walk."

"Refreshing . . . ?"

"My pistols are kept in this room, Jones. At the moment I am sorely tempted to do far more than clean them."

He could hear Jones swallow from across the room. "A walk would be most refreshing." Jones slid out of his chair and slipped behind it, walking backward toward the door.

"A long walk, Jones. *Very* long."

"Yes, Your Grace." With that, Jones fled.

"Coward," Adam mumbled under his breath. At least he wasn't as confoundedly stupid as Gordon Hewitt.

The thought of his not-distant-enough relative had Adam seething once more. He would not leave Falstone to that lack-brains. The idea was nauseating.

But marriage?

Adam felt himself tense at the very thought. She, whoever this impoverished young lady with the horde of siblings was, would run—on foot, if necessary—all the way back to her run-down hovel of a home rather than tie herself to him. One look at the tangled remains of his face and she would get that look of revulsion on her face, perhaps even faint. Others had.

He wouldn't subject himself to that. Not even for an heir.

His mind was quite suddenly assaulted by the picture of Gordon Hewitt selling the Falstone tapestries to an oily London pawnbroker, the Falstone Forest, the work of generations of his family, leveled, the lake drained. He would put none of it past Mr. Hewitt.

Adam couldn't prevent Mr. Hewitt from inheriting unless he were to provide an heir apparent to usurp the heir presumptive. And to do that, he would have to marry.

Adam muttered an impressive string of curses, though they were wasted with no one near enough to overhear and feel appropriately apprehensive.

She would run. He would offer, she would come to Falstone, then she would flee.

If, Adam amended with a sudden dawning of an idea, *she had the chance.* He merely had to find someone desperate enough to not back down.

"Jones!" Adam roared, knowing someone in the house would find the man quickly.

Someone desperate, he repeated to himself. *On the shelf. Poor. Probably homely.* In fact, it would be best if she were rather plain. Adam severely disliked beautiful people.

He'd have his heir. Whoever he married would have a title. Her family would have their fortune. And Gordon Hewitt, the cowardly, idiotic slug, would never have a chance to touch a single tapestry or tree on Falstone land.

Perfect.

CHAPTER TWO

Shropshire, England

"WHAT HAS HAPPENED, PAPA?" Persephone Lancaster asked upon seeing the worried look on her father's face. "Evander? Or Linus?"

"No, no." Papa shook his head. "The boys are fine."

Persephone breathed an audible sigh of relief. Both boys, though only thirteen and fourteen, were midshipmen in the Royal Navy—that being one of the few options available to the sons of the youngest son of the youngest son of a minor baron. That same minor baron's grandson's daughters had no such avenues by which to make their fortunes. Persephone, being the eldest, and her three sisters were destined to be penniless spinsters subsisting on the charity of their neighbors, which charity could be questionable at times.

"I have just received the most befuddling letter." Papa offered no further explanation.

Persephone waited. Father was prone to wandering, mentally and physically, and she had learned over the years to allow him time, room, and silence in which to recover himself. He continued pacing, circling the sitting room several times, which, considering the small confines of their one and only communal space, was accomplished quickly.

After glancing a few dozen more times at the missive in his hands, Papa looked up at his eldest daughter, still appearing entirely baffled. "You, my dear, have received an offer of marriage."

"A *what?*"

"An offer." Papa's shock matched hers.

"Good heavens!"

"He is incredibly wealthy and possesses an old and prestigious title."

"Good heavens!" Persephone dropped into the nearest chair.

"Yes, you've said that before," Papa said, his eyes vague in the manner they often were when his thoughts had suddenly detoured. "Certainly you can think of another reply."

"Not at the moment," Persephone muttered.

Something sparked in the back of Papa's gaze, and he became attentive once more. "What I cannot fathom is why the duke has settled on you. He cannot be even remotely acquainted with our family."

"The *duke?*" The situation grew stranger with each revelation.

"Of course, dear," Papa answered, obviously unaware he hadn't told her that bit of information. "The Duke of Kielder."

"The Duke of Kielder has asked for my hand in marriage?" She didn't believe a word of it. After all, she did not know His Grace, or any *Grace*, for that matter.

"Quite specifically." Papa began reading aloud the letter in his hands. "'Mr. Lancaster. I wish to request the hand of your eldest daughter in marriage. I am prepared to settle upon your three remaining daughters £20,000 each for their dowries and £50,000 upon yourself for the sake of yourself and your sons. The ceremony will take place October the first in the Falstone chapel. Please reply as to your intentions. Yours, etc. Kielder.'"

It was not the most romantic nor flattering of proposals, to be sure. It was remarkably presumptuous and arrogant. *The ceremony will take place* . . . There was not the slightest acknowledgment that the unforeseen offer might be declined.

All thoughts of the duke's writing style flew from Persephone's thoughts when the staggering sum of his offer struck home. "That is more than £100,000."

Papa only nodded.

"What are we to do?" Persephone's head spun at the shock of it all.

"Let us look at the question logically," Papa replied precisely as Persephone would have expected him to in former days, when "logical" was a more frequent and apt description of him. "Kielder offers a fortune beyond anything we could ever expect to come into and would place your sisters in a position to marry—something we had little hope of before now."

"That is true," Persephone admitted. "But I rather dislike the idea of being sold."

"And I despise the idea of selling you," Papa replied. "I would not view this in that way at all, though I admit it rather feels a touch like a negotiation at market, does it not?"

Persephone nodded wearily.

Papa was wandering again, so Persephone allowed her own thoughts to churn. £100,000! It was a breathtaking sum, especially when offered as the marriage settlement between two perfect strangers.

She had long ago decided on the type of gentleman she wished to marry, should she be fortunate enough to be wed. Papa was a scholar, to be sure, or had been at one time—witness the names of his children: Persephone, Athena, Evander, Linus, Daphne, and Artemis. Papa had a particular penchant for Greek mythology. While Persephone admired her father's intellect, and certainly required a husband with more than cotton between his ears, she found his frequent mental distance tiring. Papa could spend hours, days sometimes, engrossed in his studies, oblivious to his surroundings and the daughter who was standing in as mother for his other five children, Mrs. Lancaster having not survived the birth of her youngest child, now eight years old.

No, Persephone desired a husband who was attentive and companionable. Someone with whom she could talk without fighting for precedence with myths and philosophy and the haunting ghosts of the past.

After eight years of making all major decisions entirely on her own, Persephone wished for a husband who was strong and firm enough to see to his own affairs, to order his life and his home without placing the burden entirely on her shoulders.

"What is the Duke of Kielder like?" Persephone asked as her papa paced.

"Like?" Papa repeated. "Couldn't say. I've never met the boy."

"Boy?" Somehow Persephone doubted that was an accurate description. Papa likely remembered the duke from years earlier, and, at least in the moment, his mind hadn't acknowledged the passing of time. At least she could be assured that His Grace was younger than her own father. "What was his father like?" Persephone knew for a fact that a child could be remarkably different from his or her parent, but she could see no other means of learning about her would-be fiancé.

"Dull as dishwater," Papa answered. "But his mother is an active sort."

She would have asked more questions, but Papa's eyes grew distant, and she knew he'd be lost again in his own world for hours, if not days.

Persephone spent the remainder of the day pondering the strange turn of events. Her opinion shifted repeatedly. One moment, she couldn't help but be persuaded by the obvious benefit such an alliance would bring her family. They would have the funds to live comfortably, something she'd had to strive personally to achieve the past eight years and, at times, hadn't managed to succeed in. Her sisters could have a Season in Town. They would have entry into the highest circles—would have the opportunity to *choose* their life's partner.

And that recollection would inevitably remind her that she had experienced no such luxury. In fact, were she to accept the Duke of Kielder's offer, she would be selecting her husband without knowing a thing about him beyond the basics of his financial situation and his name. Suppose he were a dolt or, worse yet, a madman. The nature of his proposal made the last possibility all the more conceivable. He might prove to be every bit as inattentive as her papa could be at times.

But Papa was a kind man, Persephone would then remind herself. She could do far worse.

Then she'd wonder if the Duke of Kielder was, in fact, a kind man. He might be prone to violence or fits of temper. A married woman was completely at the mercy of her husband. Suppose the Duke of Kielder was one to wield that power? He could, and most likely would, make her miserable.

Absolutely no hope existed of receiving any other offer—Persephone knew that much. Without the £100,000 the Duke of Kielder offered, her sisters had no hope of marrying, either. Nor would her brothers be likely to find a future outside the difficult and often perilous life of a seaman.

By dawn the morning after she'd been informed of the strange proposal, Persephone was still debating with herself. If this proposed wedding were to take place the first of October, the banns would need to be posted soon. Persephone had an enormous decision to make and not a lot of time in which to decide. And she had no idea which path to take.

CHAPTER THREE

Falstone Chapel, Northumberland
October 1, 1805

EVERY FAMILY OF ANY CONSEQUENCE in the northern half of England had come to Falstone Chapel for the wedding, Adam was absolutely certain. And he wasn't at all happy about it.

"Who invited all these people?" Adam had grumbled, piercing Lord Hettersham with a freezing look when the baron had the effrontery to stare openmouthed at him. Hettersham had quickly lowered his eyes, trembling a bit as he stepped away.

"I did," Mother had explained with her unvarying calmness. "It is not every day my poor boy takes a bride."

Adam had clenched his jaw at the loathed epithet. "I assured my bride—" The word still felt awkward on Adam's lips "—that ours would be a quiet ceremony. I do not believe Miss Lancaster has invited anyone beyond her own immediate family."

"I hadn't intended to cause awkwardness, Adam," Mother answered. "I only wish to celebrate."

Adam did not feel much like celebrating. He was standing at the front of the chapel awaiting the arrival of his bride. He had yet to meet the woman who would become the next Duchess of Kielder. He'd specified that she not be at Falstone until that morning. Barton, the Falstone butler, had assured Adam that Miss Lancaster had arrived that morning as expected.

Any young lady who would willingly marry him had to have been desperate. She was most likely older than he—a lady was considered firmly on the shelf at thirty; he was twenty-seven. And, while he knew her financial situation didn't bear scrutiny, Miss Lancaster must also have been rather plain, for a pretty face could often induce a gentleman to overlook a lack of dowry.

So he was about to marry a poor, plain spinster. He could handle that.

"Wonder if the chit'll actually show up." That was Mr. Adcock. Adam would know his snivel anywhere.

Adam turned slightly to the left, sending a look of warning across the congregation, though his eyes locked with Adcock's, all the while inching the hilt of his dress sword out of its scabbard. Swords were not necessarily au courant, but Adam always carried one. Adcock knew that and knew Adam could and *would* use it.

Adcock cleared his throat a touch anxiously and kept any further comments to himself. The rest of the wedding guests shifted a little nervously as well. So Adam let his sword slip back into its scabbard. The elderly vicar, Mr. Pointer, who'd known Adam all his life, did not appear the least bit intimidated. If anything, he looked quietly amused. Adam never had been able to inspire the proper amount of apprehension in that man.

Where the devil was Miss Lancaster? Another five minutes and Adam planned to go retrieve her himself. It would not be the best start to their marriage, but he was not a patient man.

"Try not to run through any of the wedding guests," Mr. Pointer said under his breath.

The elderly cleric was one of only two people who ever dared be insolent when speaking to Adam. The other was Adam's only friend, Harry Windover, who was chuckling from his seat in the front row.

Adam would run *Harry* through if he didn't watch himself.

Then the chuckling abruptly stopped. An abnormal hush descended over the chapel.

She's decided to come, after all, Adam thought, keeping his eyes firmly fixed on the vicar, listening to the shuffling of several pairs of feet, followed by the distinct sound of two sets of footsteps approaching from behind—Miss Lancaster and her father, no doubt. He didn't look back, just waited as she approached.

After an interminable moment, Miss Lancaster reached the front of the chapel and the ceremony began.

Mr. Pointer smiled at the bride. But then he had been known to smile at *Adam,* so the man's grins were hardly a reliable reaction. Mr. Pointer would have smiled even if Miss Lancaster looked like a horse.

That thought was enough to force Adam's eyes to wander in Miss Lancaster's direction. He was prepared to take a plain bride but certainly not one who was equine. His expression, he felt certain, turned to stone in that moment. His "aged, homely spinster" couldn't possibly have been more than twenty years old. And not at all unpleasant looking. Not what the *ton* would declare a beauty, but she was decidedly pretty. *Pretty* was the last thing he wanted.

Adam cursed under his breath, turning his eyes to the vicar once more.

Mr. Pointer must have heard. He paused briefly, one eyebrow raised. Adam offered no apology and the ceremony continued. From Miss Lancaster he heard not a sound, though she couldn't help but have overheard his remark.

She was a quiet sort, then. That would probably help. Adam shifted slightly, making sure he was full profile to Miss Lancaster. She stood on his left side, which ought to keep her there long enough to complete her vows. After that she'd simply have to learn to live with her husband's face.

In his mind, Adam cursed Josiah Jones to every torment imaginable for his assurances that Miss Lancaster would be the perfect bride for Adam. Only a lady with no prospects of any kind and even fewer redeeming qualities would have fit the requirements— would have been willing to settle for what she was getting—so Adam wouldn't be blamed for ruining her life.

Miss Lancaster, however, with her pleasing looks and youth, could have looked elsewhere.

Adam half-expected her to object to the union when Mr. Pointer asked if there were any reasons why the marriage ought not take place. No one else would dare, but he knew little of his soon-to-be wife. She remained as silent and still as ever.

"Adam Richard Boyce, Duke of Kielder, Marquess of Kielder, Earl of Falstone . . ." Adam barely refrained from rolling his eyes at the ongoing list that was his legal name. Ridiculous. ". . . so long as ye both shall live?"

"I will."

"Persephone—"

Persephone? "Ridiculous name," Adam muttered under his breath.

Out of the corner of his eye, he saw Miss Lancaster turn her head the slightest bit in his direction, the first acknowledgment he'd seen from her of his presence, let alone his comments. Adam turned his eyes toward her just enough to see her reaction.

Miss Lancaster looked confused. She didn't say a word and quickly turned her gaze back to Mr. Pointer. In the next moment she answered the vicar, "I will."

Adam felt himself stiffen, realizing what came next. In a minute's time, Mr. Pointer placed Adam's right hand in Miss Lancaster's, and he was hard-pressed to keep his head turned enough to prevent her from glimpsing the scars that were the right side of his face.

He probably needn't have bothered. Miss Lancaster's eyes never rose above the level of his cravat, reconfirming his initial impression that she was a quiet, shy sort of young lady. Unfortunately, he could also see that she was every bit as pretty as he'd thought when she'd first arrived at his side.

He felt uglier than usual in that moment. Adam hated feeling ugly. He went to great lengths to avoid people who made him feel that way.

This is never going to work, he thought to himself.

* * *

Persephone managed to keep a smile plastered on her face as she and her new husband walked through the throng of well-wishers gathered outside the chapel. Obviously a duke's idea of a small, quiet ceremony differed greatly from that of the great-granddaughter of an insignificant baron.

"Madam," a deep, rumbling voice said from a pace ahead of her.

Persephone pulled her attention to the present and realized her husband was offering to hand her into their waiting carriage. He wasn't looking at her, something he'd avoided doing throughout the ceremony. Odd.

"Thank you." She placed her hand in his, stepping carefully onto the lowered step of the exquisite landau, its roof fully collapsed. She seated herself on the forward-facing seat and quickly arranged her skirts, feeling suddenly nervous at the idea of being alone, even for the length of a carriage ride, with her husband of less than ten minutes. He stepped up and sat beside her without looking in her direction.

The carriage smoothly began its forward journey. Persephone saw the duke nod to the well-wishers. She, herself, smiled as they pulled away. Most of those assembled would be at Falstone Castle for the wedding breakfast, so there need be no farewells as yet.

Persephone watched her husband as they pulled further away from the churchyard. What little of him she'd been able to see, thus far, was not unpleasant. He wore his dark hair a little long, falling in waves around his face, completely covering his ears. He had strong features, which seemed to hint at an underlying strength of character and determination. His build was that of an active man. Persephone wondered how he spent his days, whether he preferred riding or fencing.

She saw the duke's eyes dart quickly in her direction. Persephone dropped her gaze to her lap, embarrassed at being found out studying him. They continued in silence for a few more minutes before the duke spoke abruptly.

"Is your name really Persephone?" His voice wasn't raised enough to be heard by the driver over the pounding hooves of the team pulling them swiftly on their way.

"It is." She kept her voice low. She glanced up at him once more. He watched the passing landscape, face turned a little away from her.

"What were your parents thinking choosing a name like that?"

She hadn't heard him wrong during the ceremony, after all, it seemed. At first she'd told herself that he hadn't referred to her name as "ridiculous" in the midst of their wedding. Now it seemed likely that he had done just that, and only moments after muttering a curse loudly enough to stop the vicar mid-sentence.

"My father is a scholar. He is particularly fond of Greek mythology."

"Entirely too fond, it would seem," the duke said. "Are the rest of your siblings similarly afflicted?"

"In what way afflicted?" Persephone refused to acknowledge his further disparagement of her dear papa.

"What absurd names did your parents assign the other members of your family?" His tone clearly indicated he was not impressed with her mental prowess.

"Athena is just younger than I. Evander is fourteen. Linus, thirteen. Daphne will be twelve toward the end of the year. The youngest is Artemis."

"Fates save us from short-sided scholars," the duke muttered.

Artemis would surely have deemed the duke "grumpy," one of her favorite descriptors. Persephone had never met anyone who fit the word so well.

She watched him as they passed into dense forest, the road the only visible break in the trees.

"Do you have a middle name?" the duke asked, as if it were highly unlikely.

Persephone fought down an ironic smile. "I do."

"I suppose it would be too much to hope that it is something common." He still did not look at her.

"Iphigenia," Persephone said.

The duke's head turned instantly in her direction. His expression registered shocked disbelief, just as she knew it would.

He was looking at her full-on for the first time, and Persephone barely managed not to stare. For the right side of his face, from hairline to nearly the corner of his eye, was a spider's web of scarring—not hideous or frightening, but absolutely impossible not to notice.

"Persephone Iphigenia?" the duke said in something like amazement, and not the flattering kind of amazement, either. He had already returned his gaze to the landscape. "Did no one ever call you anything else?"

"Only 'Miss Lancaster.'"

"Well, I cannot call you *that*," the duke answered with an obvious grasp of the irony. "I suppose I will have to consign myself to 'Persephone.'"

"It would seem so." Persephone was baffled.

She'd never met anyone quite like the Duke of Kielder. He was gruff and not at all personable, and yet there was enough intelligence and wit in his conversation to make him intriguing. Then there were those scars, which made a person wonder how he'd acquired them, want to know more of his history.

"You, of course, will call me Kielder."

"I will not call you Kielder," Persephone answered almost immediately.

"Everyone calls me Kielder." The tension in his jaw was obvious even in profile.

"Kielder?" Persephone shook her head. "It sounds as though I am accusing you of a crime." *Killed her.* That was exactly how the title sounded.

The duke's lips seemed to twitch for a fraction of a second before his indifferent demeanor was set firmly in place once more. "You would, no doubt, prefer Agamemnon or Apollo or something along that vein."

"My papa certainly would." A smile gently tugged at her mouth. He had a sense of humor, it seemed. She'd seen him nearly smile. Perhaps the duke wasn't as irascible as he seemed, his less-than-ideal mood stemming merely from the same nerves Persephone had been dealing with all morning.

"What do you propose to call me, then?" the duke asked impatiently.

She remembered hearing his Christian name during the ceremony. "Adam?" Persephone suggested.

"No one calls me Adam."

"No one?" She hardly believed that. Certainly his family and closest friends would.

"Harry does," the duke admitted, though obviously begrudgingly.

"Harry?"

"A friend," he answered in clipped tones. "One who allows himself far too much freedom."

The journey continued in silence. The duke seemed intent on watching the passing scenery, so Persephone opted to do the same.

Despite being late morning, the forest was dim, very little light filtering down through the thick canopy of trees. It was like leaving behind the sunshine and passing into a beautiful tunnel, evergreens mingled with shrubbery, every shade of green represented in the mixture of plant life. *How deep does the forest run?* she wondered. *What sort of animals roam inside?* Persephone could picture a crystal-clear lake tucked away somewhere, or a roaring river, perhaps.

There was so much she wanted to know and didn't feel comfortable asking. Until she understood the duke better, Persephone couldn't be sure that her inquiries would be welcomed, let alone answered.

The carriage made the turn that Persephone remembered well from her arrival that morning. The woods suddenly gave way to a clearing. In the midst of the clearing was a thick, embattled stone wall, at least ten feet high with an enormous iron gate. Behind the fortified wall lay a castle, the kind children saw in fairy-tale picture books: towers with heraldic flags ruffling in the cool breeze, turrets and arrow-slits now filled in with stained-glass windows.

Once inside the outer wall, they continued past the stables and kitchen gardens. They pulled further in under the arching gateway of the inner wall and past the formal gardens.

And I am now mistress of all this, Persephone thought in astonishment. Her amazement gave way quickly to apprehension as the open landau came to a stop directly in front of the home that was now her own.

"Fourteenth or fifteenth century," Papa had said that morning as Persephone and her sisters had stared, openmouthed, at the towering walls. Persephone hadn't really heard Papa's explanation of how he'd determined the castle's age. She had simply stared, as she was doing just then.

The castle's four outer towers loomed large over her, connected to each other and the keep—the central wing—of the castle by narrow passageways elevated several stories above the ground, supported by stone arches. It was intimidating, daunting, and far more than she'd bargained for.

A footman in red and gold livery, the same colors seen in the flags, met the carriage and let down the step. The duke stepped down first, turning slightly back toward her. He kept the scarred half of his face turned the other way, Persephone noticed.

The duke extended his hand to her. With a nervous glance at the row of pristinely turned-out servants and another at the overwhelming residence spread out before her, Persephone swallowed back her apprehension and placed her hand, noticing it shook a little, in the duke's. He helped her down, never looking at her but keeping his face turned away.

This is never going to work, Persephone said to herself. She'd never been mistress of anything but her family home, and it wouldn't have even remotely filled a single story of any of the castle towers. She was not cut out for the life she'd just thrust upon herself.

The duke slipped her arm through his and walked, all dignity and aristocratic assurance, toward the castle. Persephone looked up at him, hoping for some tiny show of reassurance. She saw his eyes flick toward her briefly before settling straight ahead.

"'Adam' will be fine," the Duke said, still looking ahead. Then, almost as an afterthought, he added, "Persephone."

Not exactly a fairy-tale beginning, but it was all she had.

CHAPTER FOUR

"WHAT DID YOU DO TO JONES?" Harry asked, watching the coward's head-hanging retreat from the book room.

"I fired him," Adam said.

"Again?"

Adam didn't answer but kept his eyes firmly fixed on the roaring fire from his preferred armchair nearby.

"How many times have you fired the poor man?" Harry dropped into the chair opposite Adam's. He always made himself perfectly at home in Adam's book room, a presumption that drove Adam absolutely crazy.

Adam shrugged. "Six. Seven. And every time he sulks away like a lily-livered coward."

"You didn't pull a pistol on him this time, did you?"

"I have never pulled a pistol on Josiah Jones," Adam insisted curtly. Harry looked doubtful. "I may have held an épée to his throat once or twice, but he was never in any real danger."

"Did *he* know that?" Harry asked with a raise of his eyebrow.

"The man may have been operating under a false assumption." Adam leaned his head back casually, crossing his booted feet where they rested on a footstool. "Can't imagine why."

"Perhaps it has something to do with your less-than-pristine reputation, Adam. Rumor has it you've run through a few men in your time."

"Rumor has it I've done quite a few things." Adam rolled his eyes.

"Fought a duel on the floor of the House of Lords, for example," Harry said.

"Ridiculous."

"Shot the pistol out of a man's hands in a duel, without so much as winging him," Harry continued.

Adam nodded. "Twice."

"Bested Gentleman Jackson."

Adam smiled at the memory. *That* had been extremely gratifying.

"Bloodied Poisenby's nose at a ball." Harry was smiling. He'd been there for that now-famous occurrence.

"*Broke* his nose," Adam amended.

"Walked out of Lords in the middle of a speech by Addington."

"The man was being obtuse," Adam said.

"He was the prime minister," Harry pointed out.

Adam just shrugged. The papers had spoken of little else for several weeks after his abrupt departure from the House of Lords that day. But he'd made his point.

"And you wonder why Jones thinks the worst whenever you're angry with him," Harry said with an ironic twist to his mouth.

"He'll recover."

"I hate to even ask," Harry prefaced.

"Then don't," Adam answered.

Harry, as usual, ignored him. "Why did you let the man go this time?"

"He has apparently lost his mind."

"How so?"

"Why are you so deuced curious?"

"You provide me with constant puzzles," Harry answered. "What, precisely, has caused you to question your man of business's mental capacity?"

"He gave me some advice—"

"Ah." Harry shook his head.

"—that proved remarkably stupid," Adam finished.

"As stupid as sitting up in one's book room with one's friend on one's wedding night?" An ironic twinkle lit Harry's eyes. "Because that, Adam, is a level of idiocy far and above ordinary stupidity."

Adam clamped his jaw shut. He would spend his wedding night wherever he chose. "I stood through the wedding, endured the wedding breakfast, and spent an interminable dinner with my flock of new sisters-in-law."

"Did they stare at you?" Harry asked, unaffected by the cold glare Adam skewered him with. "It would be understandable, you know. Not having been warned."

"I ought to have written, then?" Adam didn't hold back the sarcasm in his tone. "I suppose I should have included a postscript with the proposal. 'By the way, I have a mutilated face that you will be forced to see day in and day out for the rest of your life. Hope that's not a problem.'"

"Perhaps not those precise words." Harry had the audacity to sound on the verge of laughing. "I was thinking more along the lines of, 'I should mention that I am often cranky and will probably bite your head off at every little thing. And it would be best if you came to Falstone a day or so ahead of time so you can get a good look at me before making any of this irrevocable.' That would have been a good idea, you know."

"Should I have posed for a miniature, do you think?"

Harry nodded. "Full right profile. And you should have made a list of all the rumors circulating about you, indicating those that were true, those that were exaggerations of the truth, those which were untrue but plausible, and those which were completely absurd."

Adam allowed his lips to turn up ever so slightly. "There are few rumors that would be considered completely absurd."

"She ought to have known that ahead of time." Harry sounded almost scolding. "'Twould have been only fair."

"She wasn't exactly forthcoming, either, I will have you know."

"Forgot to mention something important?" Harry asked. "Like another husband, perhaps? A third limb?"

"Her name is Persephone." Adam gave the revelation all the emphasis it deserved. Much to his satisfaction, Harry looked taken aback. "A man ought to know a thing like that about his future wife. Persephone *Iphigenia*. What a bloody ridiculous thing to name a child."

"So you are spending your wedding night in a chair in your book room because your new wife's parents had a rather classical taste in names?" Harry shook his head in disbelief. "I'm beginning to think Addington isn't the only obtuse gentleman in England."

Adam didn't care for the insinuation. "My pistols are kept in this room, you know."

"Do I look worried?" was the flippant response.

Harry never was appropriately subdued by Adam's threats. Infuriating man.

"I had a chance to speak briefly with your new bride, Adam. She was delightful. Perhaps a little quiet, but that is to be expected considering the upheaval in her life lately. I'll confess I had expected someone rather long in the tooth, rather long in the face, in all honesty."

"So did I," Adam grumbled.

"But she's a fetching thing," Harry continued. "Young and quite pretty—" Harry stopped abruptly. He gave Adam a searching look. Adam glared back, daring Harry to make some philosophical remark or assessment. Harry, as always, did just that. "You expected someone desperate and ugly and undesirable. Instead, your bride turned out to be a vast deal more than passable." Harry shook his head. "Not quite what you bargained for, I'd guess."

Adam turned his gaze to the fire and kept his jaw firmly clamped. He would not honor that assessment with a response. His marriage was no one's business but his own.

"So, because she is young and fine looking and appears to be good natured, the poor girl is upstairs, alone, probably wondering what she's done wrong, and you are down here brooding. Adam, you are completely bacon-brained."

"I should call you out for that."

"Do," Harry answered. "But not tonight. I'm tired." Harry rose to his feet. "Call me out tomorrow, would you? I'll most likely pick pistols, by the way. I'd like to see that shoot-the-weapon-out-of-my-hand trick I've heard so much about."

"I ought to lock you in the dungeon," Adam muttered as Harry made to leave.

"You should," Harry agreed, walking to the door. "No point having a dungeon if no one is ever consigned to suffer in it."

"Pack your things and take yourself off at first light." Adam's demand emerged half-hearted.

"Am I supposed to walk out of here stooped and defeated now?" Harry turned back to face Adam from his position at the threshold. "I don't think I would play that role nearly as well as Jones."

"Don't mock me."

Harry smiled. "'Night, Adam."

"'Night." *Presumptuous lout.*

"And Adam?"

"What?" he snapped.

"Give the poor girl a chance," Harry said. "Ain't her fault you ended up with every man's idea of a perfect wife. She could probably even manage to be a nag if you asked her."

So Adam threw a book at him.

Harry's laughter echoed in the empty corridor as he made his way toward the room he always occupied when he visited.

"I don't know why I keep inviting him back," Adam mumbled.

Harry had an annoying habit of interfering in Adam's life. He never found Adam remotely off-putting and always laughed off every threat Adam made against his person. Furthermore, he was precisely the sort of gentleman Adam generally avoided: easy in society, handsome, self-assured. If he'd been an idiot into the bargain, Adam would have despised him. As it was, Adam wasn't entirely sure why he *didn't* dislike him.

He'd hit a nerve that night, however. Adam found himself thinking of Persephone—*ridiculous name.* She probably was wondering where Adam was. Though, more likely than not, she would be grateful to be spared the sight of him. He certainly had no intention of inflicting himself on her.

Adam pulled himself up out of his chair. He was tired, he had to admit. And spending the night sleeping in his chair, as comfortable as it was, did not appeal to him. He walked quietly from the book room, up a flight of stairs, passing tapestries and arms and tables holding mementos passed down by generations of Boyces.

He dismissed his valet on the spot, preferring to divest himself of his wedding clothes on his own. He was finding the attire almost suffocating at the moment.

Jones ought to have known better, he thought for the hundredth time that day. Adam had been very specific in his requirements. Someone who needed his money. Someone with no other prospects. Someone who would be grateful for even a hideous husband.

Jones had chosen Persephone Iphigenia Lancaster.

Adam muttered a curse. So much for thwarting Mr. Gordon Hewitt. A young, pretty wife would want nothing to do with Adam.

Adam's eyes wandered, of their own volition, to the door connecting his bedchamber with the new duchess's.

It sounds like I'm accusing you of a crime. Adam nearly smiled at the memory of her words. He'd known immediately what she'd meant: killed her. The name did sound that way, though no one had ever said so before.

She was intelligent, on top of it all. Intelligent and witty and beautiful. And they were stuck with each other.

CHAPTER FIVE

"I DO NOT WANT TO GO!"

Persephone recognized Artemis's anguished voice, and her heart hurt at the sound. She turned toward the enormous wooden doors of Falstone Castle, where Athena was attempting to strong-arm their youngest sister into stepping outside and into the waiting carriage.

"Let me speak with her." Persephone took Athena's place beside Artemis. She took the girl's tiny, eight-year-old hand in hers. "Let's walk for a minute or two."

Artemis nodded, and Persephone led her down the stone steps to the gravel drive. Papa seemed to understand and told the driver to wait for a bit. Persephone and Artemis stepped off the drive and onto the grass that surrounded the closest of the formal gardens. When they were far enough from the carriage to not be seen, Persephone knelt on the ground, heedless of the damage she was no doubt doing to one of the dresses provided for her by her husband, and faced Artemis directly.

"Oh, my dear girl." She touched Artemis's face. "You're crying."

"He cannot make you stay here!" Artemis threw her arms around Persephone's neck.

By "he," Artemis certainly meant Adam. It must have been unfathomable to such a young child to have a sister, who had been more of a mother to her, leave their family home for good. A painful lump seemed to suddenly form in Persephone's throat. She hugged the girl back, squeezing perhaps tighter than she ought to have.

"No one is making me stay here, dearest." Persephone forced her voice to not waver or break. "Falstone Castle is my home now. But I shall send you letters, perhaps with a guinea under the seal." The bribe didn't loosen Artemis's embrace. "And you and I shall visit back and forth. You could come here and we could explore the castle together."

"*He* won't let me," Artemis answered petulantly.

"Of course he will, and we will have grand adventures. Perhaps there is a tower room where we could imagine all sorts of wonderful stories, the way we always did at home."

"Promise?" Artemis asked with a hiccup.

"I promise."

"Who will take care of me when you're gone?" Artemis stepped back a little and wiped her cheeks with the back of her hand.

"Papa will engage a governess for both you and Daphne, I imagine." Persephone tried to sound encouraging. Papa could afford a governess now, and Persephone hoped he would remember that one was needed. "And a companion for Athena when you are all in Town."

"Will you visit us there?"

"Of course."

The slightest rustling sound drew her attention a little behind Artemis. Adam stood there, watching, with a look of contemplation, mingled with the wearied impatience she'd seen on his face most of the day before. Persephone forced herself to concentrate on Artemis, knowing the girl needed reassurance.

"Persephone?" Artemis asked with a sniffle.

"Yes, my dear?"

Artemis reached out and touched Persephone's cheek, a gesture she'd employed almost from infancy, as if she needed the human contact. "Who will take care of you?"

The lump in her throat increased tenfold, and tears suddenly pricked at her eyes. Persephone pulled Artemis back into the circle of her arms and hugged her once more.

"Will you be happy even though we are gone?" Artemis asked, her head resting against Persephone's shoulder.

"When have you known me to be *un*happy?" Persephone answered.

That gained her an extra squeeze from her sister. "Then I will be happy, too," Artemis declared in a voice of determination. She pulled away from Persephone, with a look on her face that was so fierce it was comical. "But if I don't leave now, I will cry again, and I do not want to cry anymore."

"Let us promise each other not to cry," Persephone suggested.

Artemis nodded then bit down on her still-quivering lip.

"I will see you soon," Persephone said. "Be good for Papa."

"I will," Artemis promised.

"I love you, dearest."

"I love you, too, Persephone," Artemis answered, a betraying quaver in her voice. "You're the . . . b-best mama I ever had."

She wrapped her arms around Persephone's neck once more before abruptly pulling away and running back to the waiting carriage. Persephone stood and walked slowly back in the same direction. She stood on the edge of the lawn and waved as her family disappeared under the arch of the inner wall. Only after she was certain they were out of sight did Persephone allow a tear to slide down her cheek, followed by another.

"I thought you weren't supposed to cry," came a male voice from not very far behind her.

Persephone had all but forgotten about Adam in her distress over Artemis.

"Artemis is crying as well, I guarantee it." Persephone wiped the two trickles of moisture from her eyes.

"Then why make the promise?" From the sound of Adam's voice, Persephone would guess he was rolling his eyes, though she didn't look back at him.

"To lessen her pain," Persephone replied. "If my sister knew I was crying, it would break her heart."

"But you know *she* is crying," Adam pointed out, still remaining behind her. Persephone couldn't remember the last time she'd had a conversation with someone from that position.

"I know her better than she knows me."

"Ah, yes. The best mama she ever had."

Now why had Artemis gone and said that? She could have borne almost anything other than the reminder that she was to be separated from the girl whom she thought of as her own child. Persephone had raised her from the day she was born. They had never been separated.

The enormity of what she'd done by accepting Adam's proposal suddenly hit her. She'd done this, almost exclusively, for the benefit of her family. But she hadn't truly understood that in doing so, she would have to let go of them. She was leaving Artemis.

Tears streamed at an alarming rate down her face. "I've lost my baby," she cried in an anguished whisper.

Persephone knew she'd be sobbing in a moment's time if she didn't wrest control of her emotions. She could never do that unless she had a moment alone, away from the sight of the now empty archway and carriage drive.

She turned back toward Adam, to offer her excuses, to beg his pardon before fleeing. But he was gone. In her distress she hadn't heard him go. And he hadn't said a word before departing.

Her throat constricted against the sob forcing its way out. Desperate not to disgrace herself in front of any of the staff who seemed to constantly be coming and going outside the castle but knowing she'd never get to her room in time—she had difficulty finding it still—Persephone ran as swiftly as her feet would carry her through the break in the hedgerow and into the first of the formal gardens.

She ran quickly, taking turns at random and working her way deeper, behind bushes and hedges, until her lungs and feet would not carry her further. In a small outcropping, surrounded by bushes she imagined would be filled with blooms come spring, she found a small stone seat. Persephone sat, lowered her face into her hands, and did something she hadn't done since her mother's death. She wept with such force that she was certain her heart would break with the effort.

* * *

For a moment after she awoke, Persephone had no idea where she was. She forced her eyes open despite the burning. Hedges and plants surrounded the stone seat she was curled upon. And she was chilly.

Flashes of memory bombarded her hazy mind as she pieced together the morning. Her family had left. She had fled to the garden for refuge.

I must have fallen asleep, Persephone thought to herself. Her joints protested as she uncurled. She was tempted to close her eyes again; they stung and throbbed, as did her head. She had forgotten how miserable one could feel after an elongated bout of tears.

Persephone took a deep breath, wrapping her arms around herself against the slight chill seeping through even her pelisse. She must have been more tired than she realized to have fallen asleep on a stone seat. Of course, she hadn't slept much of late, especially the night before.

She'd waited up for Adam, it being their wedding night. Hours had passed, and he'd never come. Not even to bid her good night. She'd thought he would, at least, do that.

She'd sat up until the clock in her sitting room had chimed one in the morning. Light had flickered under the door that led to Adam's bedchamber. Still she'd waited. The light was eventually extinguished, and silence descended on the house. She sat at her window, watching the door. As the clock had struck two, she'd climbed into bed feeling completely rejected and utterly alone.

"You are no quitter, Persephone Iphigenia La— Boyce," she told herself. "This simply needs time." Squaring her shoulders, Persephone rose, trying to ignore the pounding in her head. "And no more tears," she instructed herself.

Persephone had ever been the optimist in her family. Every situation had a glimmer of hope, she'd discovered early in her life. They'd lost Mother but had gained Artemis. The boys had left for the sea but had become strong and sure—more so than they would have had they remained at home. She was married to a perfect stranger who seemed to want nothing to do with her, but . . . but . . . But, she told herself sternly, she had a home to call her own and the hope that he would turn out to be a friend, at least, and perhaps, eventually a good husband.

Rising with what dignity her stiff joints would allow, Persephone shook out her skirts, grimacing at the havoc she'd wreaked on her appearance. She shook her head at herself. "And I wonder why my husband has no interest in my company." More attention to her appearance, an attempt to be attractive, couldn't hurt matters.

Persephone moved along the garden trail, her mind clamped onto that train of thought. What else might she do to improve her situation? She couldn't come to know Adam if they never spoke to one another. Adam certainly hadn't made any attempts. Persephone had never been terribly bold, but she did know how to hold up her end of a conversation.

After several minutes of walking, and a few wrong turns, Persephone finally reached the garden entrance. She'd been asleep longer than she'd realized. The sky had already dimmed with approaching dusk, and the air had grown colder.

Conscious of her rumpled appearance, Persephone walked up the stone steps to the front door of Falstone Castle. The door opened at her approach.

"Your Grace," Barton the butler said, his face not revealing even the slightest surprise at her appearance.

"Thank you, Barton," Persephone answered with a faint smile, too exhausted for enthusiasm.

She crossed the spacious entry hall, still awed by the scale of everything. "I will never fit here," she thought morosely.

What had happened to the determined duchess she'd momentarily been in the gardens? Weariness, it seemed, had robbed her of her resolve. Her head throbbed with every step she took, her eyes burned anew, and her legs were ready to drop out from under her.

Persephone began to climb the wide stairs, determined to lie down at least for a few minutes. At the first-floor landing, she came face-to-face with Adam's mother.

"Good eve—" the dowager duchess's greeting ended abruptly. "Are you feeling well, child?"

"I am a little tired."

"Of course, you are," she answered empathetically. "You had a long and tiring day yesterday."

Persephone nodded.

"Do not fret yourself over dinner, dear," the dowager instructed. "I shall have a tray sent to your room. You rest."

"Thank you." With a wan smile, she stepped past her mother-in-law.

She only had to backtrack once before finding her room. She didn't even bother ringing for a maid to help her undress but dropped onto her bed fully clothed.

The tears threatened to spill again, but Persephone forced them back. She was done crying. After a night's rest she would face the future.

CHAPTER SIX

"I TOLD YOU TO PACK up and go," Adam grumbled as Harry sauntered into the book room.

"You also told me you'd call me out today," Harry replied.

"Never did. Always knew you were afraid of me."

"I've decided to shoot you in your bed instead." Adam looked out the French doors and out over the formal garden below, though little was visible in the nearly moonless night. "Go to sleep so I can load my pistols in peace."

"Your mother said the new duchess was indisposed this evening." Harry, as usual, was unaffected by threats. "Any idea what she meant by that?" He obviously thought Adam knew *precisely* what Mother had meant.

He did, actually, have a pretty good idea.

Adam had stood at the door he was standing at now for the better part of a quarter of an hour that morning, looking out over the gardens to a small alcove among the back hedgerow, where Persephone sat with her face in her hands. He knew she had been crying. It had bothered him. Quite a lot, actually.

Twenty-four hours into this ill-conceived marriage and his wife was already sobbing in the back of a garden. Watching Persephone's teary farewell with her family was enough to, most likely, convince half the staff that he was some kind of ogre holding the fair maiden against her will. And then the littlest sister—what was her name? Archipelago, or some such nonsense—had all but dissolved into a puddle there on the front lawns.

"The best mama she'd ever had," Adam muttered under his breath.

"What's that?" Harry asked.

"Nothing." One would think he'd married the girl's mother then sent her off to some orphan asylum.

"Old Jeb Handly says winter will come in early this year." Harry abruptly changed the subject. "Says we're bound to see a foot or two of snow before Christmas."

"Hmm," was all the reply Adam offered, despite Old Jeb's legendary ability to predict the weather. The man had to be approaching his eightieth year and hadn't made a wrong guess in sixty-five of those years. "Two feet of snow ought to be enough to keep you from coming to visit."

"I was born and raised in Northumberland," Harry scoffed.

"Maybe it will turn out to be ten feet and you'll never come back." Adam stepped away from the French doors and back toward his chair near the fire.

Harry grinned. "Don't worry, Adam. If you're really lucky, we'll get that ten feet of snow before I leave."

"Then I really would shoot you in your sleep."

"I'm quaking." He obviously was doing nothing of the sort.

"You should be." Adam glared across at him.

"So why was your new wife not at dinner this evening?" Harry casually studied his fingernails.

"Mother said she was indisposed." Adam infused his voice with utter lack of interest.

"She also was not at tea?"

"She was out."

"Luncheon?"

"Harry."

"Late this morning?"

"Harry."

"Earlier this afternoon?"

"You are keeping rather close tabs on her." Adam raised an eyebrow.

"Do not change the subject," Harry said. "That is a bad habit of yours, you know."

"So is breaking other men's noses."

"You've done that already, Adam. When we were fifteen."

"Then I'll straighten it for you."

"Did. We were sixteen."

"Remind me again why you're still here." Adam leaned back again and stared into the fire.

Harry shrugged. "Someone has to slay the dragon."

"And that would be me?" Adam asked dryly.

"Dragon. Lion. Ogre. Take your pick."

"I am not an ogre."

"You've convinced a lot people otherwise."

"Idiots."

"She wouldn't be the first person to hide from you."

"She? You mean Persephone?"

"I certainly don't mean your mother," Harry answered. "You could shoot a man dead in the drawing room, and she'd just smile indulgently and say, 'My—"

"'—poor boy,'" Adam finished with him. "The woman will still be calling me that when I'm eighty."

"When you're eighty, she'll be dead."

"Shut up, Harry."

"So are you inviting the Lancaster clan for Christmas?" Harry asked. Why was the man suddenly so intent on unpredictable changes of topic?

"We will be buried under several feet of snow, remember?" Adam crossed his feet on the footstool.

"So have them come early." Harry sounded quite enamored of the idea. "Then we can all be cozily snowed-in together."

"I will not have hordes of people roaming around my house." Adam tensed at the thought of the stares and the whispers, the noise and chaos. He preferred his days quiet and predictable. Harry was enough of a nuisance.

"Not even for your wife's sake? I am certain she would—"

"I am not a monster keeping her prisoner here, forcing her to stay against her will."

"I know that, Adam," Harry said.

"She chose to accept me."

"Yes, but without the benefit of the rather ingenious postscripts we composed last night," Harry pointed out. "I'm not sure she realized—"

"You think I've made her miserable already?" Adam asked, piercing Harry with a disapproving look.

"I didn't say that." Harry held up his hands in a show of innocence. "Only that she seemed to take the farewells particularly hard. You ought to have insisted her family stay longer."

"I didn't make them go."

"You didn't ask them to stay, either."

"They chose to go," Adam said with finality.

"And that's it? That's all the consideration this whole thing gets?"

"What whole thing?"

"'What whole thing?'" Harry repeated his words in a tone of utter disbelief. "You've been married for an entire day, and you've already driven your wife to her rooms."

"I haven't driven her anywhere," Adam snapped, his jaw and shoulders tensing. "She is indisposed."

Harry rolled his eyes.

"You don't believe that?" Adam asked. "You think she's in her rooms, quaking in some corner?"

"She wouldn't be the first. I'm pretty sure Addington sucked his thumb for a week after you walked out of Lords. You do have a tendency to overrun people."

"So I am the villain already, am I?" A steel-edged calm had crept into Adam's tone, and he felt a familiar surge of determination as he rose swiftly to his feet.

"Well, what other gentleman can you think of who has managed to alienate his wife within twenty-four hours? I wouldn't be surprised if you never saw the poor woman again as long as you lived. In a place as enormous as this pile of rock, she could avoid you for years."

Adam set his jaw. Wouldn't that be fodder for the laughing throngs? The Duke of Kielder commands the notice of society, the ears of his Peers in Parliament, the awe of his contemporaries, but his wife will have nothing to do with him.

Suddenly, Adam was angry.

"Where are you going?" Harry actually sounded concerned.

"My wife is indisposed," Adam flung back at him. "I am going to see for myself that she is well."

"Adam." It was both warning and question. Harry was on his feet.

"I am not going to hurt the blasted woman," Adam growled back as they both left the book room and made their way down the hall.

"Adam." That same tone.

Adam spun around, stopping Harry mid-step. "Have I ever harmed a woman?" Adam demanded. "Have I?"

"No," Harry finally admitted, with a little smile.

"I have no intention of starting now. So quit looking at me like I'm about to drown a puppy."

"Have you ever drowned a puppy?" Harry asked.

"Shut up, Harry." Why did the man like goading him? There were dozens of men in Town who would tell Harry in no uncertain terms that pushing Adam was not a good idea. There were dozens more littering the countryside.

"Is it really necessary to bother her?" Harry trailed along behind Adam.

"I am not going to be made the monster in my own home."

"Adam."

"No. Do not start using that tone with me," Adam snapped, turning down the hall that housed both his rooms and Persephone's. "Whenever you think you have some great philosophical insight into my—what was it your sister always said, my 'tortured soul'—you use that tone. It's enough to make a man want to throttle you."

He grabbed the doorknob to Persephone's sitting room.

"I cannot go into your wife's rooms," Harry reminded Adam.

"Good." Adam shut the door in Harry's face.

"I'll just be in my room," Harry said from the other side of the door. "You know, for when you get around to shooting me." Harry's footsteps faded as they retreated down the corridor.

"Jack-a-napes," Adam growled under his breath.

He turned. There was no sign of his wife in her sitting room. Adam crossed to the doorway to Persephone's bedchamber. She'd be in there looking like some frightened rabbit, apparently.

He'd married a coward. That was worse than marrying a beauty. If they ever made an appearance in Town, she'd need more than a pretty face to survive the viciousness of the *ton*.

Persephone needed backbone. He'd simply have to tell her to toughen up, to seize command of herself. Adam had done so even as a child. If he'd spent his life feeling sorry for himself, he'd be nothing more than his mother's "poor boy" still.

Adam set his features and stepped across the threshold to Persephone's bedchamber. He checked the shadowed corners first—that was where cowards tended to hide. He found her, however, curled in a ball on her bed. She was still fully dressed, wearing precisely what she'd worn that morning when bidding her family goodbye—what she'd worn in the gardens.

Persephone must have come straight from there to her room and promptly fallen asleep. She hadn't even gotten under her coverlet. The room, he noticed, was not terribly warm, despite the low fire.

"Boil and blast," Adam grumbled. He'd been ready to confront a quaking wife. Instead he'd found her sleeping, obviously exhausted, seeing as how she'd not even dressed for bed. The last thing he wanted was to feel sympathy for the woman. Emotions were best left out of any and all interactions—he'd learned that early on.

He crossed to the door, which, conveniently enough, led to his own chambers, but he stopped with his hand on the knob. It was entirely too chilly for her to sleep without at least a blanket to provide warmth.

"Now I've become a lady's maid," Adam muttered, crossing back to the bed.

He grabbed the coverlet on the side of the bed opposite Persephone. With a tug he pulled it loose then draped it across her where she slept.

Tomorrow night, he told himself, she'd simply have to remember to get under the blankets, as he had no intention of playing nursemaid again.

CHAPTER SEVEN

PERSEPHONE HAD DECIDED ON A few things. First, that she would shed no more tears for her former life. It was excusable, she had allowed, to feel some sense of loss, to shed some tears over the abrupt change in her situation. But the time had come to look to the future and not the past.

She'd washed her face quite thoroughly that morning, wishing her eyes weren't puffy from a day of crying. She donned a simple but flattering morning dress in a lovely shade of blue, deciding she would prefer to have blue eyes, her eyes being that unusual shade of hazel that became whatever color she was wearing. She had always felt more confident with blue eyes. When they were green, she felt more cast down, no doubt due to the reminder of her emerald-eyed mother. And brown eyes did absolutely nothing for her whatsoever.

Today would be blue.

Blue and puffy, Persephone sighed. She'd tried, anyway.

Second on her list of absolutely necessary undertakings was that of learning to be the Duchess of Kielder. She would be the mistress of Falstone Castle, responsible for the staff, the menu, the household expenses, and she knew not what all. Persephone had absolutely no idea how to go on. Managing a small household was one thing. Undertaking the management of a four-hundred-year-old castle and a staff the size of a small village was quite another.

Nothing would do but to seek out the only other lady on earth who could tell her precisely what was expected of her: the Dowager Duchess of Kielder.

Her stomach turning as she descended the stairs, Persephone made her way to the breakfast room. She did not relish the coming minutes. No new bride enjoys confessing to her mother-in-law that she is incompetent. But, if this life Persephone had chosen for herself was to be anything but a dismal failure, confess she must.

Right after she figured out where she was.

Persephone glanced around. She stood in a long, narrow passageway, surrounded by stone walls hung with the occasional tapestry. Recalling what she'd seen of the castle thus far, Persephone knew she could be just about anywhere. It was not the capable beginning she'd imagined when she woke that morning.

Persephone retraced her steps, only to find herself in another passageway, or perhaps the same one—she couldn't tell. Perhaps after a few more days, she would know the castle better. Two passageways later, or twice in the same one, Persephone amended her prediction to a few more years.

"Oh!" came a startled exclamation.

Persephone spun around. Standing with eyes wide in shock was a young maid, probably no more than thirteen or fourteen years old.

"Thank heavens," Persephone breathed.

"Forgive me, Your Grace!" She bobbed a curtsy. "I didn't mean to interrupt your . . . your . . ."

"I was attempting to find the breakfast room."

"But you're halfway to the north tower," the girl answered in obvious disbelief.

Persephone tried to shrug off her embarrassment.

An understanding smile tugged at the maid's mouth. "I got lost a few times when I first came," she said. "Falstone Castle is awful big."

Persephone nodded.

"I can show you where the breakfast room is," the maid offered.

"I don't want to keep you from your duties . . . ur . . . I am afraid I don't know your name."

"Fanny, Your Grace." She bobbed again. "An' you won't be keeping me from my work. Not if I'm doing what you asked me to do. You being the mistress of the house, and all."

"True." Persephone smiled a touch ironically.

"This way, Your Grace," Fanny said, and turned on her heels to walk back the way she'd apparently come.

Persephone followed at a close distance. After a minute or two, the passageway opened into a larger corridor. "This looks vaguely familiar," Persephone said, mostly to herself, eyeing the paneled walls and pointed-arch windows.

The corridor spilled onto the first-floor landing, the wide staircase leading down to the entrance hall and its fan-vaulted ceiling. A long, crimson banner hung just above the double front doors displaying what Persephone had decided upon arriving two days earlier was the family coat of arms.

The Lancasters had no family crest or motto or any of the hundreds of other things that set families like the Boyces so far above the rest of society. The Boyces had history. They belonged to hundreds of years of their own existence. No doubt there were Boyces long before the Domesday Book. The Lancasters weren't known to have walked the earth more than four or five generations back.

"I'm an intruder here," Persephone whispered to herself.

"Just this way, Your Grace," Fanny said, leading the way across the landing.

They passed the doors to the dining room where the wedding breakfast had been served, and Fanny stopped at the next door, motioning for Persephone to enter.

"The breakfast room," she said quietly, as if passing on a secret.

"Thank you, Fanny."

The girl bobbed a curtsy then quickly disappeared back down the corridor. Persephone took a deep, fortifying breath and stepped inside.

"Explain to Harry before you leave that you are not going because I forced you to do so," Adam's voice reached Persephone as she stepped into the room.

She looked up at the sound, finding him seated at the round breakfast table, obviously addressing his mother, who sat across from him and watched him with obvious motherly concern. Adam spoke over the top of a newspaper, lowered to reveal only the left half of his face. Persephone thought of the brief glimpse she'd had of Adam the morning they were married and the scars that marked the right side of his face. She wondered if he purposely hid it.

Adam continued addressing his mother. "Harry seems to think I drive every person who ever comes here away with a scythe in one hand and a flaming torch in the other."

"A regular one-person bloodthirsty mob—that's what you are." Harry's reply drew Persephone's eyes to where he sat, a few places removed from Adam. "You really ought to think about employing pitchforks when you—"

Harry looked up at that moment and spotted Persephone. He rose abruptly to his feet, acknowledging her entrance. Persephone let her eyes wander back to Adam. He had risen as well but did not look in her direction. Adam seemed mesmerized by something just outside the windows.

"Persephone!" the dowager duchess exclaimed, hurrying to the doorway where Persephone stood. Adam's mother had taken to Christian names early on, though Persephone could not bring herself to so much as think of the duchess as *Harriet.* "Are you feeling better this morning?"

Persephone nodded, color staining her cheeks as she remembered running into her mother-in-law when she was certain she looked less than presentable: red-rimmed eyes, mud-stained dress, wrinkles from bodice to hem.

"Come break your fast, dear," the dowager instructed. "Eggs? Kidneys?"

"Yes, please." She hadn't eaten a thing since breakfast the morning before and was ravenously hungry.

"Harry, will you please—"

"I will prepare a plate for her, Mother," Adam interrupted, sounding none too happy about it.

"I can—" Persephone began to protest.

But Adam had already turned to the sideboard and was placing eggs on a plate.

Persephone sat at the first empty seat she came to. A delicate china plate was placed in front of her. "Thank you, Adam," Persephone said on something near a whisper.

He picked up his paper, lying on the table near Persephone's left arm. Apparently, she'd chosen the chair next to his. Persephone looked up at him with a smile, unsure if she ought to be apologizing or looking pleased with the arrangement. The newspaper in Adam's hand crumpled under the tension in his fist. He was facing away from her, but Persephone could see the disapproval written all over his face.

"I'm sorry," Persephone said, rising. "I'll sit somewhere else."

"Sit," Adam instructed without looking at her.

Persephone obeyed immediately.

"Perhaps you should move to the other side, dear," the dowager suggested.

His right side! Persephone could have kicked herself. She'd suspected before that Adam was self-conscious about his scars. He would not appreciate having her seated at his right.

Persephone stood again, picking up her plate.

"Sit," Adam said again, a touch impatiently.

Persephone began to sit but stopped when the dowager spoke again.

"I am certain she wouldn't mind," she said to her son. "It isn't so very much to ask, poor—"

"*I* will move." Adam snatched his own plate and walked around the table to the seat furthest from the one he had occupied.

Persephone tucked into her breakfast, thinking furiously. She hadn't done well, thus far, on the goals she'd set for herself. She doubted Adam had even noticed her blue dress or her new coiffure. Not that she'd expected him to spout sonnets at her appearance. But a smile would have been nice.

She took a sip of tea. From then on, Persephone vowed she would take care never to sit on Adam's right. It was a shame, really, that he was so conscious of his scars. They truly didn't bother her. She wondered about them, how he'd come to have such extensive injuries. And she wondered if those scars were the only reason Adam had been so unhappy with her seated so near.

A knot formed instantly in her stomach at the thought that she alone had sent him to the far end of the table. Suddenly, Persephone didn't feel very hungry.

"Will you be coming to Town at Christmastime?" the dowager asked, her eyes turned to Adam.

"Of course not," Adam answered, his paper raised once more. "I never go to Town until absolutely necessary."

The dowager turned her attention to Persephone. "You must convince the poor boy to go about more in society. I would so love to have the two of you with me in London."

"I have never been to London."

The look of shock that followed what Persephone had intended to be a conversational comment instantly silenced any further words she might have produced. *That* hadn't been the right response to the dowager's invitation.

"Well, then," Persephone's mother-in-law recovered herself quickly, "in that case you absolutely *must* come." Her smile broadened to an entirely sincere grin. "I will positively love taking you around Town and introducing you to just everyone! Do come, Adam. We could all go. I am certain you could pack quickly. I could delay my departure by a day or so and we could all—"

"No, Mother," was the implacable response. "I will be forced to take her in the spring as it is."

"Forced?" the dowager replied with obvious disapproval at Adam's word choice. "The Season is such fun. How can you say 'forced'?"

"I despise London," Adam answered. "But the Queen will be put out if Persephone is not presented. And that is one bother I could do without. Thus, I shall be forced to Town."

Upsetting the queen qualified as little more than a bother to Adam? Persephone felt her less-exalted birth keenly in that moment.

"Do not let him burden you with even the tiniest amount of guilt, Your Grace," Harry said to Persephone. "He will be eager to go to London come March or April. By then he will have gone at least nine months without insulting the members of the Cabinet nor any of the Royal family and will be itching for the opportunity. He will, we can now be quite certain, blame the trip on you."

"I am not to believe that reason, then?" Persephone asked. Harry had an easy smile—one that had almost instantly brought an answering smile to her own lips. She'd needed someone to stand as reassurer.

"It seems, with Mother Harriet haring off to Town, there will be no one to explain to the new duchess how to interpret her husband's frequently misleading moods," Harry said as if deep in thought.

Persephone took a sip of tea to hide her smile.

"I suppose, as a good friend of the family, I ought to remain behind and offer my insight. Seeing as how I no longer fear the threat of your pistols, and you have assured me that you do not, in fact, brandish farm weaponry in ridding yourself of guests who overstay their welcomes." Harry rose from his seat. "I feel entirely secure in remaining at Falstone Castle indefinitely."

"Do not be surprised if you are thrown from the south parapet," Adam warned, not so much as lowering his paper.

"I am beginning to suspect, Adam, that you do not like me very much. Your Grace." Harry bowed to the dowager. "Your Grace." Then to Persephone. With a grin, he bowed to Adam. "Your Grace."

"Clod-head," Adam grumbled.

"This could get confusing," Harry said as he walked to the door. "We really ought to think of names for the three of you."

Persephone smiled. She hoped Harry did stay for a while. His optimism was infectious, and she needed every drop she could come by.

"Do not leave without saying good-bye, Mother Harriet," Harry requested.

"Of course not, Harry." The dowager smiled at him.

"Are you really leaving?" Persephone asked after Harry had gone.

"Later this morning," was the confirmation.

"Oh." That upset her plans. She had hoped for a few weeks of instruction.

"It is sweet of you to look so downcast at my departure, my dear." The dowager smiled kindly. "But it really is for the best. I am more comfortable in Town. And I think every newly wedded couple appreciates the absence of any and all of their parents." She smiled at Adam as she passed him and floated out the door with all the dignity and grace a duchess ought to possess.

Persephone managed to bite back her sigh of frustration. Her plans for the day had just, essentially, gone up in flames. Her duchess-tutor was hying herself to London. Persephone's attempts at improving her appearance had not even been noted. And Adam was sitting as far away from her as possible without actually leaving the room. He also seemed to be completely oblivious to her presence.

"Now what?" Persephone silently asked herself. And the trouble was, she had no answer.

CHAPTER EIGHT

"Haven't you any relatives willing to endure the sight of you for a few days?" Adam asked as he and Harry rode back through the outer gate of Falstone after a particularly bruising mid-morning ride.

"Is that a not-so-subtle hint that my indefinite visit is coming to a rather definite end? Or are you simply curious about the state of my relatives' affection for me?"

"I have no doubt your relatives are as heartily sick of you as I am. They, however, are far less likely than I am to draw and quarter you. Probably only because they do not have a conveniently located dungeon as I have."

"It amazes me, Adam," Harry said, keeping pace with him as they passed under the arch of Falstone's inner wall and brought their mounts to a halt at the front steps of the castle, "how you can feign such dislike for me. I am generally considered a very likable fellow."

Adam dismounted, handing Zeus's reins to one of the stable lads who'd met them there in order to take their mounts back to the stables.

"You don't think I'm all the crack?" Harry asked, with a laugh, as they ascended the stone steps leading to the solid front doors of Adam's home.

"Using cant, Harry?" Adam despised slang. "You sound more like those idiotic young London fops every day."

"And you sound more like my grandfather every day."

"I knew your grandfather," Adam reminded him.

Harry laughed. "In other words, I've offended you."

"I doubt I remind you of your rapscallion grandfather in any way." Adam handed his gloves and hat to Barton and continued across the entry hall.

"Certainly not in your choice of wife," Harry said.

Adam followed Harry's suddenly fixed gaze up the stairwell to the first-floor landing, where Persephone stood with her back to them and her head bent over as if studying something in her hands.

"My grandmother was something of a dragon," Harry went on. "Never left a fellow bellows to mend, I'd wager."

"It is generally not a good idea to tell a short-tempered man that his wife has left you breathless," Adam warned, Harry's observation inexplicably raising his hackles.

"He might shoot me in my sleep?" Harry hazarded the guess with a barely held-back laugh.

"He might shoot you where you're standing," Adam answered with a growl.

"Hmm." It was far too ponderous a sound for Adam's tastes. Without acknowledging Harry's apparent evaluation of the situation, Adam began moving up the staircase, bound for his book room.

Persephone, apparently, heard his approach. She spun around to face the gentlemen, hastily slipping something behind her back and smiling a little nervously. What was she hiding?

"Persephone," Adam acknowledged with a slight bow.

"Hello, Adam. Mr. Windover."

"We are practically brother and sister," Harry said, the slightest scold in his tone. "You really ought to call me Harry."

Adam noticed Persephone's eyes drift toward himself, as if uncertain.

"You are afraid Adam, here, will inflict some dire punishment on me for such a liberty?" Harry guessed. Persephone seemed to smile the tiniest bit. "Do not fret. I know several highly secretive passages out of the dungeons."

Persephone's brow furrowed and she spun back around, glancing once more at the paper in her hands. Adam managed not to roll his eyes. She was still using that blasted map.

Persephone turned her attention back to Harry. "There are no passages leading out of the dungeons."

"They are *secret*," Harry answered in a low aside. "You won't find them on a map."

Persephone colored up on the spot, her eyes once more shifting nervously in Adam's direction. "I . . . I . . . I just . . ."

"You've been walking around with your nose pressed to that confounded map for a week," Adam said. "I certainly hope you have the castle memorized by now."

"After a week?" Harry had the effrontery to laugh out loud. "You and I may have the castle memorized, Adam. But we practically grew up here."

"I *did* grow up here."

"Truly?" Harry looked confused, but Adam spotted the twinkle of mischief in his eyes. "I was sure you were born grown-up."

Before Adam could respond, the front bell rang. Adam reached out and snatched the map from Persephone's unsuspecting grasp. "You cannot be forever looking at this thing," he muttered. "Especially when there are other people around."

"Because it would be embarrassing?" Persephone asked quietly.

"Because it would be ridiculous."

"Not nearly as ridiculous as my getting lost four or five times a day, as I was before I had the housekeeper make up that 'confounded map.'" Persephone motioned to the parchment crumpling in Adam's fist. "And I would appreciate it if you would return it to me."

"Do you still rely on it?"

"No," she admitted warily.

Adam stuffed the map into his coat pocket. The bell rang again. Adam turned his gaze down the stairs toward the front door. "Someone had bloody well better answer that door before the entire staff is let go!" he bellowed.

"Of course, Your Grace," Barton said quite calmly from the foot of the stairs. "I was merely waiting to inquire whether or not you are 'at home.'"

"No," Adam growled.

"Very good, Your Grace." Barton, being a proper butler, turned without blinking an eye to the door and went about his duties. There was a man who understood how things are done. He performed his duties—he took Adam's threats seriously—as he ought to.

Harry, as usual, chuckled. "Planning my demise?"

Adam shot him a venomous look.

"Would you mind putting off my obviously deserved murder until after I complete my correspondence?" Harry requested mockingly. "I am sadly behind and can think of at least a half dozen people who would be sorely put out if I were to stick my spoon in the wall before writing off a final farewell."

"You can write all the letters you wish in your carriage as it pulls away from Falstone," Adam grumbled, brushing past Harry and Persephone as he continued toward the corridor that led to his book room.

"I do not have a carriage," Harry called after him.

"You can use one of mine," Adam answered without looking back.

"You are nothing if not a model of hospitality." Harry laughed as Adam stepped down the hall.

"Is he actually making you leave?" Adam heard Persephone ask, her tone one of confusion and concern.

"No. He's just cutting a sham."

Adam clenched his fists. Why did Harry insist on sounding like an idiot? "Cut the cant, Harry," Adam bellowed back at him, "and write your blasted letters."

To which, of course, Harry laughed.

Adam didn't pause but continued toward his book room.

"Adam?"

He stopped at the sound of Persephone's voice. Adam let out a breath of frustration. Couldn't he have a moment's peace?

"Yes, Persephone?" He turned just enough to see her out of the corner of his left eye. He was steps from his book room. Couldn't this have waited?

She seemed to hesitate for a moment. "May I please have the map back?"

The deuced map again. "No lady should require a map for her own house."

"Unless that house is the size of a small village," Persephone answered with something like exasperation.

"Falstone Castle is laid out logically," Adam replied shortly. This wasn't so very difficult. "All of the public rooms are on the ground level. The first floor," Adam gestured around them, "holds the living areas: dining hall, breakfast room, and so on. The second floor is the family bedchambers. Third floor, the nursery. Fourth and fifth floors and three of the four towers house the guest bedchambers. It is not so confusing that one ought to be required to carry around a map."

"Perhaps not after some time," Persephone persisted.

"You know the castle well enough to get around on your own," Adam insisted, still not looking at her full-on. "You will learn the rest far faster if you must find your way using your own observations and memory."

"I would feel more confident if I had the map with me should I need it," Persephone said. "I haven't been *relying* on it this past day or so, only checking it occasionally."

"Then you do not need it now."

"Why are you so insistent about this?" Persephone asked, her tone gaining a hint of urgency. "I don't understand. It seems such a trivial thing."

"Did you use a map in your home in Shropshire?" Adam asked, frustrated at her insistence. He was accustomed to simply being obeyed. Dukes always are.

"No, of course not."

"If one does not know a house, it cannot be one's home," Adam said.

"You wish me to feel at home here?" she asked with obvious doubt.

Feel at home? Adam instantly bristled at the sentimentality of that phrase. "I only wish for you not to stick out," he answered sharply. "There are enough reasons why our situation is . . ." He was suddenly struggling with his composure, something he rarely experienced. Adam shifted enough to be looking away from her and found it helped. ". . . ridiculous," he finally finished the phrase, "without making the flaws so obvious."

He heard Persephone take a tight breath and release it shakily. "I *have* been trying," she said. "But there is a lot to learn."

"Then perhaps you should get on with the learning and leave me be." Adam found the necessity of talking while looking away from his conversational partner grating.

"Your Grace?" That was Barton's well-modulated voice.

"What?" Adam snapped.

"Mr. Jones is below. He claims to be in receipt of a letter from you reinstating his employment and wishes to express his most heartfelt thanks." Barton delivered the message without so much as a change in expression.

"Tell Mr. Jones that if he wishes to show gratitude, he can do so by taking himself off."

"Very good, Your Grace." Barton executed a dignified bow and took his leave down the corridor, no doubt to deliver, verbatim, Adam's response.

Jones would scurry away like a frightened rabbit. Adam had some satisfaction in that knowledge, at least.

He allowed a glance in the direction of Barton's retreating back, his thoughts on the confrontation he would be missing. His attention, however, was quickly recalled when he realized Persephone still stood quite near, her gaze riveted on his face.

He would not be stared at in his own house.

"Haven't you some household duty to see to?" He turned his back once more, closing the distance between himself and his book room.

"Several," he heard Persephone answer in a tone clearly laced with resignation. "I ought to have seen to them before now. Another of my obvious flaws, I suppose."

Though he doubted her reply was meant to be barbed, it stung just the same. He hadn't intended to imply that *she* was flawed, only the idea of a marriage between the two of them.

Persephone's footsteps sounded, muted by the long, woven rug running the length of the stone floor. Adam turned his face and watched her go. She held her head high, her posture perfectly straight. But as he watched her retreat, Adam saw Persephone wrap her arms around her waist, and he knew, watching her, it was a gesture of self-comforting.

He hadn't meant to hurt her. The realization shocked him. Not so much the hurting without meaning to as the idea that he hadn't set out to cause her pain. When, he silently asked himself, was the last time he'd met someone whom he hadn't instantly felt the need to lash out at?

At what point had he grown weak and vulnerable?

Emotions had no place in his life. No place, whatsoever.

That, he reminded himself, could never change.

CHAPTER NINE

Dear Persephone,

We have been home for two days now and I am nearly dead with boredom! Athena spends all her time reading fashion magazines and practicing country dances, which she does not perform well, at all. I do not think she will find a husband dancing like she does. No gentleman wants to marry someone who dances like a cow.

Persephone smiled for what felt like the first time since arriving in Northumberland. Poor Artemis, to endure the raptures Persephone could easily imagine Athena, at the very romantic age of eighteen, indulging in at the prospect of a London Season. Athena ever was the romantic of the family. Daphne was the shy, practical one, even at eleven. And Artemis, though only eight, had the reputation for dramatics.

Papa has engaged a governess, but she will not arrive for another week. So I am running around like a heathen (that is what Mrs. Russell says) and terrorizing the neighborhood. It's lovely. I wish you were here so we could be heathens together.

When can I come explore your towers? You did promise. Do duchesses have to keep promises? I have been wondering about that.

I will have my birthday in London, Daphne says. I think that could be fun, but I am not sure yet. I will invite you. If the duke wants to come, he can too, even if he never did talk to me once while I was at his castle.

    Please write to me. Be sure to put the guinea under the seal.

Your sister,
Artemis

"You seem in good spirits this afternoon."

Persephone looked up at Harry Windover, who had apparently entered the sitting room while she was reading. "I have been reading a letter from my youngest sister, Mr.—" A disapproving look changed the words even as they left her lips. "Harry," she corrected with a smile.

"She writes with good news, then?"

"She has written a letter filled with crises, actually." Persephone smiled. "With Artemis—that is my sister's name—every little thing is a crisis. I was enjoying being reminded of that."

"You miss your family." He said it so matter-of-fact, as if there was no question of her feelings.

"And what of you, Harry?" Persephone carefully refolded Artemis's letter. "Do you miss your family, being here as long as you have been?"

"I think of Adam very much as a brother," Harry replied, "so being here is like being with my family."

Persephone studied the gentleman standing near the fireplace, warming his outstretched hands.

"How is it that the two of you have become such close friends?" Persephone would normally have been alarmed at her own audacity but was too perplexed by the man she'd married to hold the question back.

"Does it seem hard to believe because we are so different?"

"And he is so hostile toward you." Persephone sat on a sofa facing the fire, feeling her brows furrow with her confusion.

"Adam is hostile toward everyone." Harry shrugged. "It is just the way he is."

"Does he never show any tenderness of feeling?" Persephone felt her heart sinking lower with every word. She had been entertaining some hopes that Adam would improve upon closer acquaintance—that, perhaps, he was simply wary of strangers. An odd character trait, she admitted, for one who'd chosen a stranger to be his bride.

"Tenderness of feeling?" Harry pushed a log further into the fire with the toe of his boot. "Not within the last two decades, I'd say."

"And before then? Before the last two decades?"

"I met Adam at Harrow," Harry said. "Twenty years ago. I have no idea what he was like before that."

"Then you forged a friendship with someone who was . . . was . . ." How did she put it into words? She finally decided on, "Hostile?"

Harry smiled. But a different smile than he usually produced. It was sentimental, fond; not laughing or joking. "Adam saved my skin," Harry said. "First year at Harrow. I was something of a runt, and the other boys found that grounds for torturing me. Adam set them straight."

"They weren't unkind to Adam?" Persephone knew how children could sometimes be.

"They were afraid of him," Harry answered. "Even then. They still are. Everyone is."

"He would have only been seven or eight years old." Persephone tried to imagine a child Artemis's age already intimidating and hard.

"Seven," Harry confirmed. "He was a force to be reckoned with even then. The only shell in the history of Harrow, I'd guess, who ran the school."

"Shell?"

"The youngest year," Harry explained. He chuckled as if remembering something. "A few of the boys, now grown gentlemen, of course, still whimper when they see him."

"But to be so frightening when he was only a child." It was unfathomable. And not a very encouraging sign. Perhaps there wasn't a gentle side to Adam, after all.

"It wasn't that, exactly." Harry strode from the fireplace to sit on the sofa facing Persephone. "He was, still is, remarkably intelligent. And he is authoritative, the kind of man few people question. Even at seven he was very much that way. And he is unafraid."

"Unafraid? I don't imagine anyone could be entirely unafraid."

"I would wager a pony he hasn't an ounce of fear in his entire body," Harry said. "And if he does, he squelches it with alarming finality."

"There is nothing that frightens him? Nothing that intimidates him?"

Harry rose as if to leave. "Not that I've seen."

Persephone digested that as Harry made for the door. A man without fears, in control in every situation, who had been intimidating, apparently, all his life. And she, who had always been quiet and happy at home, dreaming of her future cozy family life, was married to him. What had ever led her to believe that this marriage could be remotely like the one she'd always hoped for?

"Why doesn't he ever look at me?" she asked the instant the question jumped into her mind. She immediately regretted asking. Persephone felt herself color up.

"What do you mean?" Harry stopped a step from the door.

"Never mind," Persephone whispered, knowing her face was flaming brighter than ever.

"No. There's no 'never mind' here." Harry walked back toward her. "He never looks at you?"

Persephone shook her head. "And he moves away if I sit near him. I thought, that morning at breakfast, it was only because I sat on his right side. Considering his . . . um . . ." She was getting flustered.

"Face," Harry finished for her. "Adam's mother makes a lot of fuss over Adam's scars. More than she needs to. At Harrow, when one of the other boys would sit on his right at meals or something and started staring, Adam didn't move. He made the boy who was staring move. And they always did."

"Then it wasn't because of the scars?" Persephone's heart plummeted. If his reason hadn't been the scars, then it had to have been *her*.

"I couldn't say." Harry looked genuinely perplexed.

"Oh." Her prospects were growing dimmer.

"He really doesn't look at you?" Harry asked.

Persephone shook her head. Adam hadn't once taken more than a very passing glance in her direction. He turned away almost instantly when she came into the room.

"That is strange," Harry said. "He usually faces problems head-on."

"I am a problem, then?" Persephone asked in a small voice.

Harry smiled at that. "Poor choice of words on my part."

Persephone managed the smallest of answering smiles.

"It may just be that Adam is unused to the idea of a wife," Harry offered. "He tends to get more, I don't know, *prickly* when he has a lot on his mind."

"So I should give this some more time?" Persephone felt a bit of her natural optimism returning.

"Definitely. Look at me. If I'd given up on Adam for being grumpy, we wouldn't be friends."

"How long did it take for him to not be prickly with you?" Her determination was building once more.

"He still is. But after a while he quit landing me facers every few days. I figured that was something."

"Landing you facers?" Persephone had never heard that particular phrase before.

"It's cant. Slang. Means punching a person in the face."

"Good heavens," Persephone muttered.

"Adam hates it when I use cant." Harry smiled mischievously.

"But you do, anyway?"

"That's why I do. Every time I'm in Town I try to pick up a new phrase. Drives him mad."

"Doesn't that worry you? Suppose he actually follows through with one of his threats?"

"He won't."

"How can you be so sure?"

"Adam would never admit it," Harry said, "but he knows I refuse to be bullied, and I think he respects that. He keeps trying. But I think he hopes it'll never work."

"So he doesn't like people who are intimidated by him?" Persephone rose to her feet. She needed to think about this new information.

"Doesn't *respect* them," Harry corrected.

"I guess that is a little different."

"It is a great deal different to Adam," Harry said. "Adam *likes* his mother."

"But he doesn't *respect* her?"

Harry shook his head rather adamantly. "Mother Harriet—I have called her that since I was a boy—has made something of a hobby out of pitying Adam."

"And he doesn't like that?"

"Frustrates the—" Harry cleared his throat and looked a little embarrassed. "Frustrates him."

Persephone paced the room, her brain spinning with the insights Harry offered her. "If Adam does not like people to be afraid of him, why does he go to such lengths to accomplish it?" A few of the stories she'd heard from the staff regarding Adam's rather colorful past came springing to mind: duels, brawls, grown men reduced to tears, women swooning.

"I have a few theories," Harry said. "But Adam would, literally, kill me if I posed any of them to you."

Persephone turned to look at Harry, expecting to see the joking façade he usually presented. He looked far too serious for her peace of mind.

He shrugged. "'Kill' may be a little strong. Still, Adam's motivations are not a topic I am willing to discuss."

"But I am trying so hard to understand him."

"Most people do not even try." Harry's smile was full of sympathy. "Give it some time. I have a feeling you will come up with a few theories of your own."

He bowed then walked to the door. He stopped a step from the threshold and turned to look back at her. "He really never looks at you?" he asked.

Persephone shook her head.

"Something about you has ruffled him." Harry narrowed his eyes a little. "And nothing ruffles Adam."

"Is that good or bad?" Persephone asked, suddenly concerned.

"I don't know yet." He gave her one last searching look before inclining his head and stepping out.

"Ruffled him?" Not exactly the reaction most women would wish for from their husband. "But," she told herself, "it means he, at least, is not indifferent."

Perhaps that was something she could build on. Persephone quickly reviewed all Harry had told her about Adam.

"Do not be intimidated. Do not pity," Persephone whispered. It wasn't much as far as advice went, but it was something. She thumped Artemis's letter against her open palm as she circled the sitting room.

Adam had said something the morning before, in the corridor outside his book room, about not wanting her to stick out at Falstone Castle, about not advertising her flaws. Appearances seemed to be important to him as well.

Persephone could learn to conduct herself like a duchess. She had been practicing and could improve. She'd also been spending a little extra time at her dressing table each morning, allowing her maid the opportunity to experiment with her toilette. Adam hadn't said anything, specifically, about her appearance. But it certainly couldn't hurt.

"Do not be intimidated," Persephone repeated to herself.

She still wasn't sure why he seemed to avoid her, why he, apparently, couldn't bear to look at her. But those things could be dealt with later. Persephone had a goal.

If nothing else, Adam would respect her.

CHAPTER TEN

WINTER HAD COME EARLY, JUST as Jeb Handly had predicted. It was the third week of October, and already a bitterly cold wind was whipping around Falstone. But arctic cold didn't bother Adam's faithful horse, and it didn't bother Adam. Unfortunately, biting cold also failed to intimidate Harry.

"Old Jeb really ought to seek out a position as royal weather predictor," Harry said as they cantered through the front gate.

"There is no such position."

"If Mad King George knew of Jeb's abilities, he'd have the position created," Harry insisted.

"If he heard you calling him Mad King George, he'd have you thrown in jail."

Harry laughed. The man didn't even take treason seriously.

"Jus' so, Yer Grace," a voice echoed across the paddock near the stables. "She's a bit skittish 's'morning, it bein' so cold an' all."

"Haven't you a horse who isn't skittish about cold?"

Adam's head snapped at the sound of Persephone's voice. He hadn't seen much of her in the two days since their encounter outside his book room. Part of the reason, he acknowledged, was that he'd been avoiding her. Something about Persephone made him uncomfortable.

Every other female he'd ever encountered was either instantly horrified or gave him the kind of sad look one generally reserved for injured puppies or fatally ill children. Persephone simply looked confused whenever they were in one another's company.

Adam hadn't yet decided on the best course of action. Indecision was a feeling entirely foreign to him.

"There's Atlas," the groom who was standing near Persephone suggested. *John*, Adam identified him. *John Handly. Jeb's son.* The man was good with horses. Persephone had sought out the right person if she was seeking any information about the stables. Wise girl.

"Atlas?" Persephone asked with a hint of doubt. "Who named him Atlas?"

"His Grace did," John answered, the statement almost sounding like a question.

Adam was close enough to see a smile touch Persephone's lips. "And His Grace does not think it a ridiculous name?" she asked, almost mockingly. "It being Greek and mythological?"

"I 'spect not, Yer Grace," John replied. "Named 'is own mount, Zeus. That be one o' them heathen gods, too."

Persephone looked very near to laughing. A quick glance at Harry revealed that he, too, found the revelation particularly entertaining. They were laughing at him.

Adam tensed his jaw. "Such names are *not* ridiculous for horses."

Persephone turned as he spoke, a look of embarrassed surprise on her face. Now she would slump her shoulders and tiptoe off. Adam watched and waited. But Persephone surprised him. Her jaw set, she seemed to square her shoulders and returned his gaze. "Then I had best search the forest for a sorceress who can transform me into a horse, or else I shall be doomed to spend the rest of my life in a constant state of ridiculousness."

It was a set-down, Adam knew. And yet he couldn't help feeling reluctantly impressed at her show of backbone. "You would make an atrocious horse, Persephone." Adam dismounted with his back to her.

"There are some 'obvious flaws' in that plan, then?"

Again, a barbed comment. Adam had little experience being on the receiving end of criticism. "Why, precisely, have you come to the stables?" Adam allowed a stable lad to lead Zeus back to the stables while he moved to stand on Persephone's right side.

"I was hoping to attempt to ride again." Persephone watched Alibi, who was running in a rather erratic pattern around the paddock.

"How long have you been out of the saddle?" Adam asked.

"Ten years."

"Ten years! And you were going to attempt to retake riding on *Alibi*?" Not such a wise girl, after all.

"No, Yer Grace," John quickly jumped in. Like his father, Jeb, John had few qualms about addressing Adam without invitation; it was an impertinence that didn't bother Adam in the least. He only interrupted or spoke up when the topic was one on which he was considered an expert. The man knew when to assert himself and when to hold his tongue. "She weren't wanting to ride Alibi. Her Grace had only just arrived at the paddock an' asked if the filly were ailin' or upset."

"Alibi is a fine horse in warm weather," Adam explained to Persephone, hoping to stem the tide of any rash course of action she might be considering. It was his experience that people, in general, had a tendency to do incredibly stupid things when faced with situations they knew little of. "She is confined to the stables and the paddock in the cold."

"I gathered as much from John," Persephone replied. It was something near a scold. Adam turned his head enough to look more closely at her. No one ever scolded him. "He suggested Atlas as an appropriate mount. And I am inclined to agree, his name having instantly endeared me to the creature. I am assuming the horse is, indeed, a *he,* considering his namesake was most definitely male."

"Another heathen god?" John asked her disapprovingly.

"Decidedly heathen," Persephone answered with a growing smile.

"And was you named for one o' them heathens, too?"

"A goddess," Persephone nodded. "She was abducted by the god of the dead, who held her captive in the underworld. The Greeks believed that while Persephone was held prisoner, the world was plunged into cold and darkness."

"Laws," John whistled the word through the gap in his front teeth. "And how'd the Greeks say she escaped?"

"She was eventually permitted to leave, but only for part of the year. While she is free, they believed, the world saw growth and warmth and harvests. During those months when she returns to the underworld, the earth again mourns for her."

"Such a sad story," John said.

"It was merely an attempt by the ignorant to explain the changing of the seasons," Adam grumbled.

"I have always thought it a very touching story," Persephone said, in obvious disagreement with Adam's assessment.

"That the poor gel got stolen off?" John asked her, disbelieving.

"It is a story so full of love. Her mother's love and grief is what brings Persephone back to her family. And when she returns to her loved ones," Persephone said, a look of sentimental longing on her face, "their joy is so full that the entire earth comes to life with the enormity of it."

"Laws, that is a rather fine thing to think about." John nodded. "Makes a man wish his parents had thought to give 'im a name with some kind of grand story to it. There must be loads of them stories from the Greeks."

"I will not have you rechristening my stable staff with mythological names." Adam worried at the moment that she might actually select a new name for John.

Persephone laughed, precisely as Harry would have. Harry did, in fact. He stood on Persephone's other side. If Adam hadn't kept his head turned in the other direction, he might have seen him there, and Harry's sudden burst of laughter wouldn't have been nearly so unexpected.

"Nonsense, John," Persephone addressed the stable hand. "The Bible is filled with Johns who have rather fine stories attached to their names."

John seemed to ponder that. "And them stories are true," he said, as if discovering an added bonus.

"Precisely," Persephone answered. "The story of my name may be touching, but it is not true."

Then John, he of the gapped teeth and sun-ravaged face, smiled at Persephone with so much admiration, it was all Adam could do not to yank the man off his feet by his hair. Not that it was the poor man's fault. A duchess ought not to be speaking so familiarly with a stable hand. It confused things. And Adam's duchess ought not to have been the sort of lady to inspire admiration in all and sundry, in the first place. If Persephone had been anything like what he'd expected, Adam's life wouldn't have been plunged so suddenly into confusion.

And John was still smiling.

"Are you going to saddle Her Grace's mount, or shall I be forced to do it personally?" Adam growled.

John seemed to snap to attention. "'Pologies." He pulled his forelock. "Would Atlas be suitable, Yer Grace?"

"Fine," Adam snapped.

John disappeared into the stables. Adam took a few breaths to compose himself. He'd never before had to try so hard to control his emotions. He'd always been one to hold to a steely calm.

"So you are really going to try riding again?" Harry asked Persephone.

"To be perfectly honest, I am not certain one could accurately call my previous experience 'riding.' Our neighbors, the Uptons, allowed me to ride a pony of theirs on occasion when I was a child. If memory serves, that particular pony was in his second decade and did little more than shift his weight."

"Then you have never truly ridden?" Harry sounded astonished.

"Impoverished grandsons of only slightly less impoverished barons do not keep a stable, Harry," Persephone answered with an ironic laugh.

Alibi was being led—forced was, perhaps, the more apt description—from the paddock, and Atlas was being brought out of the stables.

Adam surveyed the gelding with a critical eye. Persephone had never ridden; not if her description of that pony was accurate. Atlas was calm today. But, then, Atlas always was. He was slow, sedate, moving more like a heavy-laden work horse than the riding mount he was. It was the reason Adam had chosen Atlas as his name. The gelding moved as though he bore the entire heavens on his shoulders.

Atlas's one drawback was size. Standing more than fifteen hands high, Atlas might be too large for Persephone, especially considering her lack of experience. But Adam was certain there were no ponies in the stables. And many of the others, Alibi for instance, were not as large but hadn't the temperament for an unskilled rider.

"Fiend seize it," Adam growled. Why was it that Persephone constantly presented him with situations for which he had no solution? Adam was not accustomed to being at a loss.

"He's calm an' steady, Yer Grace," John said to Persephone, still smiling like a besotted calfling.

Adam thought he heard Persephone take a deep breath, as if to calm herself, before making her way into the paddock. Was she nervous? Horses could sense discomfort, and it made them nervous in return. Adam grew evermore uncertain about Persephone's plan.

Atlas shimmied a little as Persephone approached. She stopped, stiff and watching.

"He'll not hurt you." John encouraged Persephone on.

Adam wondered if she would continue on. Most likely, Persephone would bow out of the whole thing and skitter off. People, in general, were cowards.

"Can I give him a carrot?" Persephone asked John uncertainly.

"'Ave you got a carrot?"

Her eyes never left Atlas. "I brought one from the kitchens." She patted her coat pocket.

Adam realized, watching her, that Persephone was not dressed for riding. Where was her habit? Her riding whip? The bonnet she was wearing would not stay on should Atlas give her much of a jarring. "Ridiculous," Adam mumbled, but for once he didn't turn away from something he found absurd. Something in him wanted to know if she would mount, if she would see through what she'd set out to accomplish.

"The Uptons' pony was fond of carrots," Persephone further explained.

"Perhaps the poor thing waddled so much because he was overfed," Harry called out with a chuckle.

Persephone glanced back at him and smiled her amusement, the first true smile Adam had ever seen from his wife. It was perfect: lovely, straight, white teeth, mouth turned up symmetrically, no scars to cause grotesque pulls and puckering in her face. It was the sort of smile a man ought to be in raptures over. But Adam only felt an overwhelming frustration at seeing yet another reason why Persephone was not at all what he'd wanted in a bride.

She was laughing, and the sound pulled Adam from his thoughts.

"He didn' nip you, did he?" John asked.

"Not at all." Persephone still flashed that radiant smile. "Only surprised me."

"If you don't want him snapping food from your hands, don't bring any with you."

"I will remember that, thank you, Harry." Persephone seemed to roll her eyes. Adam nodded his approval of her response: useless advice ought to be dismissed.

"'E'll be calmer while he's eating." John motioned with his head toward the saddle and mounting block already in place.

Persephone hesitated. She eyed Atlas with obvious apprehension.

She was going to back down, Adam was certain of it. He shook his head. One didn't shrink from challenges, one faced them head-on.

Adam pushed away from the paddock fence. "If she and Atlas part company, see to it that John has her brought up to the castle," Adam mumbled to Harry and began walking away.

"Don't you even want to see her try?" The chastisement in Harry's words was too pointed for Adam's taste.

"She is backing down already. I have seen enough people quit in my lifetime without witnessing the same thing again." Adam heard the tinge of bitterness in his voice and hated it.

"I think she might surprise you."

Adam continued to walk away. But, only a few steps later, he found himself slowing his pace. Then, almost against his will, Adam looked back.

Persephone was on the mounting block, listening intently to instructions from John, while two stable hands stood nearby, ensuring Atlas kept still.

Adam stood frozen, watching. She'd been nervous, that had been apparent. And if her rapt attention were any indication, she still was. But she had come this far.

After a moment's hesitation, Persephone was in the awkward sidesaddle, attempting to arrange her inadequate skirts into some semblance of propriety. Her grip on the reins was a touch too tight, but otherwise she gave the impression of being nearly at ease.

"Hmm," Adam grunted. She hadn't run. That was unexpected.

He gave a nod of approval that stopped almost instantly at a flash of ankle from the would-be rider.

"Needs a bloody riding habit." Adam turned to make his way back to the house.

Persephone had a little steel in her. That was good, Adam thought to himself. She was going to need it.

CHAPTER ELEVEN

"Though I know you will be pained by my departure, I am for Hawick in the morning," Harry said at dinner the night after Persephone's first attempt at riding in more than a decade.

"Are you certain you couldn't leave *tonight*?" Adam raised an eyebrow, no hint of a joking smile.

Adam's treatment of Harry confused Persephone, even after Harry's explanation a few days earlier. Persephone was sorely tempted to sink lower on her chair, Adam's tone intimidating her. *Do not be intimidated,* she reminded herself. "Do you go to Scotland often?" Persephone asked, holding her head high.

"My mother's sister and her husband live in Hawick," Harry said. "They are always asking me to come for a visit."

"And I am always asking you to leave. How is it that their requests are adhered to and mine are ignored?" Adam asked, facing Harry, only part of his face even visible to Persephone.

Adam still hadn't looked at her. He'd come close that morning at the paddock, in the moments before he'd left. He hadn't stayed to watch her attempt at riding. She'd been working so hard at being brave and unintimidated. Persephone had hoped to show Adam that she wasn't nearly as flawed as he thought, to hopefully gain a grain of his respect, and he hadn't even stayed to see.

Harry shrugged. "Because I know you do not actually want me to go."

Adam didn't bother to reply beyond a look of ironic disbelief.

"How long will you be in Hawick?" Persephone asked, reminding herself that duchesses are not afraid to take up a conversation.

"I take it, then, you wish me to return?" Harry looked genuinely pleased by the sentiment.

Persephone glanced quickly at Adam. She didn't want to upset him or say something to further convince him she was unsuitable.

Adam's eyes darted quickly toward her before he just as quickly looked away again. "Harry will come back regardless of how you answer," he said dryly. "He's one of those friends who never disappears for long."

Persephone smiled a little. Adam had called Harry his friend, even though his tone was disapproving. She wondered if he even realized what he'd said. Harry seemed to, though. He actually winked at Persephone as if to say, "I told you."

"You had better be suffering from an uncontrollable muscle tic," Adam grumbled, still seemingly concentrating on the food on his plate.

"Completely uncontrollable." Harry's smile belied his words.

"Good. Otherwise I would think you were just winking at my wife."

"And if that were the case, you would be forced to call me out. Too bad I'll be gone in the morning."

"Certainly you mean, 'Good thing I'll be gone in the morning,'" Adam corrected, taking a bite of beef.

"On the contrary." Harry's casual demeanor did not slip in the least. "I would rather enjoy being called out by you. Gives a fellow a certain distinction to have survived a duel with the infamous Duke of Kielder."

"Who says you would survive?"

Harry did not appear concerned. "You would shoot the gentleman you only just referred to as a friend?"

"I never called you anything so mawkish," Adam grumbled.

"And now you're using cant?" Harry asked with mock surprise. "Are you feeling well, Adam?"

Persephone thought she heard a, "Shut up, Harry."

All conversation ended at that point, Harry looking remarkably pleased with himself, Adam looking as disgruntled as ever. She watched their reactions unfolding with such an enormous lack of understanding that she felt completely out of place.

"Your Grace." Barton's voice broke the silence as the last remove was brought into the dining room. He set a calling card at Adam's right arm.

Persephone craned her neck slightly, hoping for a better look. She sat too far distant to read the inscription but saw that the corner was turned down. A visitor at Falstone Castle?

"Where have you put him?" The tension in Adam's jaw didn't bode well.

"In the drawing room, Your Grace."

"He, no doubt, has come with luggage." Adam's annoyance could hardly have been more obvious.

Who could the visitor possibly be?

"Quite a lot of luggage, actually, Your Grace," Barton confirmed.

"Is it snowing, Barton?" Adam asked.

"No, Your Grace."

"Then throw him out." Adam tossed the card onto the table beside him.

"His conveyance was obtained on the road, Your Grace," Barton said. "It has already departed."

"He can walk." Adam was perfectly serious.

He wouldn't throw a man out into the night, Persephone said to herself.

"Very good, Your Grace." Barton made the appropriate bow and turned to quit the room.

Persephone felt a rising panic. "Barton," she called out to him, stopping his departure.

"Yes, Your Grace." Barton faced her and dipped his head.

"Who is the visitor in the drawing room?" She saw out of the corner of her eye that Adam was looking at her. If his expression weren't so full of shock, he might have appeared disapproving. *Do not be intimidated,* Persephone reminded herself.

"Mr. Gordon Hewitt, Your Grace."

"What is your argument with Mr. Hewitt?" Persephone asked Adam, turning her head to look at him. Adam immediately looked away. And he did not answer. She glanced at Harry, hoping for some information.

"Mr. Hewitt has had the effrontery to be the heir presumptive." Harry gave her a knowing look.

"He is family?" Persephone asked, her shock growing.

"Unfortunately," Adam muttered.

Persephone sat in complete indecision. She couldn't imagine throwing a member of her family out of her house. And, yet, Adam seemed so insistent. *Do not be intimidated.*

"Is it absolutely necessary, Adam, for Mr. Hewitt to leave Falstone tonight?" Persephone quickly covered the nervous break in her voice.

"Obviously you haven't met the man." Adam's tone fairly crackled with dryness.

"Would it be such an imposition for him to remain for the night?" Persephone forced herself to continue. "You could just as easily insist that he depart in the morning."

Silence reigned in the room, stretching out uncomfortably. She clenched her hands in her lap to stop their nervous shaking. Never had a man so intimidated her, but she was determined not to let him see that.

Adam tapped his fingers on the table, his mouth set in a tense line, his countenance that of man pondering something. She couldn't tell if he was angry.

Maybe Harry was wrong. Maybe shows of courage and determination didn't garner Adam's respect but his condemnation.

What have I done? Persephone silently asked.

Harry and Barton seemed entirely unaffected by the tense silence, as if Adam's disapproving mood were a common occurrence, which, Persephone quickly acknowledged, was probably the case.

"Excellent suggestion, Persephone," Adam quite suddenly said. "I do believe Hewitt may liven up the castle during Harry's absence." Adam turned to Harry. "How long do you intend to be in Scotland?"

"A fortnight or so." Harry sported a mischievous grin.

Adam nodded as if in approval. "Barton." Adam's usual authority asserted itself in full measure. "Put Hewitt in the Orange Chamber."

Barton bowed his understanding and left the dining room.

Harry sputtered in an attempt to stifle a laugh. "He'll never last the fortnight."

"He'll last," Adam insisted. "But he'll hate every minute of it. The West Tower is only slightly more welcoming than the dungeons."

"I am actually sorry to be missing this," Harry said.

"Hewitt will not make a return visit." Adam nodded decisively. "And he'll leave mewling like a kitten."

Persephone actually regretted her interference when faced with the satisfaction on Adam's face as he contemplated the apparent misery of Mr. Hewitt. It seemed she'd only made things worse.

* * *

Two gentlemen were in the breakfast room when Persephone arrived the next morning. One was Adam. The other was a stranger to her.

"Persephone." Adam rose as she entered. "Come and meet our cousin, Mr. Hewitt." He motioned her into the room.

She moved a little warily to where Adam stood, his arm extended to her. "Persephone, may I present Mr. Gordon Hewitt of Yorkshire, eldest son of my father's cousin. Hewitt, this is my wife, the Duchess of Kielder."

The look of shock on Mr. Hewitt's face was unmistakable, as was the satisfaction that turned up the side of Adam's mouth that she could see.

"How long ago were you married?" Mr. Hewitt asked Persephone after Adam had filled a plate for her and she had seated herself, at Adam's insistence, directly beside himself.

"On the first of the month." Persephone proceeded to feign a great deal of interest in her toast.

"Forgive me for not attending," Mr. Hewitt said. "I fear my invitation must have gone astray in the post."

"Tragic," Adam answered with obvious sarcasm.

"And where do you hail from, Your Grace?" Mr. Hewitt asked Persephone.

"Shropshire." Her determination to be courageous failed her miserably, leaving her response quiet and uncertain. She was confused. Adam's obvious dislike of his cousin bewildered her, though not nearly as much as her husband's sudden attentiveness.

Mr. Hewitt seemed quite pleased with her answer. "My mother's family are in Wales, and so I have often passed through Shropshire. It is, perhaps, the most beautiful of counties."

Persephone smiled at that. "It is, indeed, but then, my opinion is terribly biased."

"Biased, it may be," Mr. Hewitt replied, looking kindly at her, "but it is also entirely accurate."

Images of her home and environs passed quickly through her thoughts, and Persephone found herself sighing. "I shall miss the River Severn." She hadn't admitted as much out loud since leaving her childhood home.

Mr. Hewitt was all empathy. "And, in another month or so, I fear you will miss the milder weather of Shropshire as well."

"Milder? The weather in Shropshire can be quite extreme."

"*Can* be," Mr. Hewitt acknowledged. "The weather at Falstone *is* extreme. Especially in the winter."

"Have you been here often, then?" Persephone felt herself warming to Mr. Hewitt's easy conversational style.

"Actually, no." He seemed a little embarrassed. "I came several times as a young man. But only once in the past ten years."

"Only once?" He was the heir presumptive. It seemed strange that he would visit so seldom.

"Yes. After another cousin's passing placed him in the role of heir presumptive." Adam made the observation in a tone of obvious disapproval.

Mr. Hewitt shook his head. "My family had not returned to Falstone Castle after my father died," he explained. "As he was our connection to the Boyces, we felt it would be rather presumptuous to visit without him."

That confession struck a chord with her. "My mother passed when I was young, and we do not see her family as often as we once did."

Mr. Hewitt nodded. "Precisely."

"Were you planning to ride again this morning?" Adam interrupted the exchange, addressing her with less of his earlier pleasure and a great deal more of his usual shortness.

"Yes, I was." Though she was still sore from the previous day's attempt, Persephone intended to give it another go.

"I will accompany you to the stables." The offer sounded more like an order.

Do not be intimidated, she reminded herself. "Thank you."

"Do you ride, Your Grace?" Mr. Hewitt asked.

"I certainly hope so," she answered.

Adam cleared his throat in what sounded like a stifled laugh. Persephone turned and looked at him, knowing she was smiling and hoping he was as well. She'd made him laugh, certainly he could appreciate that.

But Adam didn't look amused or pleased. He looked the same as ever: indifferent, perhaps a touch disdainful.

Persephone stopped her instant dejected reaction with the reminder that he had laughed. Almost. And she'd shown him she could be courageous. He still didn't look at her, except out of the corner of his eye. And she didn't fully trust the sudden friendliness that had been in his tone when she'd first arrived. But he *had* laughed.

Adam held his left arm out for Persephone to take, which she did, rising from her seat. "Mr. Hewitt." She nodded her leave of him.

"Your Grace." Mr. Hewitt returned the acknowledgment. "It was a pleasure to meet you."

Adam didn't speak a single word as he led her from the castle, past the formal gardens, under the arch of the inner wall and to the paddock and stables. John Handly was there to greet them, probably having spotted their approach long before they arrived. Falstone was nothing if not expansive. Two stable hands led Zeus and Atlas from the stables. Persephone smiled to herself at the irony of those names.

"Did Atlas behave himself yesterday?" Adam asked without preamble.

"Do you mean did he try to throw me off?"

"He didn't, did he?" Adam actually sounded concerned. Could it be that he cared in some tiny way?

"He was perfectly well behaved," Persephone answered. "Though probably thoroughly bored."

"You weren't jumping fences, then?" Was that a joking tone?

"Only small fences." She borrowed a page from Harry, choosing to reply with a witty rejoinder. Harry insisted that Adam held him in respect. Adam himself called Harry his friend. "We'll be tackling the outer wall this morning."

Another suspicious throat clearing. How Persephone wished he would smile. Smiles had been commonplace in her home growing up.

Persephone realized something in that moment. She wanted Adam's respect. But she wanted to see him smile as well. She wanted him to be happy. And she had no idea how to accomplish that.

"Will you stay and watch my attempts at staying in the saddle?" Persephone tried to make the question sound casual.

"Zeus would never stand for anything so sedate," Adam said.

"Sedate as clearing the outer wall?" Persephone hoped Adam saw the humor in her reply.

He didn't seem to. "Enjoy your lesson," was the extent of his reply.

A moment later, Adam was mounted and riding out the enormous iron gate that marked the entrance to Falstone Castle's fortified courtyards.

Her goals for this marriage, she was beginning to realize, would not be easily achieved. She only hoped they were attainable.

CHAPTER TWELVE

"I DIDN'T POISON THE PORT." Adam and Hewitt sat in uncomfortable silence after dinner the night after the interloper's arrival at Falstone. "It's actually quite good."

"Yes, of course." Hewitt cleared his throat nervously and raised the glass of red liquid shakily to his lips.

Adam managed not to roll his eyes. How could this man possibly be related to him? He had no backbone whatsoever.

"Delicious," Hewitt croaked out, seemingly surprised to find he was, indeed, still alive.

In an apparent effort to please his host, Hewitt threw back his entire portion and promptly found himself in the midst of an all-consuming bout of sputters and coughs. "I . . ." He coughed, making an almost pained face. ". . . that was . . ." He cleared his throat several times. ". . . delicious." Hewitt wiped a tear from his eyes. "Delicious."

"Yes." Adam nodded, taking a more moderate portion from his own glass and watching Hewitt quite as if nothing untoward had just occurred. "What brings you to Falstone?" Adam set his glass on the table and turned his intense gaze on his cousin.

Hewitt went just a touch pale. *Coward.* "My—my mother." His voice even cracked as he spoke, despite his being several years Adam's senior. "She suggested I stop on my way back to Yorkshire."

"Unless you were returning by way of Scotland, I seriously doubt Falstone was 'on your way' to Yorkshire."

Hewitt cleared his throat and looked very much as if he wished for another glass of port, sputtering or no. "I did tell

Mother that." Hewitt tugged at his cravat. "She felt certain you wouldn't mind."

No doubt she also wouldn't mind if Hewitt fingered a few things to take back with him to the bevy of "G"s at home.

"How do you find your accommodations?" Adam propped his elbows on the table, interlocking his fingers and resting his chin on them, keeping his eyes glued to Hewitt's face. The scrutiny made Hewitt fidget. People always revealed more than they planned when they felt uncomfortable.

"The Orange Chamber is . . . is very . . ." Hewitt finally decided on "quiet."

"Quiet?"

Hewitt looked away. The Orange Chamber could be very quiet—it being the most remote of the castle's fifty-plus guest chambers.

"It has a fine view," Adam added. The Orange Chamber over-looked the back courtyard of Falstone, where the remains of a still-usable gibbet and stocks stood. Adam wondered if Hewitt recognized what he saw out his bedchamber windows.

"Yes," Hewitt said quietly.

Adam stood. "Let us join Her Grace in the drawing room."

Adam let his eyebrows furrow as he led the way from the dining room, Hewitt only a few steps behind him. The man was as much of an idiot as he had been on his last visit, even if he had refrained from summing up the value of his future acquisitions. Probably because there was nothing left for him to assess.

A footman opened the drawing room doors as Adam and Hewitt approached, effectively warning Persephone of their arrival. In fact, she watched the door as they entered, a smile touching her face, though not the blinding smile she'd offered Harry the morning before.

Adam felt an inexplicable twinge of regret.

"I am afraid we haven't much to offer by way of entertainment," Persephone said to Hewitt. "I am hardly a musician, nor am I much of a conversationalist."

The apology grated at Adam. She ought not to feel the need to apologize to Hewitt. He was the interloper, the uninvited guest.

Hewitt ought to be whimpering and sniveling and taking himself off in a fit of devastation at her very presence. Persephone's arrival at Falstone, as far as Hewitt knew, spelled the end of any hope the G. Hewitts had of getting their hands on the Kielder legacy.

"Then we must simply speak of Shropshire, Your Grace." Much of Hewitt's early discomfort dissipated. "I passed through your home county only this week, you must realize."

"Did you, indeed?" Persephone's eyes widened with obvious pleasure. "How did you find Shropshire?" She motioned for Hewitt to take the chair near the sofa where she sat.

Silently daring both Hewitt and Persephone to gawk at him, Adam took his seat directly beside his wife and attempted to appear enthralled by their discussion of various types of trees and wildlife. He found, however, that his gaze, which he intended to have shifted between Hewitt and Persephone as they spoke, kept returning to his wife.

He hadn't seen her so animated in the three-plus weeks she'd been at Falstone. Harry had occasionally brought a twinkle to her eyes. But she seemed to have come alive under Hewitt's influence.

Adam didn't like it at all.

"Both boys are on the *Triumphant,*" Persephone said to Hewitt.

"Both together?"

"My grandfather called in a few favors, I believe," Persephone said. "Linus was so young when they left. We all felt better knowing Evander would be with him."

"I doubt Evander was much older."

Persephone shook her head. "He was twelve."

"A little young to be starting in the navy," Hewitt acknowledged.

"Far too young for my comfort." For the first time, Adam heard worry in her tone. She'd spoken of her brothers before, but never with such feeling. Why had Hewitt inspired such confessions when he, her husband, received little more than a laundry list of information about her life and family?

Because that is the way it should be, Adam reminded himself. He begged confidences from no one.

"They are in the Atlantic, then?"

Persephone nodded. "Not far from Spain, last I heard."

"There is a great deal of activity in that part of the world just now."

"Do not remind me," Persephone said. "I worry over them almost constantly."

"Each has the other to look after him, though." Hewitt offered an understanding smile. "And, if my understanding of our naval men is accurate, they will find a great deal of loyalty in their ship-mates as well."

"Yes, thank you." Persephone returned his smile. "That does put my mind a little at ease."

Hewitt's smile grew, until his eyes met Adam's, and then the smile disappeared in an instant.

That was much better.

* * *

Hewitt had been at Falstone for three days, and Adam was only refraining from strangling the man by sheer willpower. He sniveled and slumped when taken one-on-one but regained his equilibrium in Persephone's presence. Adam watched for any signs of infatua-tion but found none on either side, which was extremely fortunate for Hewitt. Else he would quickly find that not all the rumors about the Duke of Kielder were exaggerations.

Despite theirs being only a budding friendship, Persephone's and Hewitt's ease with one another did not sit well with Adam because, he told himself, it would be impossible to get Hewitt to resent Persephone's presence if he liked her so very much. Hewitt was supposed to see her as a threat, as the one person who could prevent his obtaining his inheritance. Then, when Hewitt was at his most dejected, Adam could throw him out, content in the knowledge that Hewitt would never return.

Adam had taken pains to sit beside Persephone at every oppor-tunity in Hewitt's presence. He was finding it was not much of a chore. She would occasionally produce one of her magnificent smiles, or she would laugh with real enjoyment, and Adam found himself very nearly smiling in response.

Adam grew more adept at maneuvering their relative positions so his unmarred side was exposed to his picturesque bride.

It did occur to Adam on one or two occasions to wonder at his insistence at keeping his scars from her. He hadn't hidden them since his childhood. He had decided then not to allow his deformities to cow him, to not let others use his pain as a weapon. But from the moment he'd seen Persephone in Falstone Chapel, he'd been unwilling—practically *unable*—to give her the opportunity to be disgusted by him. And she hadn't been. Yet.

Hewitt hadn't choked on his port at dinner, Adam noticed as they walked to the drawing room on the third night of Hewitt's sojourn. At least he had improved in that respect. He had, however, quickly backed out of the sitting room that afternoon when Adam had pulled out his dueling pistols. He'd only intended to clean them. *Coward,* Adam remembered with a smile.

Stepping through the drawing room doors, Adam's eyes automatically sought out Persephone. She did not smile up at them at their arrival as she had the last two days but remained seated, bent over a paper in her hands.

Adam tensed. She hadn't obtained another map, had she? He strode across the room, determined not to let Hewitt see her studying the layout of her own home. Upon closer observation, Adam realized the paper was filled with writing, a letter, perhaps.

She seemed to take notice of his approach and looked up at him. Her eyes filled with tears even as more coursed down her face. She looked between Adam and Hewitt, her eyes almost pleading for something, but what, Adam couldn't say.

A sudden surge of sympathy clamped his mouth shut. He did not want emotional attachments, he did not want to feel sympathy or concern.

Hewitt spoke first. "Good heavens. What on earth has happened?"

"There has been a battle." Persephone's voice shook.

Her brothers. Adam felt his stomach knot.

"One week ago," Persephone said.

October 21, Adam calculated in his head.

"Near Cape Trafalgar." Her words were halting and difficult to discern. "The *Triumphant* sustained heavy losses."

"And what of your brothers?" Hewitt asked the question on the tip of Adam's tongue.

The tears picked up pace as her chin began to quiver.

No. Adam sat beside her on the sofa, at a loss.

"Evander is dead."

CHAPTER THIRTEEN

SEVEN DAYS HAD PASSED IN a haze of emotion and grief since word had come of Evander's death at Trafalgar. The great Admiral Nelson had perished during that battle as well. Early estimates were placing the number of dead at more than four hundred with the wounded numbering three times that many. Evander's name had appeared on the first list of the fallen to reach London, one of Papa's uncles having sent word to Shropshire and to herself as soon as he'd read it. Linus's fate remained unknown.

In Persephone's mind, Linus appeared the same way he'd been when he and Evander had left home headed for the sea. He'd tried so hard to appear brave, but his eyes were filled with fear and apprehension. Good heavens, he'd only been a boy, a mere eleven years old. The same age then as Daphne was now. How had she ever allowed him to go?

And now he was alone, having faced the horror of war and, more likely than not, witnessed the death of his brother.

Persephone sat in her corner of the garden where she'd come the day after her wedding to cry out her grief. She felt she ought to have been crying again, but she lacked the energy to allow the grief she felt to express itself further. She had come not to cry but to find solitude.

Since the night that word of Evander had come, she'd been faced at practically every turn with an empathetic Mr. Hewitt and a quieter than ever Adam. She was heartily sick of the both of them.

What she truly wanted was her family.

Persephone closed her eyes, blocking out the dim light of approaching winter. Papa must have been beside himself with grief. Persephone had all but raised Evander from the time he was six, after Mama had died. Her grief pierced her. She could not even begin to imagine the pain of a true parent for his child.

The girls must be at a loss, since none had ever possessed the ability to understand their often-incomprehensible father. He tended to wander about when his mind was burdened, seemingly unreachable. She alone had known how to reach out to him when he was so distanced. But she was too far away to do so now.

And Linus. Was there no one to help Linus?

A shadow passed over Persephone's face. She opened her eyes a sliver. Adam, looking as displeased as ever, stood before her, a long, narrow package tucked under one arm.

"Good afternoon, Adam," Persephone said wanly. She hadn't wanted company.

"Forgive me for intruding." Adam seemed to have read her thoughts. He indicated the package he carried. "This came for you, and I wanted to explain."

"Explain?"

Adam held the package out to her, his mouth set in a grim line. She took it, laying the package across her lap. Adam seemed to grow more uncomfortable. The tension in his jaw increased, his eyes darting between the package and a nearly bare rosebush, all the while avoiding looking at her.

"Please sit, Adam." Her request surprised even herself.

"I am fine," Adam replied gruffly.

For a moment she opted to acquiesce but in the end convinced herself to show a little backbone. "I am not asking for your comfort, Adam, but for my own. I have no desire to strain my neck looking up as you loom over me."

He raised an eyebrow in obvious surprise, but after a moment's hesitation he sat on the stone seat beside her. Persephone hadn't realized how small it was until he was sharing it with her. The contact—for there was actual contact, so small was the seat—proved surprisingly welcome. She needed to feel the comfort of another human being near enough to touch. She needed to feel less alone.

"I have sat as you asked. Now will you open the box?"

She recognized the tone of command. Why did he do that? Order people about when he could just as effectively *ask* for something? She looked more closely at him. As always, he didn't look at her. She could see little more than his left ear and jaw. His demeanor spoke volumes of his discomfort. If she didn't know better, Persephone would think Adam was embarrassed, maybe even shy. But neither description fit the Adam she knew.

"You said you wanted to explain about the package," Persephone reminded him, still watching for any change of expression, any reason for his discomfort.

"*After* you open it," Adam muttered.

Good heavens, he did seem embarrassed. Persephone shook that confusing thought from her head and pulled at the twine. Adam tapped the palm of his hand on his knee, his jaw working as he studied another bare flowering shrub. Not only embarrassed but nervous, it appeared. What in the world was in the package?

Persephone felt a little nervous, herself. She pulled back the paper. The package contained some sort of garment. She ran her finger down what appeared to be the collar but, with her gloves on, could tell very little of the fabric or make. She slipped the glove off her right hand and touched the blue fabric again. Wool, she decided, but by far the softest wool she'd ever touched.

"I ordered it before you went into mourning." Adam's voice was edged with what anyone might interpret as anger, but Persephone thought she heard frustration in his tone. "It ought to have been black, or gray at the least. Considering."

"You ordered this for me?" Persephone brushed her hand down the garment, still amazed at its softness but even more amazed at the unforeseen gesture.

"You cannot ride without a proper riding habit." Adam employed the tone he used that generally made her feel rather slow-witted.

She shifted her gaze and watched him closely. He looked briefly at the habit then let his eyes wander to the right, his head moving with his eyes. Still, his hands fidgeted, his body tensed as if poised for flight. He spoke casually but seemed anything but unaffected. His demeanor and his tone did not precisely match. Why had she never noticed that before? Was this a new discrepancy? Or had she simply been unobservant?

"A riding habit," Persephone quietly repeated, laying her hand on the collar and buttons that she now recognized as the latest fashion for riding habits, having endured Athena's raptures over the latest issue of *La Belle Assemble* in the weeks leading up to her wedding. "You must have great confidence in my ability to learn to ride. Thus far I am proving a very poor pupil."

"You were quite a bit better yesterday," Adam countered, still looking away.

Persephone allowed the tiniest of smiles. He had watched her. She'd had no idea.

"I think it the perfect color," Persephone said. "It may not be black, but it is a very deep blue, quite nearly black. And I can use it after my period of mourning is complete. Evander—" Her voice broke on the name. "—was a very practical boy, considering his youth, and would have approved."

"The boots will take longer," Adam said.

"You've ordered boots as well?"

"Your house slippers are hardly appropriate for riding." His tone gave the impression that he had just rolled his eyes, though with his face turned away, she couldn't see.

"I haven't been wearing slippers." A hint of a laugh entered her voice. She hadn't smiled in a week. How had her gruff, usually grumpy husband managed to pull a laugh from her?

"You might as well have been. You must have true riding boots. They should arrive in the next week. Rogers, in York, is sending a hat. Your gloves are coming from London, so there is no saying how long that will take."

"Gloves from London?" Persephone had never owned anything made in Town. Even her wedding dress has been fashioned by a seamstress closer to Shropshire.

"A good pair of gloves cannot be overestimated." Adam rose rather abruptly.

"I have no idea what to say, Adam," Persephone whispered, her hand brushing the habit but her eyes fixed on him.

"It is not necessary for you to say anything." He held his hands fisted at his side. "I only wished to explain why it was the wrong color."

With that, he left, forehead furrowed, jaw tight.

Persephone shook her head in disbelief. She never would have guessed that Adam would think to order her a riding habit, let alone boots and gloves and a hat. Then to go to the trouble of explaining why it did not take into account her sudden state of mourning. In any other man it would have been a thoughtful gesture. Coming from Adam, it was nothing short of utterly confusing.

She lifted a sleeve, rubbing the soft wool against her cheek. He'd been uncomfortable, that much was certain. And though no one would believe her—she hardly believed herself—he'd given every appearance of embarrassment. The Duke of Kielder, who, if rumor and her own observations were to be believed, cared not at all for his fellow man, had been uncomfortable being found out in an act of kindness.

The fidgets he'd so conspicuously been trying to hide reminded Persephone forcefully of her sister Daphne. She, too, grew antsy around others. But, then, she was painfully shy.

"Good heavens," Persephone whispered. Could the angry, snapping, aloof man actually be covering his own shyness? It seemed absurd, and yet . . .

"Adam!" she called out, clutching the riding habit to her as she hurried down the path she'd seen him take. "Adam!"

Only a few feet from the garden's entrance she saw him. He'd stopped and looked over his shoulder in her direction. She could make out the very edge of the scars that crossed his right cheek, Adam having presented her with his left side as always.

Embarrassed, she thought, with an inward shake of her head. Why hadn't she seen it before? He had at least a touch of shyness— she would be willing to wager a thousand pounds on it, more even.

"Adam," she said, just a little breathless from her run.

He didn't reply but watched her with that same aloof expression that she had begun to doubt was completely sincere.

"Thank you, Adam," she said quickly. "For the habit. I—"

Adam shook his head. "You needed one." He dismissed her gratitude. "No duchess should ride around the countryside with her ankles exposed."

So he was uncomfortable with gratitude, was he? *Interesting,* Persephone thought as Adam walked back toward the house. *Very interesting.*

Persephone watched Adam at dinner that night and in the drawing room afterward. He acted the same as he always had, no hint of discomfort or embarrassment. Why was that? Did she alone make him uncomfortable? Or was it the gifting that had unnerved him? Perhaps she had misinterpreted his mood.

How she wished Harry were back. He would be able to advise her.

"You seem thoughtful, Your Grace," Mr. Hewitt said, breaking into her thoughts.

"I suppose I am."

"Have you heard from your family?" He spoke with as much gentleness as any woman could desire when the weight of a lost sibling and an unreachable husband sat on her heart. "You must certainly wish for their nearness at such a time."

Persephone answered with nothing more than a small smile and retook the book she'd been pretending to read all night. While she appreciated Mr. Hewitt's attempts at solicitude, she found that he had the uncanny ability to bring tears to her eyes with his kindnesses. She had no desire to cry at that moment.

"I believe you are distressing the duchess." Adam's voice came quite suddenly from near Mr. Hewitt's chair. Persephone looked up. Adam stood at Mr. Hewitt's arm. "I suggest you take yourself off."

Mr. Hewitt cleared his throat nervously and rose hastily from his seat. "I am a little weary, at that." He eyed Adam with obvious apprehension. "Perhaps I should retire for the night."

"Excellent notion, Hewitt."

Mr. Hewitt scurried away—Persephone couldn't think of another word for the way he hied himself from the room—and Adam took the seat he'd vacated. They were now occupying chairs directly opposite one another. He would be forced to look at her, Persephone realized.

She lifted her eyes once more from her book only to find his gaze fixed, as always, to his right. "Look at me!" she felt like screaming. She was miles from her family, in a castle that felt nothing like a home to her, with no one to talk to, to feel a connection with, and he would not so much as look at her.

Frustration bubbling up inside, she raised her book once more and said, "Mr. Hewitt was trying to be consoling."

"He was making you teary again," Adam countered. "I got the distinct impression you did not wish to cry tonight."

Now how, Persephone wondered, had he come to that conclusion?

CHAPTER FOURTEEN

HE NEVER SHOULD HAVE BOUGHT the bloody riding habit. Adam threw open the glass-inlaid doors of his book room, inviting the sting of cold night air. It had been a whim, he told himself. Persephone had needed a habit. He could just as well have left ordering one up to her. Why he'd taken it upon himself, Adam couldn't say. And, of course, he'd made a mull of it.

That was what came of acting impulsively. He'd sent out the order that first day Persephone had attempted to ride. He hadn't even waited to see if she stuck with the undertaking. And, as if anxious to add to his folly, he'd also sent out orders for boots, gloves, and a riding hat. Her measurements had been taken by a highly recommended seamstress in York, should she require anything be made. That circumstance had made making a fool of himself far too easy.

But, unbidden, came the image of Persephone brushing her fingers along the fabric of her new habit. He knew the wool was particularly fine, he'd seen it on his last trip to York. Its quality was, in fact, the reason he'd specifically requested the habit be made from that bolt of wool.

"A person ought to be comfortable when riding," Adam told himself firmly. His choice had nothing to do with the fact that he'd known, almost instinctively, that she would be delighted by the softness of it. He never indulged in that sort of sentimentality.

A howl cut through the silence of the night. Adam glanced out over the forest, the home of England's only remaining pack of wolves. If one insisted on complete accuracy, the pack in Falstone Forest were not technically wolves. Over the centuries since the forest was planted, the wolves who had lived there mingled with feral dogs that had found their way inside. But the resulting mongrels looked and acted like wolves, so the word stuck. Besides, if any man in England ought to have his own personal pack of wolves, the Duke of Kielder ought. So he never corrected the locals. Wolves he wanted, so wolves he had.

Another howl pierced the air. The pack was more vocal on winter nights than any other time of the year. The scarcity of food, no doubt, required they hunt more than in milder seasons. Being confined to such a small stretch of woodland significantly limited their sources of nourishment. The pack always ended the winter fewer in number than it had begun.

Other than the wind, which seemed never to cease from November on through the winter, and the occasional sounds of the pack echoing from the forest, winters were quiet at Falstone. The nights, Adam had found long ago, could be completely silent otherwise.

"I wonder what Persephone will think of that." The moment he spoke the thought, Adam clamped his mouth shut. Had he lost his mind entirely? At what point had he begun to care what other people thought of his home?

He spun around, slamming the doors shut behind him. He would not turn into a sentimental fool. He didn't care what others thought. Of him. Of his home. Nothing anyone said impacted him in the least—hadn't for years, in fact. That, he told himself as he stepped inside his bedchamber, was not going to change.

Except that he couldn't seem to get out of his mind the memory of Persephone stroking that wool. She really had appreciated it, noticed its softness.

Adam flung his jacket on to a chair, followed by his waistcoat.

Persephone had seemed sincere when she'd thanked him for it. Not that he'd wanted her gratitude. Gratitude could be as painful as pity.

Where had that ridiculous thought come from?

Somewhere in Falstone Forest another wolf howled into the night.

"Precisely," Adam grunted and dropped onto his bed, having dismissed his valet, something he'd been doing more often lately. He hadn't altered his routine in ten years or more. Now he was buying his wife clothes on a whim, cutting his ride short to watch Persephone's riding lessons, lying awake on his bed, not bothering to change into his nightshirt, listening to the wolves break the silence of the night.

"I'm losing my bloody mind." It was not a comforting thought.

Adam closed his eyes and took a deep, calming breath. He seldom needed to calm himself. Adam prided himself on never being truly riled or out of control. Few people would believe as much, most being convinced he was apt to snap in a fit of rage or anger. But he never actually lost control of his emotions.

Frustration threatened to overwhelm him: frustration with himself, with the sham of a marriage he'd brought on himself, with his own stupidity in allowing another person's judgment to take the place of his in a matter as important as choosing his wife.

His father wouldn't have done anything so brainless. The Old Duke, as most of the Falstone staff still called Adam's father, had been decisive and strong and unyielding, never vacillating over a decision or being cowed by another person's disapproval.

Dukes, Adam had learned early on, were authoritative and strong. They didn't worry about being liked. They didn't hide from the world, no matter how much they wished to. Dukes knew their responsibilities and carried out their duties to the letter. They commanded attention. And they were never weak.

So why, over the past week, had Adam, seeing Persephone's visible pain at the loss of a brother so young and so obviously dear, found himself wishing he knew what to say, what to do when tears crept into her eyes or when she seemed to suddenly retreat into herself?

Tears are weakness. He'd been told as much many times. Weak and vulnerable. Dukes are neither. Duchesses, neither, he would guess. Adam had never seen his mother cry. She looked pityingly at him, but she never shed a tear. He'd assumed Persephone would be the same. Now he didn't know what to do.

His door scraped open. Had Hewitt come to murder him in his sleep? The thought brought a laughing grin to Adam's face. The man really was an idiot. Obviously he didn't realize Adam kept a gun in his room.

"Adam?"

No. That was Persephone. What the deuce was she doing in his bedchamber? Adam kept himself still, not opening his eyes or indicating he was awake. Maybe she would go away.

A howl echoed outside. On its heels came the sound of Persephone taking a shaky breath. "Adam?" she asked again.

He didn't answer. A second howl filled the silence. Adam heard Persephone's footfall, soft and quiet. He opened one eye just a sliver. Was she leaving? No. She had merely crossed to his window, pulled back one of the heavy velvet curtains, and peered outside.

What was she looking for? A third wolf call answered Adam's unspoken question. Persephone let the curtain drop on the instant and took another haggard breath.

"Why won't they stop?" she whispered to herself. She sounded genuinely worried.

She was afraid of the wolves? That was hardly sensible. The pack was out in the forest, while she was within the walls of the castle. What harm could they possibly do?

"You are fine," he heard Persephone say to herself.

Adam managed to stop the smile that wanted to spread across his face. She had some steel to her, he had to admit.

"They're far away," she continued softly, moving slowly back toward the door connecting his bedchamber to hers. She looked more like a little girl than a duchess, wrapped as she was in a thick blanket, her bare feet peeking out beneath the edge. "They can't possibly—"

Another howl.

Something like a whimper escaped from the retreating blanket, and before Adam had a chance to even contemplate what she was doing, Persephone climbed onto the opposite side of his bed, curled into what looked like a ball of blanket.

Yet another poorly thought-out plan of his had backfired. If he'd simply answered her when she'd come in and sent her back to her room with a flea in her ear, he wouldn't be in such a predicament. She was in his room, one of his sanctuaries, one of the places no one ever came. And she was acting like a coward.

She had tried, he told himself, then just as quickly dismissed the obvious justification.

"I'm sorry, Adam," she suddenly whispered. For a moment he thought she realized he'd only pretended to sleep. To be found out shamming his wife was rather humiliating, a feeling he was not accustomed to. But she continued on, much to Adam's relief. It seemed she believed she was apologizing to her sleeping husband. "I am trying to be brave."

She, apparently, never gained any courage. Persephone remained wrapped in her cocoon on his bed all that night. Adam knew she hadn't left—he'd hardly slept. He was unaccustomed to the sound of another person breathing in his room—not to mention the little noises she made while she slept, and the fact that she moved several times an hour.

Sometime before dawn, Persephone awoke. Adam did as well, and watched, though he feigned sleep, as she walked slowly and quietly from the room, still wrapped in her blanket. It seemed as if she didn't want him to know she'd been there.

The wolves, he noticed, were silent. Adam wondered if Persephone would have remained if they'd still been howling. Was she more afraid of them or of him? He was used to being feared, but, inexplicably, he almost hoped she found the wolves the more fearsome possibility.

* * *

"Of course you must see to your mother," Persephone said to Hewitt that afternoon as one of the Kielder coaches was being loaded with the man's mountains of traveling trunks. Other than an extra dose of awkwardness when Adam had first encountered her earlier in the morning, Persephone gave no indication that anything out of the ordinary had occurred the night before. So she didn't plan to admit to her fear or her unexpected remedy? Adam didn't know what he thought about that.

He listened to the exchange as he stood beside Persephone, deliberately placing himself where Hewitt was certain to notice his close proximity to his wife. Let Hewitt leave with the picture of marital bliss, feigned though it was—fresh in his mind to make him uneasy all the way back to York.

"I hope she is not terribly ill," Persephone said.

Hewitt shook his head. "My mother fancies herself ill when I have been gone longer than expected."

Rather tied to the apron strings, wasn't he?

"That must impact your ability to travel freely." Persephone seemed quite empathetic to Hewitt's cause, as if he hadn't brought most of the inconvenience on himself by putting up with his parent's nonsense as he had.

Hewitt nodded.

Adam shook his head. "Haven't you any brothers capable of tending her?" Hewitt had obviously never thought the problem through very well.

A nervous cough preceded Hewitt's reply. If only the man would grow a spine and learn to speak up for himself. Thinking of that slug of a man as the next Duke of Kielder positively nauseated Adam.

"My brothers are quite capable," Hewitt said, still that faint hint of apology in his tone. "But as the eldest son, I feel, morally, ethically, it really is my responsibility. My duty."

So Hewitt did have an ounce of conviction in him, after all. Adam hated to make the begrudging concession, but he was never one to deny giving credit where it was due. Hewitt was still an idiot—reference the rather pathetic conversation they'd had over port the night before.

"The woods in this part of the country are quite impressive," Hewitt had said. "To think the Druids, themselves, may well have walked beneath those very trees."

"Provided the Druids had the ability to travel across time," Adam had answered dryly. "Falstone Forest has only been in existence for four hundred years."

How could a man so ignorant of the traditions surrounding Falstone and the Kielder holdings possibly be in line to inherit them? Idiot.

"Do come visit again," Adam heard Persephone say to Hewitt. Before he had a chance to contradict her invitation, Hewitt was passing beneath the inner arch and on his way from Falstone.

Persephone looked up at Adam, her expression unreadable. "He can no longer see you."

Adam raised an eyebrow in inquiry. What had that comment signified?

"You need not keep pretending that you enjoy standing beside me." She turned and slowly, with almost tangible dignity, made her way through the enormous front doors of Falstone Castle.

Gone, it seemed, was the quaking figure who had hidden from wolves during the night. Adam appreciated her courage—he always applauded shows of spirit—but the stinging rebuke she'd served him along with it struck home with more force than he cared for.

"Should have tossed her off the bed with the first noise she made." But he heard in his voice something he hadn't heard in years: a threat that came across as completely hollow.

CHAPTER FIFTEEN

"Adam?" Dinner had been completely silent through the first three courses, and, with dessert all but finished, Persephone felt the tension acutely.

"Another complaint, Persephone?" Adam replied with deceptive calm. Persephone could hear the anger just below the surface. "I have refrained from standing anywhere near you all day."

How had she allowed her tongue to get away with her? They'd reached something of an accord in the garden the day before, over his unexpected gift. Now he was on his guard again, borderline hostile and cynical.

"I am sorry for what I said." Persephone hoped he heard the sincerity in her voice. "I really haven't been myself these last few days."

In the little more than a week since news of Evander had arrived, Persephone had been completely at loose ends. One moment, she felt calm and quite in control; the next, she was either weeping with unbearable sadness or angry or exhausted beyond all reason. It was unnerving. And, worst of all, she felt completely alone in her suffering.

Seeing Mr. Hewitt, who had been her one source of empathy throughout the horrific ordeal, depart had pushed her past her limit, and she'd spoken a thought she'd never intended to voice. She'd noticed Adam's tendency to hover nearby when Mr. Hewitt was in the room. At first she'd allowed herself the flattering thought that Adam had developed a preference for her company, followed by the equally heady sensation that he might be a touch jealous. She'd soon noticed, however, that Adam's attentions dwindled back to nonexistence when Mr. Hewitt was not nearby.

It hadn't taken a great deal of thought to understand what actually lay behind the odd behavior. Adam intended to convince Mr. Hewitt that theirs was a happy marriage—one that would, no doubt, destroy his claim to the Kielder title. She'd been nothing but a puppet in Adam's ongoing efforts to upset and belittle his cousin.

"Harry wrote today." Adam spoke quite as if Persephone's apology had never been uttered.

She lowered her eyes to her trifle. "I hope he is well." She managed to squeeze past the sudden lump in her throat.

There she went again, emotions swinging like a pendulum. Adam had certainly been indifferent before. Why this particular moment of apathy should so undo her, Persephone could not say.

"He is remaining in Scotland for a week longer than anticipated," Adam said.

"Harry must be enjoying his visit with his aunt and uncle." Her voice dropped to little more than a whisper. Trying to muster another bit of volume would surely reduce her to tears.

She had apologized, blast him! Couldn't he have had the civility to acknowledge that?

Adam continued eating with as little discomfort as one could possibly have. He didn't care at all. This was the man she'd been so certain only the day before was kind and shy underneath his harsh exterior? How had she been so blind, so gullible?

Oh, why had she ever left Shropshire? She could have been at home at that very moment with her family, with a sympathetic shoulder to cry on, surrounded by people who cared deeply for each other.

Persephone rose hastily to her feet, fighting back a flood of bitter, lonely tears. "Excuse me," she said, her voice shaking. She ran in an unladylike manner from the room.

One of the first things she'd learned about the castle was how to get outside. While outside, she could orient herself far easier than when indoors. But orientation was the last thing on her mind as she fled the drain of Falstone Castle for the sanctuary of her garden. It was the only piece of Falstone she, albeit secretly, claimed for herself. That alcove of greenery had shared her deepest sorrows in the month she'd been the Duchess of Kielder. No human being could lay claim to such an involvement in her life during the short weeks she'd been at the castle.

She dropped onto the patch of earth directly in front of her bench, laid her arms across the stone seat, and dropped her head onto her arms.

"I just want to go home," she cried. "I need my family."

Quite as if she hadn't wept more times than she cared to remember over the past week, Persephone sobbed as she sat there on the cold, damp ground.

Evander was far too young to be gone. He'd not even reached his fifteenth birthday. Someone ought to have been looking out for him. Someone ought to have been keeping him safe. He should have been at school with nothing more threatening than exams and teachers.

Persephone had married to secure his fortune. What good was that fortune now?

Her throat burned, her lungs shuddering with each breath. She could not regain control of her sobs.

Something dropped onto the stone bench near her face, rustling and whooshing as it did. She raised her head from her arms just long enough to look. She could make out only a pile of brown fabric. Persephone laid her head back on her arms, just looking at the material through the tears that continued to fall.

"You didn't bring a coat." Adam's clipped tone was easily recognizable.

The lump of wool, apparently, was her brown coat.

Her breaths continued to shudder. Words were not possible.

"That's all." And his footsteps began sounding a retreat.

It was such cold civility. Any one of her family members would have urged her to return to the house, offered words of solitude, or simply sat beside her in empathetic silence. Persephone turned her head away from the lump that was Adam's sole offer of comfort: a coat he'd dumped on the seat beside her.

"I want to go home," Persephone whispered in agony to herself.

* * *

Adam watched as Persephone continued to sit on the cold earth, head turned away from the coat he'd brought her, as if she had no intention of putting it on. "It won't do you any good on the bench," he muttered under his breath. He stood not more than twenty paces from where she sat, close enough to see her shudder.

He'd brought her the coat. What more did she want? He had no idea why she'd left—she'd *run*. Adam knew she was upset about something. He'd seen her out in the garden where she always went to cry, on the ground, at night, without a coat. He'd made an effort. And she couldn't be bothered to put the bloody coat on!

"What more do you want?" Adam muttered. He knew exactly what she wanted. He heard her say as much only moments before. She wanted to go home.

No doubt to be with her family in her grief. Adam wondered for a brief moment if his mother would grieve so all-consumingly should he meet an untimely end. They'd never been close, so he couldn't really say. It was an insight into himself with which he was not at all comfortable. Would anyone cry for him the way Persephone wept for her brother?

"Hewitt won't," Adam muttered. Every one of the Brothers "G" would rejoice should Adam be struck down by a bolt of punitive lightning.

Harry might miss him once in a while. Persephone certainly wouldn't. Except during the occasional round of howls from the Falstone wolves. She might think of him then.

Adam's eyes drifted back to Persephone. She had made no move to leave. She still didn't have her coat on.

"Foolish woman," Adam mumbled. But he was already retracing his steps to where she sat.

Her sobs had relented somewhat. Adam actually felt relieved to hear some steadiness return to her breathing. Only because he disliked crying, he told himself.

"You'll catch an inflammation of the lungs," Adam told Persephone after he'd stood uncertainly over her for more than a few awkward moments. "Everyone in London will accuse me of poisoning you."

A strangled sort of laugh broke Persephone's silence. Adam couldn't remember making anyone, other than Harry, laugh. But Harry laughed at everything. Persephone seemed more selective.

He had the sudden, impulsive desire to wrap that deuced coat around her, carry her back into the castle, and deposit her safely in front of the largest fire he could find, where she could thaw out. He shook his head to dislodge the thought, but it wouldn't be dismissed.

Opting for a compromise, Adam lifted her coat—it looked serviceable enough, no doubt a leftover from her days of poverty— from the bench. "You'll be warmer inside," he told her, knowing what would have been a gentle invitation from a decent sort of husband had come across as an order from him.

But she seemed willing to comply. Persephone shifted from her position, sitting back from the bench but not looking up at him.

"With Hewitt and Harry gone, the castle will be quiet." Adam tempered his tone in a way he hadn't in some time, and didn't plan to again soon. "You can find a . . . private spot and . . . do . . . whatever it is you do after you cry."

"I usually sleep," Persephone answered quietly. "And wake up with a headache."

"Sounds awful."

She nodded and slowly rose to her feet. Adam handed her the coat, which she did little more than drape over her shoulders.

"Then why cry?" It seemed a rather ridiculous thing to do, knowing ahead of time what the end result would be.

"Generally, I can't help myself." Persephone wiped her cheek with the palm of her hand.

She, then, hadn't learned the art of securing a tourniquet around her emotions.

"Come on, then." Adam felt ever more uncomfortable now that the dim light of the half-hidden moon and the light spilling from the castle windows made Persephone's continued drip of tears visible. He led the way out of the garden, hearing her footsteps behind him.

He knew he probably ought to have said something, but he couldn't think of a single thing worth verbalizing. Empty reassurances about her brother's bravery or heroism wouldn't ease her pain. Saying he knew how she felt would be a bald-faced lie. Professing any tender attachment or caring concern on his part would be no less untrue. Adam cared for no one. Just as no one cared for him.

Persephone's little sister, the tiny one—Artemis was her name, he thought—had asked who would take care of Persephone, before Artemis had left for Shropshire.

Adam heard a shaky breath on the path behind him and thought he could picture the girl's tiny face—one so much like her sister's, her mouth twisted in a line of disapproval, brow furrowed with worry the way it had been during that brief conversation.

No one, it seemed, was watching out for Persephone.

CHAPTER SIXTEEN

IT WAS A VERY GOOD thing Adam slept so deeply, Persephone thought to herself over her breakfast tea the next morning. The wolves hadn't been particularly loud the night before, but she hadn't felt well. As predicted, her head had begun to ache not long after she'd retired to her bed. While the tears had stopped, she still had an ache in her heart that might very well never go away.

She'd walked slowly, quietly to the connecting door of their bedchambers, just as she had the night before last. Again, Adam didn't respond when she whispered his name. She'd tried several times. Convinced he slept, Persephone did as she had the previous night. Wrapped tightly against the cold, she'd climbed onto his bed, careful not to wake him.

Odd that being near him allowed her to sleep so quickly. She had always shared a room with Athena. Perhaps she simply needed the reassuring familiarity of another person in the room. Yet, comforting as it was in the moment, she knew a very real fear that should Adam discover her there, he would not find the intrusion welcome.

"You've missed your riding lesson this morning." Adam's voice suddenly sounded from the doorway of the breakfast room.

Persephone looked up in momentary alarm. She shook her head inwardly. He couldn't possibly know what she'd just been thinking. She managed to make sense of his statement and forced a reply. "I am afraid I overslept." She'd tiptoed back to her room at first light, determined to leave before Adam realized she'd been there.

"And how is your head this morning?" Adam still stood in the breakfast room doorway, his eyes slightly diverted, looking out the windows behind her.

"My head?"

"You said last night that your head hurts after you've been crying."

He'd remembered that? "It does ache a little," she admitted, surprised but not unpleasantly.

"There is an apothecary in Sifton," Adam said. "I could send one of the grooms for some powders."

Too shocked by his unforeseen offer to verbalize a reply, Persephone shook her head.

Adam hovered a moment longer, as if trying to decide on his next course of action. When had she ever seen Adam appear uncertain? The answer came in the form of a memory of the two of them sitting on a bench in her garden the day Adam had given her the riding habit. He'd seemed remarkably uncertain then and uncomfortable. Very much like he appeared standing just then in the doorway.

"Do you use this apothecary often?" Persephone asked the first question that came to her mind.

"I am seldom ill." He made the declaration as if it were a matter of pride, a tremendous accomplishment. "But he is utilized when someone on the staff is unwell."

"Sifton is nearby, then?" Persephone asked, pursuing the topic in the hope that Adam would fully enter the room, perhaps come sit by her. She was still unaccustomed to eating her meals alone. And, she had to admit, he intrigued her. He'd been autocratic and strictly civil the night before in the garden. At that moment he seemed very nearly human.

"Sifton is almost an hour's ride," Adam said. "Kielder Village is closer but has no apothecary, nor a physician, for that matter."

"How far away is the nearest physician?"

Adam still hovered, still avoided looking at her.

"There is a surgeon living in Hawick." His reply was characteristically short. "The town of Sifton has a physician, but he is useless."

Another person evaluated, judged, and dismissed by Adam. The physician probably wasn't *entirely* useless. Persephone had come to realize in the month she'd spent at Falstone that, while often harsher than necessary, Adam's evaluations of others held more than a grain of truth.

He'd described Harry as a friend who took too many liberties. That, to a degree, was accurate. Harry was his friend. And, compared with every other person Adam knew, Harry was familiar and comfortable with him in the extreme. Adam didn't seem to understand that Harry's behavior was normal and acceptable for a *friend*.

Persephone had heard Adam describe Mr. Hewitt as a "spineless idiot." Again, the label proved harsher than warranted. But, she had to admit, when compared to Harry, Mr. Hewitt did come across as too easily intimidated. And, when compared with Adam, who Persephone had begun to realize was remarkably sharp, Mr. Hewitt didn't impress one as overly intelligent.

"John, at the stables, indicated that Atlas can be saddled whenever you would like to have your riding lesson," Adam said after the silence had stretched on. "Though it does look like Falstone will shortly have rain—snow if the temperature continues to drop."

"I am not sure I am up for a ride today, anyway."

"Are you certain you do not wish for some powders?" For a moment, his eyes darted to her face. He actually looked concerned.

Persephone hadn't expected that. It was, by far, the most encouraging sign she'd had from him in some time. "Rest is all I really need. But thank you for offering." She smiled, hoping to break through his icy exterior.

Again her gratitude seemed to unnerve him. He gave a crisp shake of his head before stepping from the doorway and disappearing down the corridor.

Persephone laid her napkin on the table and rose from her seat, making her way to the doorway. She knew Adam would not still be there—that he had, no doubt, retreated into his book room already. Still, she looked down the empty corridor in the direction he'd gone, wondering if he had any idea how perplexing a man he was.

Why did he keep people at a distance? Why did he go to such lengths to appear uncaring when he had shown her—inadvertently, she was certain—twice that he did, indeed, care, at least a little? And if he did care even the slightest bit, was that not reason enough to try to make their marriage work?

A faint knock echoed along the walls of the stone corridor. Persephone had never before lived in a house so large that a knock on the front door sounded, when heard from a few rooms away, like little more than mice in the walls. The knock was followed immediately by an almost frantic ringing of the front bell.

She moved quickly down the corridor and onto the front landing. Adam stood at the head of the staircase, watching as Barton opened the front door.

"Urgent message for His Grace," a breathless voice said.

Persephone looked at Adam. His expression hadn't changed, but something in his demeanor had tensed. Despite the subtle change, Adam remained calm and in control.

"Your Grace." Barton bowed and handed Adam the missive.

Adam nodded, and Barton made his way back down the stairs. Persephone watched Adam read, feeling herself tense as Adam's jaw noticeably clenched. He finished the letter in less than a minute.

"Barton!" he called out. The butler reached the foot of the stairs in an instant, awaiting instructions. "Send word to the stables to send up the chaise." Adam walked down the stairs. Persephone followed close on his heels, her concern growing. "And send someone to Sifton for Mr. Johns."

"Yes, Your Grace." With a look, Barton sent one of the footmen out the door to deliver the message.

"Are you leaving, Adam?" Persephone asked as they reached the bottom stair.

"Almost on the instant." To Barton he said, "Tell Mrs. Smithson to prepare Mr. Windover's usual room."

"Harry?" Persephone's heart pounded. "Is something the matter with Harry?"

Adam turned toward her, seeming to forget in his anxiety not to look at her. "He's taken ill at an inn between here and Hawick."

"Is it serious?"

"Apparently so."

She pushed down a surge of panic. "What do you plan to do?"

"Go retrieve him, of course." His words were clipped and tense. "If the stables ever send my carriage, that is," he snapped, pacing to a front window and peering out impatiently.

"I'm certain they are doing the best they can." She crossed to the window where he stood and gazed out along with him. "It has begun to snow," she said, alarmed anew.

"Precisely why I wish to make an immediate start."

"But is it safe?" Persephone watched the sprinkling of snow as it continued to drift to the ground. "If the snow should begin to fall faster, you might become stuck."

"I can reach the inn before then." Adam turned toward Barton as he arrived with Adam's caped greatcoat.

"But you might be snowed in." The very idea alarmed her. Suppose the inn was not well heated? Suppose he didn't reach the inn in time? Her heart lurched at the thought.

Adam just shrugged.

"How will I know you are safe?" Hundreds of possible scenarios flashed through her mind.

"If I do not return for the night, you can assume I am holed up in the undoubtedly flea-infested hostelry Harry has chosen to take ill in."

"I will assume no such thing." Persephone turned from the window to look up at him. How could he think she would be so easily appeased? "Simply not returning will tell me nothing. You could just as easily be half-frozen on the side of some road or devoured by wolves or ill yourself."

"I have driven these roads for years," Adam said dismissively. "I have never once broken down."

"You have to promise me you will be careful." The insistence in her tone surprised her.

"Persephone." Adam said in way of censure, but he looked more surprised than upset.

"If you don't promise me, I will worry." She worried already. He may not have been the husband of her dreams, but she cared what happened to him. And, despite his gruff demeanor, she knew he was kind and gentle, at least in moments. He'd brought her a coat, bought her a riding habit, asked after her well-being.

"Why would you worry about me?" As the chaise pulled in front of the castle, he made his way to the front doors.

"Why wouldn't I?"

Adam turned back to her once more, actually looking at her for the second time in a matter of minutes. He seemed so utterly, completely confused by her show of basic human compassion. "No one has ever worried about me, Persephone." It was a simple statement—no self-pity, no bitterness or a sense of having been wronged.

"Someone does now," Persephone said.

His brows furrowed, his eyes betraying his confusion. "Don't."

Persephone smiled a little at that. "I'm afraid I can't help it."

"Like crying?" he asked, the tiniest hint of lightness in his tone.

Persephone nodded, remembering their conversation from the night before.

"Worrying will probably give you a headache as well," Adam warned, as Barton opened the front doors.

"Then spare me the headache and promise you will be cautious." She followed him out, the cold air chilling her on the spot.

Adam looked back from the chaise as he alighted the step. "I will be cautious," he said.

Even though he'd looked a touch annoyed, that concession stuck with Persephone as the hours dragged on. It hadn't precisely been an acknowledgment of her concern, but he hadn't completely dismissed her worries, either. He had promised to be careful. Persephone was certain that once Adam gave his word, he could be depended on to abide by that promise.

Dusk came without any sign of Adam or Harry. Mr. Johns, the apothecary from Sifton, had arrived in time to take dinner, though as the hours passed and the snow began falling once more, it became obvious he would not be leaving Falstone that evening.

"Oh, Adam," Persephone whispered, feeling tears stinging her eyes once more. She watched the front drive from the tall windows of the library. The snowfall picked up pace, the wind blowing more fiercely. Adam had not returned.

At what point should she stop watching? Persephone didn't know how far from Falstone the inn sat nor how long the journey could be expected to take. Suppose Adam was caught in the dark of night only miles from home? It was bound to be an extremely cold night. And there were the wolves.

"Please," she pleaded quietly with the heavens. "You've taken Evander. Please do not take my husband as well."

As if in answer to her prayer, the barely distinguishable silhouette of a traveling chaise made its way to the front steps of the castle. In the light that spilled from the castle windows, Persephone watched as Adam stepped from the door of the carriage.

Even as she breathed a sigh of relief, Persephone spun from the window and moved quickly from the library, down the corridor to the first-floor landing in time to see Adam, directing two footmen behind him, step into the entry hall. She'd worried for him more than she'd thought she would, and she'd missed him terribly, considering he probably hadn't thought of her once in all the time he was gone.

"Take him directly to his chambers," Adam ordered the footmen. "Is Mr. Johns here?"

"Yes, Your Grace," Barton answered.

"Send him to Mr. Windover's chambers."

Harry, pale and inert, was carried past where Persephone stood on the staircase. He was more obviously ill than she had expected him to be. Even the sight of Harry being bodily carried to his room didn't prevent Persephone's eyes from returning to Adam. He looked a little pale as well.

Adam's eyes lifted to meet hers for a moment. Persephone thought she heard him let out a tense breath. It was the tiniest hint of vulnerability, but it pulled at her heart. Finally, she'd seen some indication that Adam might need her.

She took the steps between them at twice the speed she would have otherwise. "You're home." Persephone allowed her relief to be heard in her voice.

"I told you I would be careful." His usual gruffness nearly disappeared in the weariness so heavy in his tone.

"I suppose I should have believed you." Persephone wished they were comfortable enough with each other to reach out to him, to comfort him the way she would have any other member of her family.

"Yes, you should have."

"You look cold," Persephone said. Why did conversation between them have to be so awkward?

"I am freezing."

"You should change. Something warm and dry."

"Harry—"

"Mr. Johns will see to Harry."

"Are you to be my voice of reason, then?" Adam asked, almost chuckling. He reached out a hand and briefly touched her cheek.

It was so unexpected, Persephone involuntarily flinched. Adam pulled his hand away on the spot, his mouth tightening to a tense line.

"Your hand was cold," Persephone said, wishing he would reach for her again.

"My apologies," he said rather formally. "If you will excuse me, I have been told that I ought to change out of my cold, wet clothes."

"I am glad you have returned, Adam," Persephone said as he stepped past her. She laid her hand on the cheek he'd touched.

It was the first time in a month that anyone, other than the stable hands who helped her mount, had intentionally touched her. She hadn't realized until that moment how deeply she'd craved human contact, how much she'd missed the simple gesture of being touched.

Adam had been so gentle, so kind, in that brief moment. If only, she thought to herself, he could be that way more often.

CHAPTER SEVENTEEN

ADAM FLUNG HIS DAMP CRAVAT toward his valet. The boots had been the first thing to come off. Adam vaguely remembered a pair of woolen stockings his nurse would put him in on cold winter mornings. Whatever had happened to Nurse "Robbie?" He hadn't thought of her in years. She used to sing some ridiculous song to him about a boy the size of a thistle. He used to ask her to sing it over and over, and she always did.

What had brought back that memory? Adam wondered, buttoning up a clean waistcoat. It was a far more sentimental thought than he usually indulged in.

Adam shook it off. His valet approached with a claret-colored jacket, one Weston had been particularly proud of. He often wore that jacket in Town. It was the latest cut and fashion, and deucedly uncomfortable. Generally speaking, he willingly endured the minimized range of movement required to cut an impressive figure—impressions were everything in society. But in that moment, for the first time in memory, Adam cared not at all how impressive he looked.

"Not the claret, Hansen." He nearly smiled at the look of shock on the face of the man who'd been his valet for ten years. "The brown wool."

Hansen's eyes doubled in size. Adam actually did smile at that. At the sight of Adam smiling, Hansen's jaw dropped. Adam shook his head, holding back a chuckle. "Harry doesn't care what I'm wearing," Adam said, unsure why he was explaining himself. "And the wool will be warmer."

Hansen nodded mutely and returned to the wardrobe to seek out the usually overlooked jacket.

Walking down the corridor to Harry's chamber, Adam felt excessively pleased with his choice. He might actually thaw out from the hours-long drive to retrieve his one and only friend.

"He looks remarkably ill." Persephone's voice floated out Harry's bedchamber.

Adam approached slowly. In the back of his mind the memory surfaced of Persephone standing at the top of the staircase, obviously relieved to see him.

"Mr. Windover will recover easily enough," Mr. Johns said. "I've sent Cook instructions for a tisane."

Adam stood in the doorway of Harry's bedchamber, watching Persephone.

"Then I am certain he will be fine," Persephone said. "My husband has expressed his confidence in your abilities. Just this morning, in fact, he spoke quite highly of your competency."

"Did he, indeed?" Mr. Johns sounded genuinely surprised by the praise.

Adam was a little surprised by it as well. He may have expressed his confidence in the apothecary to Persephone but had hardly expected her to reiterate his words.

"That means a great deal." Mr. Johns still sounded a bit taken aback. "His Grace is not known to be extravagant in his praise."

"No, he is not," Persephone confirmed.

"Hm," Mr. Johns said, something between a chuckle and an expression of surprise.

When the apothecary drifted back toward Harry's bed, offering instructions to Harry's valet, Adam stepped inside.

"Adam." He couldn't tell from Persephone's tone if she was happy to see him or not. A blush spread across her face, and her eyes almost immediately lowered.

Because he'd touched her, Adam assumed. He hadn't intended to. It had been an impulse, one he had uncharacteristically acted on.

She'd flinched, immediately backed away from his touch. She'd said something about his hand being cold, but Adam felt certain that was not the reason.

"Mr. Johns seems quite confident that Harry will recover," Persephone said.

"That is reassuring."

He forced his eyes toward Harry but found he wanted to keep watching Persephone. Was she afraid of him? Repulsed? Indifferent? Somehow he couldn't imagine Persephone being indifferent to anyone. Unlike himself, she seemed to feel something for every person she met.

"The fever is not dangerously high," Mr. Johns said. "I have provided some powders that should help bring him around."

"Thank you, Mr. Johns." Adam couldn't remember the last time the apothecary had spoken to him with so much ease. Generally he stammered and sputtered.

Mr. Johns smiled as if Adam had offered him a compliment. "A couple days in bed should put him to rights. I've instructed his man on treatment and administering the tisane."

Adam had never seen Mr. Johns look more confident. Could a simple compliment heard secondhand change a man so much?

"Then we should probably let Mr. Windover's man see to him," Persephone suggested.

"I haven't had a chance to check on him myself."

"I think you can trust Mr. Johns, Adam. Bringing Harry here was the best thing you could have done." She stood directly beside him, looking up into his face. Adam looked away, knowing what she would see if he didn't. "Letting him rest would be the second best thing."

"You really think he will recover?" Adam asked Mr. Johns.

"Absolutely."

"Well, then, I suppose I would be well advised to listen to my wife and let him sleep." Adam shook his head at his easy agreement. He wasn't usually one for being led.

"I have found that listening to my wife is always advisable," Mr. Johns answered with a smile.

Mr. Johns was married? The apothecary had been coming to Falstone for eight years or more, and Adam hadn't, until that moment, even known he was a married man.

"You've been out in the cold all day, Adam," Persephone said. "You should get some rest as well."

Quite to Adam's surprise, Persephone took his hand in hers and gently led him from the room. As if he were a mere child, Adam followed without comment all the way back to his bedchamber.

"I will have the kitchen send you up a hot dinner." Persephone stepped back from his doorway.

Adam couldn't think of a response. He wished she yet held his hand, wished she hadn't already stepped away. He'd never known another person whose proximity he missed so immediately.

What was happening to him? He, who needed no one—who kept the world at arm's length—wished Persephone would remain.

He'd spent the better part of his journey to the Boar and Dagger thinking of Persephone's parting words. She'd made him promise to be careful. And he had been. At any other time he would have told James Coachman to spring the team in hopes of reaching Harry faster. Instead they'd taken a more sedate pace.

And as Harry had slept on the trip back, Adam had thought of Persephone again. He'd imagined her waiting at the door for his return, happy to see him, perhaps greeting him with an embrace. It had been rather far-fetched and completely uncharacteristic. Yet the image had refused to be dismissed.

He'd even been disappointed when Barton had opened the doors of Falstone Castle and Persephone hadn't been there. But not two steps inside, he'd seen her up on the landing. Then she'd all but run down the stairs.

Who could blame him for reaching out to her? It had been an idiotic thing to do, he acknowledged with a frustrated shake of his head. He was simply tired and overwrought after hours in a snow-storm to retrieve his friend, who'd proved even more ill than he'd anticipated.

A good night's sleep, Adam told himself. That was all he needed. In the morning he'd be himself again.

CHAPTER EIGHTEEN

A LONG, CLEAR HOWL PIERCED the darkness for the third time in only a few minutes. Adam held his breath. Apparently the moon had broken through the clouds enough to provide the pack with some light.

"You're a sop," he told himself, even as his eyes darted again to the connecting door between his chambers and Persephone's.

It must have been nearly one in the morning. Persephone had likely already fallen asleep and hadn't even heard the noise that, apparently, unnerved her so entirely. If he'd realized the pack would be silent for so long, he might not have been so insistent they return to Falstone so soon after reaching the Boar and Dagger. The inn hadn't proven as run-down as he'd anticipated, though the innkeeper was every bit as grasping and dishonest as the letter from Harry's valet had hinted.

Adam could have handled the man for one night—he still had every intention of seeing that Mr. Smith's business practices were looked into. Any innkeeper who required a fee before allowing a sick man to send for a physician was not at all the sort of businessman Adam wanted in the vicinity.

Nevertheless, Mr. Smith and his shady business weren't the reason for Adam's haste. Neither was concern for Harry's well-being nor the ever-growing drifts of snow. It was Persephone and those ridiculous wolves. Not that he'd believed they were going to devour him on his return trip as she had so comfortingly predicted. All the way to the inn and all the way back he kept thinking of how greatly she feared the pack—feared the *sound* of them—and how, for some inexplicable reason, she seemed less afraid with him nearby.

Adam shook his head at his own uncharacteristic actions. Her fear was irrational, completely and utterly nonsensical. He ought to have sent her back to her own rooms that first night and forced her to face them. A person couldn't go through life afraid of things that weren't threatening. It would be better for her in the long run.

If she came in again—Adam's eyes darted back to the still-closed door—he'd simply tell her so. He'd send her back through the door with instructions to show a little fortitude.

Adam heard the door scrape open. His eyes were closed in an instant.

Why in heaven's name did he feel nervous?

"Adam?"

He reminded himself of his intention to send her away. Adam didn't say a word.

Persephone's footsteps sounded quietly as she crossed the room.

What am I doing? Adam demanded of himself. He'd made a decision, chosen a course of action. But he wasn't sticking to it. He *never* changed his mind once he'd come to a conclusion.

The bed shifted, and Adam knew Persephone had climbed in again. She'd done so the past two nights. If he opened his eyes, he would, no doubt, see her wrapped in a blanket, curled in a ball, sleeping on her side.

A wolf howled from the distant forest.

Persephone seemed to sigh, a sound of immediately recognizable relief. "Oh, Adam," she whispered, and somehow Adam knew she wasn't actually addressing him, "you've married a coward."

Adam wanted to tell her she wasn't the coward she'd labeled herself. He'd seen her mount Atlas when she'd had no previous experience with riding. She'd lived with him for weeks without once turning into a trembling heap. That was a rare accomplishment.

She feared the wolves, which didn't really make sense. But Persephone had found a way to deal with her fear. That showed a remarkable amount of intelligence, a character trait Adam valued highly. Persephone wasn't exactly what he'd wanted in a wife, but she had her good points.

She'd been in the room less than five minutes when Adam realized she'd fallen asleep. Strange how her being in his room seemed to relax her, when it only made him tense. Perhaps it was the fact that she was not a peaceful sleeper. There was the frequent movement, coupled with little noises at regular intervals.

"At least," Adam whispered almost silently, "she doesn't snore."

There was nothing for it but to try to sleep. Adam opened his eyes and turned his head in Persephone's direction. She was little more than a mound of blankets. Persephone slept on her side, as always, with her back to him. Adam could make out nothing but her hair. It was brown, too dark to be blonde. His hair was black. It seemed as good a combination as any.

Adam shook his head, pushing out a breath of frustration. Why the blasted blazes was he analyzing their hair colors? He really was losing his mind!

He shifted so he faced the canopy that hung over his bed. He slammed his eyelids shut and commanded himself to sleep. Like every person who ever received an order from the Duke of Kielder, he obeyed. He hadn't expected sleep to come so easily and never would have predicted the dream that followed. Adam *never* had nightmares.

Fog rolled in, dense and biting—the frozen kind that nipped at every exposed inch of flesh. Adam rode Zeus, the horse's hooves crunching through a frozen layer of day-old snow. From the shrouded distance a howl echoed among the trees. Adam heard the sounds of the pack on the move. Snow had, no doubt, driven their prey underground, and the pack, in its hunger, seemed to be growing more aggressive. Their howls had sounded closer to the castle lately.

"Go on, Zeus," he urged the unusually skittish stallion. They were still miles from Falstone. He had no desire to be lost in the forest with fog rolling in.

A growl echoed off the trees. More growls joined it. Then barking.

"The pack is hunting," Adam muttered to himself. The idea made him uneasy, nervous. He was armed, of course . . . Adam was always armed.

A long, bone-chilling howl signaled a chorus of identical calls. Somewhere in the midst of the chorus of voices, Adam heard a snort he recognized at once as equine, followed by a horse screaming, the way the more aggressive stallions did if put together in the paddock. It was a fighting sound.

Adam didn't like it. Zeus didn't either. His mount was fighting him with every step as Adam made his way toward the increasingly hostile sounds of the pack and the frantic noises of a horse Adam felt certain had found itself in their midst.

There was no reason for a horse to be in the forest. The nearest stables were at Falstone, and the grooms never lost sight of an animal long enough for it to wander from the gates. Falstone Chapel was several miles further, but Mr. Pointer kept his cattle securely inside the vicarage barn when not in use.

Adam's heart began pounding. Something was not right.

He pressed Zeus on.

The howling gave way to barking, snarling, the sounds of predators on the hunt. The horse's sounds grew more erratic, less aggressive, and more frightened.

"On, Zeus!" But the horse resisted.

Between trees and through fog, Adam followed the sounds as they grew louder. His heart pounded. For the first time in years he actually felt fear. Still he kept on, as fast as the fog and Zeus's uncharacteristic nervousness allowed.

Suddenly the sounds were all around him. The pack had surrounded him. He could hear them but couldn't see a single wolf through the thickening fog.

A rasping Adam recognized as strangled breathing joined the other noises echoing madly through the air. He knew it was the horse.

He urged Zeus closer. Close enough to see through the fog, a horse struggled to stand, bloodied and breathing loudly, harshly. It was saddled but riderless. Adam's eyes darted around, but the fog didn't reveal his surroundings.

He moved closer still. When had the horse lost its rider? Before or after the pack had arrived?

Suddenly, Adam panicked. He recognized the horse. Atlas. With a sidesaddle.

"Persephone!"

Adam sat bolt upright in his bed, heart still pounding, breathing as heavy as if he'd run the length of Falstone's outer wall.

"Persephone." Her name came out breathless, laced with the panic that still hadn't subsided with waking.

She wasn't lying on the bed where she ought to be.

"Persephone?" he said a little louder, looking around the room, which was strangely well lit and bright.

Adam jumped from the bed and moved swiftly to the connecting door. He pulled it open, the tension in his shoulders almost painful.

"Persephone?" She wasn't in her bedchamber. "Perse—!"

"Adam?" Persephone stepped through the doorway to her dressing room, dressed for the day.

He covered the distance between them in a few long strides. He grasped her upper arms, holding her still as he looked her intently over, still half-convinced he'd find her bruised, perhaps bloodied. Other than obvious surprise and even a little alarm, Persephone appeared to be whole and unharmed.

For the first time since seeing Atlas without her in his dream, Adam felt some of his tension seep away. Never had he been so frightened for another person as he had been in the past few moments. And all on account of a stupid, stupid dream.

Adam released Persephone's arms. "Ridiculous," he muttered to himself and walked away. A dream! He'd never been unnerved by a dream in his entire life.

Adam slammed the door shut behind him as he returned to his own bedchamber.

"Ridiculous! Bloody ridiculous!" He'd have hit something if everything in the room hadn't been made of either solid stone or hardwood. Breaking his hand wouldn't change the fact that he'd just acted like a blasted idiot.

And a coward into the bargain, letting a dream frighten him. *Worry* him, he corrected. *Concern.* He was never frightened by anything. *Not ever.*

"Adam?" If he had merely been concerned, he wouldn't have felt so relieved at hearing Persephone's voice from just behind the closed door.

"What?" he snapped in frustration.

She didn't answer immediately. Adam could sense her hesitation. She seldom seemed intimidated by him. It ought to have felt like a victory.

It didn't.

"Harry seems a little better this morning." Uncertainty filled her voice, so quiet it barely penetrated the door between them.

Adam let out a frustrated breath. He knew that hadn't been what she'd originally intended to say. He paced back to the closed door. "I am glad he is improving." Adam leaned against the wall but didn't open the door.

"So am I." She still hadn't stepped away. Adam could picture her just on the other side of the wall.

"Are you planning to ride this morning?" he asked, closing his eyes.

"I am."

"I'd rather you didn't," he said.

"But—"

"I would rather you didn't." He forced his tone to become stern, unyielding, then all but held his breath as he awaited her reply.

"I won't if that is what you wish." An obvious question mark lingered at the end of her response.

It was a completely irrational request made in response to nothing more than a dream, albeit it an extremely vivid one. Yet, he felt palpable relief at her acquiescence. He actually started breathing again.

"I'm losing my bloody mind," Adam grumbled and walked away from the door.

CHAPTER NINETEEN

PERSEPHONE STOOD IN FRONT OF the full-length cheval mirror in Harry's room. She'd come to check on him, only to find him quite soundly sleeping. She tipped her head to one side, carefully scrutinizing her reflection, searching for the fatal flaw.

It was the black dress, perhaps. Her eyes were brown when she wore black. But, she thought, her eyes had been brown before, and it hadn't seemed so horrible then. Maybe her eyes weren't the problem.

She leaned closer to the mirror, tilting and turning her head. Her nose *was* a little too small. "Cute as a button," her mama used to describe it. But duchesses weren't supposed to have button noses.

Then there were the freckles. No home remedies had entirely cured her of those. Persephone supposed she was a trifle on the short side, though she'd never thought that so great a flaw that it couldn't be overlooked.

She let out a breath of frustration. Flaws were easy to find when one was looking. Or perhaps she simply had more of them than most people. That thought brought a grimace to her face.

"I get that look a lot." The weak, raspy voice came from behind her.

She turned around. "Harry?"

He appeared to be improving but still looked pale and ill. He attempted a smile. The miserable failure of that expression told Persephone volumes about the state of his health.

"We've been worried about you." She crossed closer to him, tugging the bell-pull as she passed it. His valet would appreciate knowing Harry had awoken.

"It's all been a ploy to get attention," Harry rasped, sitting up a little. A cough cut off any further comment.

Persephone poured him a glass of water from the pitcher on a bedside table, handing it to him and waiting as he took a sip.

"Why were you so displeased?" Harry asked after a sip. He took another then added, "When you were looking in the mirror?"

She took the glass from him and helped him lie back down. "It was nothing." She shook her head and set the glass back on the table.

"That wasn't nothing," he whispered.

Bless Harry. Even when he was terribly ill, he tried to be helpful. "Do you think I'm ridiculous?" She'd asked the question before she could stop herself.

"Ah, lard buckets." Harry breathed out the homegrown curse on a chuckled whisper that quickly turned into a cough. His valet came into the room in time to hear the latter and began immediately fussing over Harry. From around the ministration of his servant, Harry managed to say, "Adam once described St. James's Palace as 'ridiculous.' It's his favorite word."

"You need your rest," Persephone said. To Harry's valet, she added, "If there is anything at all that he needs, do not hesitate to ask."

"Thank you, Your Grace."

It's his favorite word. Persephone thought about that as she made her way downstairs to the sitting room.

She'd never seen St. James's but doubted the royal palace could be described as "ridiculous" by anyone other than Adam. Yet she didn't doubt that he had, indeed, found the probably impressive structure entirely unsatisfactory.

Was it any wonder, then, that she, too, fell under that category? She'd been thrown completely off guard when Adam had approached her in her room that morning. She'd immediately begun mentally revisiting her departure from Adam's bedchamber.

Had she left behind something that had given away her presence there? Had Adam realized what she'd been doing the past few nights? Was he angry?

Then he'd taken hold of her—there'd been something almost frantic in his grip—studying her minutely. She'd frozen under the intensity of his evaluation. What was he seeing? He'd answered her question after less than a minute.

"Ridiculous."

"Your Grace." Barton's voice interrupted her memories. "You have received a letter."

"Thank you," Persephone answered automatically. Barton held the missive out to her on the silver salver he always used to deliver the post. She took it and laid it on her lap without looking at it.

Harry had been trying to tell her that what Adam considered ridiculous didn't always match what others might label that way. But that knowledge didn't particularly help. The truth remained: Adam had looked her over and didn't like what he saw.

Where was the Adam who'd given her the beautiful riding habit? The one who'd brought her a coat when she'd gone into the cold without one? The Adam who had touched her so gently, so softly only the evening before? In those too-brief moments, he'd been the type of man she'd once dreamed of marrying.

The letter on her lap drew Persephone's attention. She recognized the handwriting instantaneously: Artemis's. Persephone sighed, worry she hadn't realized she'd been feeling suddenly released. Artemis hadn't written in weeks, not since before word of Evander's fate at Trafalgar had reached Falstone.

Dear Persephone,
I wish you weren't so far away.

Tears stung her eyes. True to character, Artemis had dispensed with the expected social pleasantries and had cut straight to the heart of the matter.

"So do I," Persephone whispered.

*Everyone is sad. I know if you were here, you could make
everyone smile again. Watching them makes me sad. I don't
remember much about Evander. Athena says that I shouldn't
say that because it sounds unfeeling. How can the truth be
unfeeling? I wish you were here to explain that to me.*

*Our new governess doesn't approve of reading about
haunted castles. I don't like her.*

*Is your castle haunted? When can I come see your towers?
Our governess says your house won't be as black as ours because
Evander isn't the duke's brother. Is that true? I wish I could go
there. I am sick to death of black and people who cry all the time.*

Are you happy? I wonder about that.

*Papa wanted me to write something in my letter for him
to tell you, but he can't remember what it was. He says he'll
write you a letter later.*

I miss you. Tell me when I can come.

*All my love, and an extra hug,
Artemis*

Are you happy? Leave it to Artemis to ask a question so pointed.
With all the obvious difficulties at home, the upheaval she was
apparently dealing with, Artemis certainly didn't need to know
that her sister, her mother in many respects, was at times painfully
unhappy and growing increasingly lonely.

She held the letter in her hand as she made her way to the
stairs and up to her rooms.

Papa was going to write to her? Persephone hoped he would
but had no expectation of actually hearing from him. She worried
that his wandering mind left him neglectful of the family. Was he
even capable of looking after them?

Persephone sat at the writing table in her sitting room, pondering the dilemma before her. She did not at all approve of lies,
white or otherwise. But if she wrote to Artemis and told her that
she spent her days fluctuating between resigned and unhappy, the
girl would be heartbroken and, worse, worried.

Dear Artemis,
How happy I was to receive your letter.

She had, indeed, been quite happy at hearing from her dear little sister. Persephone bit her lips together, thinking.

Do not worry over your memories of Evander. You were quite young when he left home. If you wish, I shall share my memories with you, and then you will know him as well as I do.

Persephone blinked back the tears that started afresh in her eyes. The pain of her brother's loss was still raw. Every mention of Evander brought worries for Linus.

I do not know, dearest, when you can come to visit me at Falstone Castle. I understand the weather here in wintertime is quite unpredictable. Perhaps in the spring, or after the London Season comes to a close. I imagine summers in Northumberland are magnificent.

Artemis simply couldn't come anytime soon. Adam's mood swings, coupled with Persephone's confusion and frustration, would destroy any illusions the girl might harbor about her sister's happiness. Persephone could not allow the child to return to Shropshire worried over the situation at Falstone.

What else would set Artemis's mind at ease?

I have my own horse to ride. His name is Atlas. He is quite large but also very gentle. I ride nearly every day and am beginning to feel more confident in the saddle.

Adam bought me my very own riding habit, and it is quite the loveliest habit I have ever seen. I am to have riding boots from London as well.

Persephone furrowed her brow. Would it not put all their minds at ease to know, albeit incorrectly, that she found herself happily situated? One less family member to worry about would be beneficial all around.

> *We have had company of late. Indeed, Falstone has not been without visitors this past month. I am used to the close connections of our neighborhood and so have appreciated enjoying some of the local society.*

Persephone winced at the massive exaggeration. The visits of Mr. Hewitt and Harry hardly qualified as enjoying society.

Before she lost her nerve, Persephone quickly finished her letter.

> *We have lovely gardens here that I will show you when you visit.*
> *Please write again soon. I miss you. Please tell Athena and Daphne and Papa that I love and miss them.*
> *Be good for your governess, and do not worry over the haunted castles. You and I shall overindulge our love of such things when we are next in company.*
> *I love you, my dearest little Artemis.*
>
> *Your loving sister,*
> *Persephone*

She sat back in her chair, feeling drained and heavy.

"Forgive me these lies," she silently prayed. "But I cannot make my sister unhappy."

* * *

"Harry was as impertinent as ever when I saw him an hour or so ago," Adam said during the fish course of dinner that night. "I take that as an indication that he is recovering."

Persephone nodded her agreement. She felt undeniably nervous. She'd attempted to improve her appearance. There was no avoiding black, however. If her wardrobe color had been the culprit that had rendered her "ridiculous," she could do nothing about it.

Adam, it seemed, had drained his reservoir of conversational topics. The meal continued in silence. How would her family members interpret the awkward meals at Falstone?

How would she have described those meals in her lie-riddled letter? *We have become quite comfortable enough to pass a quiet evening in one another's company.*

The lie sat uneasily on Persephone's mind, and yet she knew she would never have offered an honest evaluation to her family.

"I had a letter from my sister today," Persephone said into the silence.

"Which sister was that?"

Persephone felt sorely tempted to not continue. Why did he so often seem uninterested in what she said? "Artemis," Persephone answered quietly.

"The youngest?" Adam concentrated on his plate of food. But, Persephone told herself, he had at least remembered which of her sisters Artemis was.

"Yes."

Adam continued eating.

Pretending he had shown an interest, Persephone continued. "She dislikes her governess, but not for any legitimate reason. I'm afraid she feels a touch weighed down by the continued state of mourning around the house. She has requested, again, to be able to come here to visit."

Persephone saw Adam stiffen at that revelation. He didn't want Artemis to come, apparently.

"I suggested the spring or summer," Persephone said.

Adam didn't answer beyond a "hmm." Not very promising. Perhaps Artemis's plans to explore the Falstone towers had been doomed from the beginning.

"Of course, nothing has actually been planned." Persephone tried to keep the disappointment from her voice. She would see her family in Town, she reminded herself. And that was only five months away.

Five months.

Persephone bit back a sigh. How could she possibly last nearly half a year as lonely as she was?

CHAPTER TWENTY

"WHAT IS THAT INFERNAL NOISE?" Adam grumbled, standing on the first-floor landing.

"I believe that would be described as lively conversation, Your Grace," Barton answered quite straight-faced. But Adam hadn't missed the irony in his tone. Barton had never before broken the slightest bit from his proper butler's demeanor.

"And who," Adam answered quite severely, "is responsible for all of this 'lively conversation?'"

A twitter of a laugh rang through the entrance hall. *That* was a sound with which he was unaccustomed. Adam raised an eyebrow.

Barton cleared his throat, sounding almost as if he barely held back a laugh of his own. "Mrs. Pointer." He managed an almost serious tone.

"No doubt the vicar is here as well," Adam said.

"No doubt." Again he detected a hint of dry humor in the butler's tone. What had gotten into the man?

"Are you feeling quite yourself today, Barton?" Adam genuinely wondered if perhaps Barton was a little touched in the upper works. The man had to be at least sixty. He'd been a footman at Falstone when Adam was a boy, elevated to butler while Adam was away at Harrow.

"I assure you I feel better than I have in years, Your Grace." Something in Barton's expression marked it as a significant statement.

Another twitter echoed up from below. "It sounds as though Falstone is infested with birds," Adam muttered.

Just then Mrs. Smithson, the housekeeper, followed by a footman and trailed by two maids, reached the doors of the drawing room below. The footman bore a large silver tray, laden with every type of finger sandwich and sweet cake imaginable. Mrs. Smithson bore the silver tea service.

"A full tea?" Adam felt rather shocked, not having seen such a thing at Falstone since the days before his mother had relegated herself to the ranks of guest at the family seat. "For the Pointers?" It seemed a little overdone for only two guests.

"I believe Cook was exceptionally excited at the prospect of preparing a tea tray once more," Barton answered. "It has been a while, Your Grace."

His words held censure. But Barton knew how Falstone was supposed to be run.

"How is it that the vicar and his wife came to be in the drawing room?" Adam used the tone his mother had often called his "duke voice." He'd perfected it some time around seven years of age, and it had never failed him, except with Harry, but Harry was the exception to most rules. "I do not recall altering my requirement that all guests be informed I am 'not at home.'"

"The vicar quite specifically asked for *Her* Grace." Most of the cheek had left Barton's voice, though he certainly wasn't quivering with concern. Adam had always liked that about Barton—he knew precisely how to act, but he had backbone. "When I presented Her Grace with Mr. Pointer's card, I thought she would actually run down the stairs, she was so pleased to have callers."

Adam felt a momentary prick of guilt at that. If Barton had been turning away callers, then Persephone hadn't had any company, either. *She* might actually wish to see people. A picture of the Falstone drawing room filled to overflowing with the neighborhood elite, curious and barely tolerable, flashed through Adam's mind. That would never do.

"How long have the Pointers been here?" Adam asked Barton, who still hovered nearby, as he walked slowly down the staircase.

"Only a few minutes, Your Grace."

"A few minutes is more than most get," Adam reminded no one in particular. Falstone was his home, where he determined the rules. He had long ago declared that there were to be no visitors, no callers, no formal teas for neighbors pretending politeness for the chance to gape and stare and slake their thirst for gossip fodder.

"Cream, yes." Mr. Pointer's voice reached the drawing room door as Adam stepped inside.

Persephone filled the vicar's teacup and handed it to him. Mr. Pointer noticed Adam's entrance and smiled at him. Only Mr. Pointer, and perhaps Harry, would dare smile when he knew he'd broken one of Adam's cardinal rules. Adam gave him a pointed look of warning, which had no visible effect whatsoever.

"Would you like a cup of tea, Adam?" Persephone asked, apparently seeing him enter.

Adam turned to face her. "No," he answered, unable to completely keep the exasperation from his voice.

Persephone smiled serenely back at him, returning to her duties as hostess, and placed a small slice of lemon cake on a plate for Mr. Pointer. Something in her demeanor seemed different from what he'd seen lately, but Adam couldn't identify it.

"It is a pleasure to see you again, Your Grace," Mr. Pointer offered conversationally.

"I doubt that."

Mr. Pointer smiled as if he were quite thoroughly amused. Mrs. Pointer appeared on the verge of fainting. Her teacup had begun to rattle. Adam hoped she put the blasted thing down before it went crashing to the floor below.

"What, precisely, is the reason for your presence here?" Adam stood over the visitors, his mouth set in a very serious, interrogative line.

"A social call, of course," Mr. Pointer said.

"Of course?" Adam repeated, making his doubt obvious in his tone. "And why 'of course,' Mr. Pointer? When, in the fifteen years you have served as vicar here, has Falstone Castle received visitors?"

"Not once, Your Grace." This conversation seemed to be entertaining to the vicar.

"And what, sir, led you to believe that had changed?"

"Wishful thinking?" Mr. Pointer hazarded the guess with barely masked amusement.

"There will be no callers at Falstone Castle." Adam's tension at the idea of hordes of gaping guests at Falstone affected his tone. "Not today. Not in the future."

"Falstone is not receiving, Your Grace?" Mr. Pointer asked, as casually as if he were inquiring after the weather. "Or *you* are not receiving?"

"It is the same."

"Forgive me, but it is not." Mr. Pointer rose, placing his cup and saucer on an end table nearby. "Thank you for your hospitality, Your Grace."

Mr. Pointer no longer addressed Adam. The vicar crossed past him to Persephone. Adam followed the man's progress with his eyes.

He hadn't been able to identify what had been different in Persephone's face earlier, but seeing her now, he knew. He knew because it was no longer there. She had been brighter, more alive and less haunted. Now the aura of sadness that had seemed to envelope her lately had returned.

"Do come ag—" Persephone stopped mid-word, her eyes darting anxiously at Adam then back at the vicar. "Thank you for—" She stopped again. With a look of disappointment, she finally settled on, "I will see you on Sunday."

Mr. Pointer gave her a look filled with empathetic concern. "Smile, child."

Persephone did. A smile shouldn't look *un*happy.

"Wait," Adam grumbled, annoyed with himself for his uncharacteristic ability to be influenced. "You might as well stay and finish your tea." He knew he didn't sound welcoming but didn't remotely care. He could do without the dramatic exit Mr. Pointer obviously meant to enact. And, blast it all, Persephone looked near tears, and she hadn't cried in days. "Cook will be offended if the tray is sent back untouched."

He expected Mr. Pointer to smirk. He was enough like Harry to do just that. The vicar looked intrigued, perhaps even a little surprised, but didn't smirk. As if the man hadn't known precisely what he was about leaving in such an overblown manner. Mrs.

Pointer hovered half-in, half-out of her seat, rear end jutting awkwardly over the deep red upholstered sofa.

"Perhaps you would like to try some of these fine cakes." Mr. Pointer moved quite casually back to the seat he'd vacated beside his wife. "Or a cup of tea."

"A dram of brandy might be more helpful," Adam muttered.

"Do sit, dear," Mr. Pointer said to his wife, as if Adam had made no comment. "And do try the lemon cake. Delicious."

Persephone didn't miss a beat, offering a plate with a slice of the praised cake to the vicar's wife with a polite smile.

"Thank you." Mrs. Pointer's voice shook. Adam almost wished she'd produce one of her twittering laughs. People who quaked in his presence quickly lost their appeal.

Persephone moved to his side. "Are you sure you wouldn't care for some tea?"

Adam shook his head. The sooner this visit came to an end, the better. He still couldn't believe he'd allowed it. He never permitted visitors.

"I didn't know, Adam," Persephone said, just louder than a whisper, her eyes darting quickly to the Pointers before returning to him. "If you'd rather they leave—"

"Let them finish their tea." He shook his head slightly at his continued illogical behavior. She'd given him the perfect opportunity to throw the Pointers out as he'd originally intended.

But when Persephone rewarded his lunacy with a bright smile, Adam felt nearly glad he'd slipped from his usual approach to life.

"I thought no one wanted to meet me." Persephone kept her voice to a whisper, obviously going to lengths to keep their conversation too low for the vicar and his wife to overhear. "Bridal visits are expected. But there hadn't been any callers. I didn't realize they were being turned away."

She could just as easily have sounded accusatory. Instead, she seemed relieved.

"They probably never came in the first place." Adam surprised himself by so willingly discussing the situation. What did he care how Persephone felt about the rules? But that rang entirely false.

He wanted her to understand, wanted her to know that *she* hadn't been rejected. It was an odd impulse for him, but he kept on. "Every family in the surrounding area knows Falstone is closed to visitors."

Persephone shot another look in the Pointers' direction before saying, quietly, "But I could go visit the neighbors."

Adam's stomach clenched on the instant. "No. They would be expected to return the visit."

"But I—"

"I will not have Falstone overrun by people."

Persephone hesitated, a war of emotions in her eyes: confusion, indecision, frustration. In the end, she managed to look neutral. "Of course not. Thank you for allowing the Pointers to remain. I have been enjoying their visit."

Adam felt like an ogre. The law gave him the right to dictate everything in his home. But his conscience began to decree otherwise. Persephone's acquiescence had obviously been reluctantly given.

And why shouldn't she wish for visitors, for society? She had nothing to fear at their hands, no reason to reject the company of virtual strangers. He, on the other hand, knew precisely how it felt to be stared at, whispered about. The animals at the Tower of London's Royal Menagerie had nothing on Adam when it came to being a spectacle for the callous and curious.

"You, of course, owe Mrs. Pointer a visit," Adam conceded, still unsure why he found himself so easily undone by the downcast look in her eyes, why he even discussed this in the same room as the Pointers. Such conversations belonged behind closed doors without witnesses. "I understand she entertains half the county on a regular basis."

"I could meet our neighbors that way, then." Persephone's tone remained hesitant and cautious, almost as if she were asking a question rather than stating a fact.

"If you want to." Adam shrugged. He'd met the neighborhood and wasn't particularly impressed.

The smile returned to her face. Adam had to force back an answering one. He knew his face looked particularly disfigured when he smiled, the asymmetry made painfully obvious.

By the time the Pointers departed, Adam had no more desire to grin. They'd quickly settled in, looking completely at ease. If they were entertaining any thoughts of returning, they would be sorely disappointed.

Mrs. Pointer filled Persephone's ears with news of the neighborhood. Mrs. Somebody-or-Other was rumored to be Increasing again, and Mrs. So-and-So was said to be redoing her drawing room in the French style and wasn't that terribly unpatriotic. Adam was bored to tears.

Her parting comment, however, left Adam wincing. "I do hope you will attend the assemblies, Your Grace." Mrs. Pointer smiled at Persephone. "Once you have passed your deepest mourning, of course." The vicar's wife acknowledged Persephone's black dress with a nod of empathy. "I understand there hasn't been a Duke and Duchess of Kielder at our local assembly in thirty years."

Adam nearly tossed the woman into her carriage himself at that point. He'd bent enough to allow the Pointers to visit. But he did *not* dance.

CHAPTER TWENTY-ONE

"And Mrs. Adcock grew up in Shropshire as well," Persephone told Harry as they sat in the sitting room after dinner a week after the Pointers' visit to Falstone. Harry, though still not entirely his usual energetic self, had recovered sufficiently to join her and Adam for meals and wander from his room during the day.

"You've met Mrs. Adcock?" Adam jumped into the conversation. He didn't sound pleased.

"At the vicarage." She'd made the three-mile journey twice in the past week. A handful of ladies from the area had been present on her first visit. More than a dozen had greeted her upon her arrival that afternoon. "She extended an invitation to us to take supper with them."

Adam looked thunderous on the instant.

"She seemed to be expecting me to turn the invitation down," Persephone quickly added. "So I had little difficulty in doing so."

He relaxed a trifle.

Persephone tried to keep her disappointment buried. The Lancasters had ofttimes dined with the families in their neighborhood. She missed that interaction, missed knowing that she had friends nearby.

"Who else was at the vicarage?" Harry asked.

Thankful for the approval she heard in his tone, Persephone took up the conversation again. "Mrs. Milston and her daughter. Lady Hettersham." Adam mumbled something unintelligible at that. At least he was listening, Persephone told herself. "Miss Greenburrough."

The sitting room door opened, cutting off the list Persephone had only begun to relate. Barton entered with his familiar silver salver bearing a rather thick letter.

From Artemis? Or Papa, perhaps? Persephone watched his entrance with eager anticipation. Barton stopped at Adam's side.

So not from home, after all. Persephone tried to refocus her mind but found the task nearly impossible in her disappointment. The longer she was away from her family, the more she missed them.

"What did you think of our resident spinster?" Harry asked.

For a moment, Persephone fumbled over the question but then realized he referred to Miss Greenburrough, whom she'd mentioned meeting during her visit that afternoon.

"She was very quiet, so I was not able to form much of an opinion of her." Miss Greenburrough's head of gray hair had reminded Persephone so forcefully of her grandmother that she felt certain she would like the lady.

"Persephone." Adam cut into the conversation. He held his letter out to her.

"It is for me?"

"It is addressed to me," he answered. "But it will explain the other letter."

"The other letter?"

Adam all but dropped the letter into Persephone's lap, at which point she realized that along with a single sheet of high-quality parchment was a second, sealed letter. She began with the opened missive.

> *Your Grace,*
>
> *Lord Barham, First Lord of the Admiralty, has relayed to me your inquiries regarding two midshipmen aboard the HMS* Triumphant. *As captain of the* Triumphant, *I will make every attempt to provide you with the information you seek.*
>
> *Midshipman Evander Lancaster, as you have been informed, succumbed to injuries sustained at Trafalgar and,*

*as with most lost at that time, has been buried in a cemetery
on Gibraltar alongside his fallen shipmates.*

Midshipman Linus Lancaster—

Persephone held her breath. How long she had waited to have
news of Linus. Her uncle's inquiries had produced nothing. She'd
alternately pictured him lost at sea and horribly injured or ill.
There would be no more wondering now, and in a way that frightened her.

"Go on, Persephone." Adam apparently noticed her hesitation.
She would have expected impatience from him but heard none in
his voice. "It is not bad news."

*Midshipman Linus Lancaster sustained only minor
wounds in that battle and remains aboard the* Triumphant.
*He will, of course, be granted shore leave when we return to
home port. Our navigator has begun tutoring young Lancaster, as he has found the lad to have a natural aptitude for
nautical mathematics.*

*The Admiralty has instructed me that should Mid-
shipman Lancaster wish to leave the navy and return to his
family, he will be permitted to do so and receive an honorable
discharge from the Royal Navy. Should he remain, however, I
am further informed, upon completing the required six years
of service, a lieutenancy will be purchased for him.*

*I have enclosed a brief missive from Lancaster to his
sister, the Duchess of Kielder.*

*I am pleased to have been of service in this way to Your
Grace and remain,*

Your humble servant, etc.
Captain Gregory Hattfield, HMS Triumphant

Persephone eagerly grabbed the letter sealed and lying on
her lap. She studied the handwriting but didn't find it familiar.

Evander had always written in behalf of both brothers. Could this truly be a letter from her baby brother? The brother she'd feared for weeks was lost forever?

She pressed the letter to her heart, fighting back a fresh flood of tears. She hadn't cried in days.

"I thought you said it was good news," she heard Harry say under his breath to Adam.

"Oh, it is." Persephone quickly answered for him. "I am only . . . oh, overwhelmed, I suppose. My brother Linus is alive and well, you see."

Harry smiled at her. "That is good news."

"I will probably weep like a baby when I read his letter," Persephone said with an amazed laugh, the shock of actually holding a letter from Linus, almost as if he were back from the grave, had her wits at loose ends. Persephone stood, still clutching the letter for dear life. "If you will excuse me, I'd rather do so without witnesses."

Harry and Adam rose as she did. Only then did Persephone realize that Captain Hattfield's letter had fluttered to the ground when she'd risen. She scooped it from the floor. "I am sorry, Adam," she said, unsure why she kept smiling like a ninny. "I've dropped your letter."

He shook off her apology. "It is truly more yours than mine."

She realized in that instant just how true that statement was. Adam, according to the letter, had written to the Admiralty inquiring after her brothers. How had he known her uncle's attempts were proving fruitless? What had inspired him to take up the effort? The First Lord of the Admiralty himself had become involved, all resulting in the precious piece of paper Persephone knew she would treasure always.

Adam was uncomfortable with gratitude; Persephone had seen that before. But she couldn't possibly let such an enormous gesture go unrecognized. She felt almost giddy with relief and budding joy.

"This is by far the kindest thing any person has ever done for me." Persephone knew she was gushing, but she couldn't seem to help herself. She knew Harry wouldn't mind, would likely simply smile. He had, in fact, quite tactfully wandered to a far window, allowing her to offer her gratitude in relative privacy. "Thank you, Adam." She ignored Adam's immediate dismissive gesture. "Thank you so, so much."

She felt like spinning, the way she had as a little girl when ending a game of bowls the winner. Then she would jump up and down and squeal in delight. And Papa would lift her into his arms and demand a kiss as recompense for his disappointment in being trounced so thoroughly.

In that moment, Persephone felt the same heady feeling of triumph, filled to overflowing with gratitude toward the gentleman who so often seemed not to care one ounce. He did. She knew he did. He cared enough to write a letter, and that letter had brought her the one she still held to her heart.

"Thank you," she said once more, stepping to where he was and lightly kissing his left cheek, placing her hand on Adam's chest for support.

She felt her face heat at the gesture of gratitude but did not regret her actions. She needed him to know that what he'd done went beyond the ordinary polite interest most people took in the suffering of others.

Relieved that he, at least, didn't object to her offering, Persephone smiled a little shyly and stepped away, determined to run all the way to her rooms and devour Linus's letter.

She didn't manage a single step. Adam reached for her—something he'd never done before—and with a look of intense determination, he pulled her back to her previous position, hand pressed to his chest.

He kissed her. Not on the cheek, not a friendly greeting, but a kiss unlike any she had experienced before, made even more remarkable by the fact that it was entirely unexpected.

Persephone felt certain that, even outside in the dead of night during the winter, if Adam were to kiss her that way again, she wouldn't feel a hint of cold. It was warm and comforting and unsettling.

As abruptly as he'd pulled her to him, Adam released her, stepping back. He looked shocked, even confused.

"You do that very well," Persephone heard herself whisper. Then, mortified that she'd spoken the thought out loud, she stepped further away from him. "I . . . um . . . I'll just go . . . read my letter."

"That would be a good idea." Adam sounded oddly distracted.

Persephone didn't need to be told twice. She stepped from the sitting room, head spinning, heart hammering.

Suddenly Persephone understood why her dear friend Harriet Upton had allowed their lifelong friend George Sanford to kiss her in the apple orchard three years earlier. And, she thought as the heat spread through her cheeks, it was no wonder Harriet had married him a few short months later. If George had kissed Harriet the way Adam had kissed Persephone, it was only a wonder that Harriet had had the ability to speak clearly enough to accept his proposal.

*　*　*

Adam dropped into his chair the instant Persephone left the sitting room. What the devil was wrong with him? He'd just kissed her. And for no particular reason, except that he'd wanted to. He couldn't even explain to himself *why* he'd wanted to.

Yes, he could. Because she'd kissed him. No one had ever kissed him, except Nurse Robbie when he was a little boy. But why had Persephone's gesture inspired him to return the offering? He didn't like not knowing why he'd done something. If he didn't understand it, he might do it again.

"I just kissed Persephone," Adam muttered to himself, too confused to say much else.

"I noticed."

Adam gave Harry a disapproving look. "You were supposed to be politely looking elsewhere." Why was it Harry always seemed to be witness to Adam's most distressing moments?

"I think Persephone noticed as well." Harry ignored Adam's grumbled comment. "Which is a good thing, by the by. If she hadn't even realized you were kissing her, one would begin to wonder about your technique."

"Shu—"

"I know, 'Shut up, Harry.'" He laughed.

Adam had been regretting the letter he'd sent to the Admiralty almost from the moment he'd posted it. If Persephone's uncle had been able to provide her with even a modicum of information about her brothers, then he wouldn't have been required to intervene. That, of course, didn't explain why he'd taken the extra step of informing the Admiralty of his intention to purchase a lieutenancy for Linus when the time came. With Adam as his sponsor and the Admiralty behind him, Linus could make a fine career for himself in the navy, if he chose it.

It made sense. But Adam still couldn't explain why he'd involved himself.

"Persephone seemed happy with her letter." Harry cut into Adam's thoughts.

Yes, Adam thought, biting down a smile. She had seemed very happy.

"Considering you handed it over to her, I am assuming it was not a request by a secret admirer for a clandestine meeting."

"It was a letter from her brother."

"The youngest one, the one who was missing?"

"No, Harry," Adam answered sarcastically. "The one who is dead. Of course the younger one."

"That's a rather harsh tone to take with someone only days out of his deathbed. A man who politely stared out the window while you accosted your wife."

"You neither kept your eyes diverted nor were in any danger of succumbing to your cold. If I thought for a minute a cold could do you in, I personally would shove you into Falstone Lake during the next snowstorm."

"A refreshing swim could be nice." Harry nodded.

Why did the man never take any of Adam's threats seriously?

"I am going to assume, based on Persephone's rather warm response, that the news of her brother was not only good but arrived courtesy of you, somehow or another."

"In a moment of insanity I sent a letter," Adam grumbled.

"And knowing you, you probably went straight to the Admiralty." Harry laughed. Almost immediately he reined in his amusement. "You did, didn't you? That got results, I daresay. Even the Royal Navy bows to the Duke of Kielder."

"That's treasonous, Harry."

"But true. A letter from the Duke of Kielder could overthrow a kingdom." Harry looked thoroughly amused. "It certainly closed up the Boar and Dagger in a trice. I heard Smith, the innkeeper, was none too pleased with that."

"He was a scoundrel," Adam said. "Any man who would charge a pound a piece for quill, ink, and paper, so a sick man could send for medical help, then provide him with no nourishment while he waited, ought not be running an inn."

"From what I've heard, he was livid when the magistrate shut down the inn," Harry said.

Adam shrugged. Mr. Smith of the Boar and Dagger would certainly not be the last person he'd make livid.

"Like I said—" Harry smiled "—the Duke of Kielder could run the country with a simple snap of his fingers."

Adam would never have said so out loud, but Harry was more correct than he realized. Should he choose to, Adam could have more influence over the course of the war with France than the Crown and the rest of Parliament combined. But he had enough problems.

For one thing, he had a wife whom he had inadvertently discovered he very much enjoyed kissing. He hadn't foreseen that complication. He'd always intended to remain as unaffected and undisturbed by his wife as he was by everyone else.

He felt confused and indecisive. He had no idea why he'd kissed his wife and no idea what he meant to do about it. Except keep his distance.

CHAPTER TWENTY-TWO

So much for distance.

The wolf pack had begun early that night. Either Persephone's nervousness at their noise had rattled him or the pack had drawn closer to the castle than usual. They were louder than they used to be. And Persephone was closer now as well. She'd tiptoed through the door only a few moments earlier. After her usual whispered "Adam?" she'd hurried, much faster than on previous nights, to the bed and climbed up.

A particularly menacing howl erupted outside. Adam heard Persephone quietly groan. "They're getting louder," she whispered to herself.

This was the precise reason he'd decided to stay away from his wife. Hearing the distress in her voice, Adam felt sorely tempted to reach out and touch her. He found himself wondering if she would feel less afraid if he held her hand. He quickly dismissed that thought. She'd probably run from the room as fast as her legs would carry her.

Adam felt the bed shift as Persephone changed positions. She did that a lot during the night. It had bothered him at first, but the last couple of nights he'd found himself waking up if she hadn't moved in a while. He'd peek, convinced she had left the room, only to inevitably spot her in her mountain of blankets. Then he'd lie there, watching to be certain she still breathed. Which only proved he was losing his mind. Only an idiot would jump to such a far-fetched possibility.

"Thank you for my letter, Adam," Persephone whispered. He could tell she had turned to face him. She didn't usually.

He was so tempted to open his eyes. Why? He had decided to keep his distance. How much greater distance could a person achieve than being sound asleep?

"Linus sounds happy," Persephone continued, her voice never rising above a whisper. "He didn't mention Evander, which worries me a little. It was always his way to avoid topics that were upsetting. But he did promise to keep writing."

Why did Persephone feel more comfortable talking to him when he was asleep?

"I hope Linus writes to Papa. He and the girls will be worried about him as well."

Adam felt her shift again, and then a bundle of blankets brushed his arm. That distance he meant to maintain was disappearing quickly.

"Thank you, Adam," she said once more. "I know you don't like it when I thank you for the things that you do, but I really am grateful."

Persephone seemed to settle in after that—the only problem being that she settled right beside him.

At what point had Persephone begun to smell like lavender? At what point had Adam learned what lavender smelled like?

Soon, Persephone began making those noises that meant she was sleeping. Adam opened his eyes. She couldn't have been more than inches from him.

Lavender. Adam shook his head. He would never have thought he would notice something like that. Or notice that a lock of Persephone's hair had fallen across her face. That had to be driving her absolutely mad.

What was he thinking? Persephone was asleep. She wouldn't even notice her hair.

Adam, however, couldn't seem to notice anything else. Even in the dim glow cast by the embers in his fireplace, her hair seemed to shimmer. Cautiously, slowly, he reached out and touched a wisp of it. *Soft.* Adam brushed her hair back from her face.

She really was too pretty to be married to him. Did she regret accepting him? He hoped she didn't.

She'd said she had enjoyed kissing him. Those hadn't been her exact words, he acknowledged. She'd said he kissed well. *Very* well, Adam amended.

Deuce take it, he wanted to kiss her again.

Adam flipped abruptly on to his other side, shifting as he did to the very edge of the bed. Distance, he reminded himself. That was vital.

Persephone had the uncanny ability, he was discovering, to leave him thinking and doing things he would otherwise never think or do. And his thoughts had begun to dwell on her more than could possibly be healthy.

He vowed, as he lay there uncomfortably on his side, to keep a room's length between them from that moment on. During the day-time, at least, he corrected. The wolves frightened her, after all. He'd simply hang off the end of the bed until the pack learned to keep quiet.

Part of him hoped they never did.

* * *

For a moment, Persephone felt nothing but shock. She'd been riding, that much she remembered.

"Persephone?" Adam's voice came at her from what felt like miles away.

She blinked a few times. The world around her would not come into focus.

"Persephone?" Adam sounded rather urgent.

"Adam?" A few more blinks and she could make him out. He knelt beside her, which meant she was lying on the ground. And he looked worried. "What happened?"

"Honeycake threw you," Adam said. "Are you hurt? Can you sit up?"

"I don't know." Persephone felt extremely confused. She couldn't decide if her bewilderment came from the fall she only vaguely remembered, or the fact that Adam was touching her face and looking at her as though he were genuinely worried.

"Let me help you," Adam said.

He'd never offered to do anything for her before. He'd brought her a coat once, and more or less threw it at her. Adam slipped a hand underneath her and lifted her with no visible effort to a seated position, still not releasing her.

"Does anything hurt?"

Persephone shook her head, unable to look away from him. She'd never seen him like this: fretting and nervous.

"Why were you on Honeycake?" Adam ran a hand down her arm, as if checking for breaks. "Honeycake is less docile than Atlas. You aren't ready for a challenging mount."

"Atlas twisted a knee." John had told her as much when she'd arrived for her daily ride.

"And you? Did you twist or hurt anything?"

"You asked me that already."

"A person can be killed being thrown from a horse." Adam helped her to her feet.

"Not at a walk." Her wits gradually returned as her head slowed its spinning.

"No, I guess not." Adam had never before sounded so distracted. He didn't look away. Six weeks of seeing nothing but the side of his face, and suddenly Adam was staring at her. He touched her face once more, so gentle, so caring. Persephone closed her eyes. Why couldn't he always be this way? "You're certain you aren't hurt?"

"I imagine I will be sore." She leaned her face into his palm.

"I don't ever want you to ride Honeycake again," Adam said into Persephone's left ear. The last time he'd been that close to her, he'd kissed her. Persephone felt her face flush at the memory. "You will stay on your feet until Atlas is available again."

"Yer Grace," John Handly's voice interrupted.

Persephone bit back a sigh of frustration. To her surprise, Adam didn't pull away. She felt his arm wrap around her and pull her closer to him. She opened her eyes and found herself eye to shoulder with him. She didn't let the opportunity pass by, but laid her head on Adam's shoulder, pleasantly surprised to feel him hold her tighter.

"Is Her Grace well?" John asked.

"I don't want my wife riding Honeycake," Adam said, that tone of authority in his voice.

"Honeycake is usually very calm. I can't explain it. It was almost like something spooked 'er."

"I do not want Her Grace on Honeycake."

"Yes, Yer Grace." John pulled respectfully at his forelock.

Persephone closed her eyes once more, savoring the feeling of being held. She'd always imagined the comfort of being in the arms of her husband. So few of her schoolgirl dreams had proven accurate during the short weeks of her marriage. She was determined to prolong the moment as long as possible.

"See to Honeycake," Adam instructed John. Then, bending his head toward Persephone, he said, "Your abigail can have a hot bath prepared for you—that should help with any stiffness."

"There really is no need for this much fuss," Persephone said, thoroughly enjoying every moment of fuss.

"You'll disagree when you are too stiff to come down to dinner." Adam led her from the paddock.

"This is very kind of you, Adam."

"Nonsense." He dismissed her gratitude, just as she knew he would. His arm remained around her waist. "You've been thrown from a horse, Persephone. Any decent gentleman would be concerned."

"Then thank you for being decent." She leaned against him as they walked.

"You're welcome," Adam answered with noticeable unease. But, Persephone realized with a smile, he hadn't brushed away her gratitude. It wasn't an enormous stride, but it was something.

"Her Grace has had an accident," Adam informed Barton the moment they passed through the doors of the castle. "Have a hot bath brought to her dressing room and have Cook prepare a pot of her bruise ointment."

"Of course, Your Grace." Barton hurried off to follow through with the orders.

Persephone was actually smiling by the time they reached her room. Other than while holding her letter from Linus yesterday, she had seldom smiled since coming to Falstone.

"The kitchen can send up a tray if you would rather not come down for dinner." Adam grew more distant.

"Adam?" She looked up at him. He shifted his face away. "When Atlas is well again, can I come riding with you and Harry?"

"Atlas can't keep up with Zeus," Adam said.

"Couldn't you rein Zeus in a little? Or let me join you at the end of your ride, when Zeus has slowed down."

"You should keep to the paddock." Adam stepped back a little.

Persephone followed, staying close to him. He'd held her so lovingly, so tenderly. Why was he moving away? She wanted him to hold her again, to make her feel wanted and needed, if not precisely loved. "I would like to try riding out," she said. "Atlas wouldn't throw me like Honeycake did."

"I'd rather you not take that chance."

"But you would be there." She reached out, laying a hand on his chest. He stiffened. Persephone forced herself to stay as she was, despite the disappointment she felt at his apparent displeasure. Why had he grown so suddenly distant? Had she only imagined him warming to her, at least a little?

"That is no guarantee—"

Something about that admission, about the vulnerability in his voice, tugged at her heart. She tipped her head up and laid a soft kiss on his lips. He didn't pull away but didn't seem to be returning the gesture. Hoping against hope that he wasn't as disinterested as he seemed, Persephone reached up and touched his face with her hand.

Fast as a flash of lightning, Adam had hold of her wrist and pulled her hand from his face. She stepped back from him, surprised but mostly disappointed.

"I'm sorry," she whispered, hurting at his rejection of her affections.

Adam released her wrist and turned away. "The bath should help," he muttered as he walked away. "And the ointment."

"Adam," Persephone called after him.

He didn't turn back.

Persephone sighed. Obviously she'd misinterpreted his concern. She'd most certainly misunderstood his kiss the day before. He'd kissed her with what she'd falsely interpreted as tender feeling. That he didn't welcome her kisses had just been made painfully obvious.

In those brief moments when Adam had held her after her accident, Persephone had felt stirrings of affection. But he'd pushed her away. She didn't understand him, didn't know what to think about Adam, about their marriage.

She'd always thought that affection would grow between them. She'd hoped that the tenderness she'd seen in him just moments before would remain. Instead he'd grown distant and cold. She'd taken a risk and reached out to him, only to be rejected.

It wasn't in her nature to give up entirely, but for the life of her she couldn't help feeling discouraged.

CHAPTER TWENTY-THREE

ADAM THREW OFF HIS BLANKET and sat up in bed. The wolves had been howling for nearly an hour. Where the deuce was Persephone?

He got out of bed. She ought to have come in already. She'd never waited so long before. Adam crossed to the connecting door but turned back without touching the handle. He was being ridiculous. Persephone was probably sleeping.

She hadn't come down to dinner. Maybe her fall had been more serious than he'd realized. Adam crossed back to the door again but stopped directly in front of it.

If Persephone wanted to come in, she would have. She certainly wouldn't want him going into her room. Adam shook his head and stormed back to his bed.

"Ridiculous," he snapped at himself, flinging himself down.

Adam closed his eyes, determined to fall asleep. But he couldn't clear his thoughts of Persephone. Gad, she'd scared him half out of his wits. He and Harry had been back from their ride for a quarter of an hour, and instead of going straight to the castle like he should have, Adam had stayed to watch Persephone ride.

He'd been impressed seeing her on a more difficult mount than Atlas. Then that blasted horse had thrown her. Adam didn't think he'd ever run as fast in all his life. When she didn't get up right away, he'd panicked.

What a sap he'd turned out to be. He should have handed her over to one of the grooms, should have kept his distance like he'd told himself he would. But he'd been worried.

Adam opened his eyes again. 'Twould be pointless to pretend he was going to sleep. Persephone was cutting up his peace. Seeing her lying still on the ground of the paddock had been more unsettling than the letter he'd received about Harry's illness. It had been more panic-inducing than the dream he still remembered so vividly about the wolves.

She'd kissed him. *She* had kissed *him*. At first he'd been too surprised to do anything but stand there, smelling her. Then she'd touched him. Touched those blasted, bloody scars, exactly the way Mother always had when he was little. She would run a finger down the longest one, the one that followed his jaw. "My poor boy," she'd say.

Adam wanted no one's pity.

"I'm sorry," Persephone had said. She might as well have offered a "my poor boy." A man comes to his wife's aid after she's thrown from a horse, and what does he get in return? Pity. He'd all but carried her back to the house, but Persephone didn't see him as her champion. All Persephone saw were the scars.

"It is too blasted quiet in here," Adam grumbled, sitting up again.

A howl sounded outside. Adam watched the door. It didn't open.

"This is ridiculous." Adam got to his feet again. He couldn't sleep, and he knew deuced well it was because Persephone wasn't there.

He hadn't had insomnia since childhood. The first few weeks after Mother had moved to London, he hadn't been able to sleep. Nothing Nurse Robbie said or did had helped. He'd eventually learned to force himself to sleep—not an easy feat for a six-year-old.

Mother never had come back. Persephone was going to.

Adam marched to the connecting door and opened it. Persephone wasn't asleep, Adam realized, seeing the bed empty. He found her in the next instant, sitting on the window seat, holding back the thin, blue curtains and gazing out into the darkness.

"Persephone." He kept his tone detached and neutral.

She jumped at the sound of his voice. "Adam!" Persephone turned to look at him, dropping the curtain.

"Aren't you asleep?" Adam asked, feeling like an idiot for posing such a pointless question.

"I couldn't seem to get to sleep."

"Are you stiff from your fall?" The memory of her accident flashed quickly through his mind.

Persephone shook her head. A howl echoed outside the window, and she visibly tensed. She turned to the window, pulling back the curtain once more.

"They are loud tonight," Adam said.

Persephone nodded mutely.

"How long do you plan to sit at that window and worry over the wolves?" Adam fought down a surge of empathy for Persephone. He knew how nervous the howling made her.

"Until they stop," she answered in a tiny voice.

She meant to sit there all night instead of coming into his room, where she would actually be able to sleep? No point in both of them being awake.

Adam crossed to her bed and pulled off the blanket. He reached her at the window and draped it over her shoulders.

"Adam?" Persephone looked up at him, so obviously confused.

"You should have come in when the wolves first started." Adam made his way to the door.

"Come in?" she repeated.

"And curled up on the bed." He stopped at the door and turned toward her, waiting.

"You knew?" Persephone whispered, her face paling noticeably. "I . . . I thought . . . I thought you were asleep."

"Asleep?" Adam answered, with an ironic raise of his eyebrows. "That's the problem."

"Problem?"

"I can't sleep." He shook his head at the ridiculousness of it. "You've ruined the room for me."

"What do you mean, I've ruined it?" Her forehead creased with confusion.

"My bedchamber used to be quiet. Then you started coming and making all those noises—"

"Noises?"

"When you sleep."

"I make noises?" Her pallor began to pink.

"And you move," Adam added. "Constantly."

"Good heavens," she whispered, pressing her hands to her cheeks. The blanket slipped to the floor.

Adam let out a frustrated sigh and crossed back to her.

"I have never been so embarrassed in all my life." Persephone turned away from him. "I was so sure you were asleep."

Adam picked the blanket up again and wrapped it around her. *Lavender.* Adam stepped back. Distance, he reminded himself.

"You must think I am an absolute coward," Persephone whispered. "And presumptuous. And . . . and . . ."

Adam held his hand out to her. She stood there, silently, just looking at his hand. Adam let it drop. Obviously, she didn't want his company any more than his own mother had, any more than every other person he'd ever known.

Adam walked away, moving to the door. He should never have come in. The Duke of Kielder begged favors of no one. He'd learned to force himself to sleep once—he could do it again. And he didn't care!

"Adam?"

He stopped on the spot.

"Do I really make noises in my sleep?"

He nodded.

"Loud noises?" She sounded uncomfortable.

"No." He shoved his hands into the pockets of his dressing gown. "Like . . . like a puppy. Little noises."

"And that doesn't bother you?" She wore the blanket wrapped around her precisely the way she had every night for weeks.

"I've grown used to it." He found himself too uncomfortable with the conversation to continue looking at her.

"I don't want to bother you." She sounded closer.

"You won't."

"All right."

"All right?" Adam looked over his shoulder at her.

"The wolves don't bother me as much in your bedchamber." Persephone even smiled a little. She passed through the connecting door.

"Are they quieter in there?" Adam followed her through the door.

"No," she replied. "The way I've figured it, if the pack ever actually makes it into the castle, they'll eat you first."

Adam was grateful he walked behind her. That comment brought a smile to his face before he could stop it. One look at his disfigured smile, and they'd be right back to "I'm sorry" and "my poor boy."

A minute later they'd returned to the established routine. Persephone lay curled in a ball, securely wrapped in her blankets. Adam could feel himself growing tired already.

How was it that in only a few weeks he'd come to depend on her for something as vital as sleep? Adam had promised himself after Mother had left twenty years ago, he would never depend on anyone.

"People depend on dukes. Dukes do not depend on people," Father used to say. He'd never said that before Mother moved to Town.

"Good night, Adam," Persephone said from the ball of blankets.

Nurse Robbie used to say that: *Good night, little Adam.* No one else ever had. Adam closed his eyes. He could almost picture her rocking beside his bed. Why were memories of his one-time nurse suddenly flooding back? In twenty years he hadn't thought of her once, and in the past month those memories wouldn't stop.

"Good night, Persephone," Adam muttered in reply.

What was happening to him? He'd made a fool of himself over Persephone's fall earlier. He ought to have stayed calm and detached.

He was chasing down his wife, practically begging for her company. He needed her nearby just to sleep.

Now he had turned mawkish over a childhood memory.

Adam rubbed his eyes. Maybe it was a temporary illness, something that would pass.

"Adam?"

Why was it that when Persephone said his name like that, quiet and uncertain, his heart seemed to thud a little harder? He shifted his eyes enough to look at the talking ball of blankets. As usual, she faced away from him.

"What?" he asked, managing not to snap at her in his frustration.

She hesitated. For a minute Adam thought he had offended her, and it bothered him. Giving offense *never* bothered him. What the blazes was happening to him?

"Why did you decide to get married?" She whispered the question, but without tears, without any threat of erupting emotions. It seemed almost as if Persephone was truly just curious about his motivation.

"At the time it seemed like a good idea."

"Does it now?"

How did he answer that? In a lot of ways it had turned into a horrible idea. Married life hadn't turned out the way he'd anticipated. His plans had been for a wife desperate enough to marry that she wouldn't care one way or another what her husband was like. And when a man married a desperate, uncaring woman, reciprocating those feelings was easy.

But he had married Persephone. Instead of life as usual at Falstone, he wondered about her and worried about her. She was supposed to have been plain and unappealing, but was pretty—more than pretty, really, with an aura of determined joy about her that was unlike any person he'd ever encountered. She attempted to smile through tears. She stood up in adversity. She wasn't cowed or browbeaten.

She wasn't what he'd wanted. A lady like her, he was discovering, could not be easily dismissed.

"Mrs. Adcock said you would." Persephone's reply caught Adam off guard. In his reflection, he'd almost forgotten her there.

"Said I would what?" It felt strange talking to a pile of bedclothes.

"Regret marrying me."

Adam felt his jaw tense.

"At the Pointers' several days ago, Mrs. Adcock said to Miss Greenburrough that most gentlemen who pay for a wife regret the purchase in the end. It was blatantly obvious she referred to our marriage settlement."

Adam's entire body tensed. He knew Mr. Adcock was a jack-a-napes but hadn't realized how well suited he and his wife really were.

"Mrs. Adcock had mentioned her sizable dowry at least a dozen times, so I happened to ask Lady Hettersham, loudly enough for Mrs. Adcock to hear, whether or not it seemed odd that some ladies found it necessary to offer money to a prospective bridegroom in order to bring him up to scratch. No gentleman would accept a horse so ill-recommended that he had to be bribed to accept it."

He laughed. Adam Boyce, Duke of Kielder, actually laughed out loud. He could not remember once, in the past twenty years, laughing out loud at anything.

"I thought Mrs. Adcock's tea would come flying out her ears—she looked so livid." Persephone laughed as well. "Mrs. Pointer was hard-pressed to maintain her countenance. She later informed me that Mrs. Adcock had been singularly proud of her dowry for years. Lady Hettersham very much doubts Mrs. Adcock will be as fond of mentioning that as she has been—at least amongst the ladies of the neighborhood."

"You compared her to a horse? I doubt even I could have produced such a cutting retort." He chuckled again. "Well done, Persephone."

"I have not pulled caps with anyone in years." Persephone giggled.

Giggled? Somehow Adam had never pictured that sound coming from a grown woman. And, stranger still, he found himself smiling at it.

"I felt like a regular warrior." Laughter rang in her tone. "Perhaps before I next call at the vicarage, I should try on one of the suits of armor for size. I could check the armory for a jousting lance and simply unseat my adversary as she rides up to the vicarage. I would be the terror of the neighborhood."

She laughed at that. So did Adam. Until that moment, he hadn't realized how good it could feel to simply laugh. And at what? A fanciful picture of his wife riding around the neighborhood knocking people off their horses.

"If it comes to full combat, let me know." Adam heard the smile in his tone. "I am rather handy with a crossbow."

Persephone laughed. Knowing he'd made her laugh was, for Adam, a strangely satisfying experience.

"Maybe Harry could be our page, and we could go conquer Adcock Manor."

"Harry would make an abysmal page." Adam shook his head. "But he might be trusted with a battle ax." It was, beyond a doubt, the strangest conversation Adam had ever had: lying in the dark, talking to a lady wrapped cocoon-like in a blanket, planning a medieval-style siege of a neighboring estate.

"Mr. Hewitt could be page," Persephone said, then burst out laughing.

Adam smiled into the darkness. "You have finally hit upon an occupation at which he could excel."

"The four of us would make a wonderfully fearsome team," Persephone said with something between a sigh and a yawn. "You see, Adam, marriage to me might not be such a terrible thing for you after all."

There was no answer to that.

CHAPTER TWENTY-FOUR

SOMETIME BETWEEN ADAM BLATANTLY REFUSING to return her obviously unwelcome kiss and their remarkably unusual discussion the night before about laying siege to Adcock Manor, Persephone had realized something she'd only vaguely acknowledged before: she was trying to make her marriage fit the dreams she'd always harbored about her future.

She'd spent countless hours, as all girls must, imagining a dashing young gentleman riding into the neighborhood, falling desperately and wonderfully in love with her. He would offer his heart, his home, his devotion. There would be love and tenderness. They would be the best of friends. They would raise a family and chickens—she wasn't sure why the chickens, but they'd always been clucking merrily around the yard whenever she'd pictured her future home. They would be surrounded by friends and family.

In the nearly two months she'd been at Falstone, none of that had appeared. Waiting for it, continuing to dream of it, was making her miserable. She could not make Adam fall in love with her. She could not transform him into the man she'd dreamed of—the man whom, admittedly, she had seen glimpses of in him. She could not force Falstone Castle to be warm and inviting. There would be no visitors. The chickens were clear on the other side of the inner wall. And, as far as she could tell, they would never have children.

She had been purchased, just as Mrs. Adcock had insinuated. For what purpose, Persephone could not say—other than to make

Mr. Hewitt worry over the state of his inheritance. That was hardly a fulfilling role to play for the next few decades.

So Persephone had come to a monumental decision. The one aspect of her childhood dreams she could even remotely imagine herself still achieving was friendship. Last night had been a start.

He had come to her room looking for her. After the initial mortification of being found out at sneaking into his room every night had subsided a little, she'd realized that his presence there was a step in the right direction.

She remembered with a stab of hurt, he had as much as admitted that he regretted marrying her, that he no longer viewed marriage as a good idea, something he'd apparently felt before meeting his bride.

But he'd laughed. He'd laughed with her over something absurd and lighthearted—something that could now be a joke between just the two of them. That sort of connection built friendships.

It wasn't what she wanted, Persephone realized despite her very sound reasoning. She still longed for a loving husband, a growing family, a true home. She wanted love. Other than her family, who were several counties away and feeling more distant all the time, she did not seem likely to have it.

So friendship, she firmly told herself, would simply have to be enough.

"His leg's still not up for riding, Yur Grace," one of the grooms said, snapping Persephone from her thoughts.

"Poor Atlas," Persephone replied. The groom nodded what seemed to be approval but kept his head lowered. Persephone didn't know this particular groom well. The few times she'd encountered him, he'd been quiet and shy. "Is he better at least?"

The groom nodded again. "Yes, Yur Grace."

"Well, then, I hope he—"

Thundering hooves pulled her attention to the front gate of Falstone. Adam and Harry had just ridden through and were reining in their mounts. Harry looked better than he had since his return.

Persephone smiled at the two gentlemen as they approached. Harry returned the gesture. Adam unbent enough to acknowledge her with a slight dip of his head.

Friends greet each other, she reminded herself when the urge to simply leave grew stronger.

"Welcome back," she said as they approached. Adam hadn't walked away, something she chose to view as encouraging.

"A good morning to you, Persephone," Harry offered with an informal bow.

"Good morning, Adam." Persephone watched him closely. Would today be a friendly-Adam day or a grumpy-Adam day? It was almost impossible to predict.

"Good morning." Adam was pointedly not looking at her. Why did he do that? Did he realize how frustrating that was? "How does Atlas fare this morning?"

She held back a sigh. "I'm afraid he's not yet up for a ride." Persephone glanced toward the groom to whom she'd spoken, but he had gone off, no doubt having plenty of work to occupy him. "I suppose we shall be forced to postpone our siege."

Adam's lips twitched. Had Persephone not been watching him closely, she would have missed it. She had expected him to not acknowledge their conversation in any way other than that, and yet she was grateful for even the small reaction.

Harry's eyes darted between the two of them, his look one of intrigued confusion. "You two are planning a siege?"

Persephone let her eyes dart to Adam. He didn't look at either of them. In fact, Adam seemed remarkably interested in watching John Handly lead Buttercup through her paces. He would have to give her more than that. Persephone's dreams had been whittled down to mere friendship—she had to have more than silence between them.

Then Adam's eyes shifted toward her, for the briefest of moments. And his lips turned up in the slightest, most fleeting smile. Almost before Persephone had registered what she'd seen, Adam turned back again to watch the filly bounding around the paddock. But it had been enough to make Persephone smile in return.

"Why do I get the feeling my presence is not particularly appreciated just now?" Harry spoke with a touch of amusement.

"I would think, Harry, that you must feel that way often," Adam replied dryly. He turned from the paddock, walking away. "But if you go now, you'll have plenty of time to pack."

"Ah, but you'd miss me." Harry laughed, following Adam.

"I never miss anyone." Adam did not pause nor look back nor seem to care if Harry followed.

He certainly wasn't missing *her,* Persephone thought as she watched the distance between them grow. George Sanford, one of her two best friends all the years she was growing up, had always remembered to offer his arm. He'd never once left Persephone behind to walk alone.

Persephone let out a whoosh of air. It condensed in front of her face. She rubbed at her cold, probably pink nose and turned back toward the paddock. Buttercup continued acting up. John Handly seemed rather content to let the troublesome horse get out her frustration.

Lucky filly. She, at least, could snort and pound her hooves in frustration. Persephone could do little more than stand out in the cold and wonder if she'd given up everything the day she'd accepted Adam's suit.

"An unhappy filly, wouldn't you say?"

Persephone looked up to see a vaguely familiar face smiling a lopsided, gap-toothed smile as he watched Buttercup kicking and snorting.

"It would certainly seem so." Why did the man, dressed as an undergardener, look so familiar to her? She watched Buttercup snap her vicious-looking teeth at John. "Perhaps her disposition is bad."

The man turned down his heavily lined mouth and shook his white-haired head. "Came here a few months back. Badly treated, she was. She don't trust people. Figures they was bad to her once, they'll be bad to her again."

"But John would never hurt her." Persephone watched Buttercup continue to storm about.

"Don't matter." The old man sucked a breath through his sparse teeth. "She won't give him a chance to. She'll fight him 'til holy perdition."

Persephone colored a little at the unaccustomed sound of such a coarse phrase. "It seems a lost cause. Why does John keep at it, I wonder?" Buttercup attempted to kick John, who managed to skirt the flailing hooves.

"There ain't no lost causes, Yer Grace," the man said, looking at her full on. His face was lined, but his eyes were bright. "Every creature has someone who could save 'em if only they would try."

Why did Persephone get the feeling she was missing something vital in this extremely odd conversation? "So is Buttercup more afraid or more angry?"

"Afeared." The man nodded with emphasis. "Been afeared fer years."

"I thought you said she'd only been here a few months."

"Used to be different." The man turned to face the paddock once more. "Didn't go after every person that came near. Friendly like."

"What happened?" How did he know so much about Buttercup? Had he accompanied the horse from her previous owners'?

"Got torn apart. Left behind." The man leaned against the fence and watched the ongoing power struggle out in the paddock. "Decided to bite before anyone bit first."

"That is tragic."

John stood closer to the troubled creature than he had a few minutes before, approaching slowly and cautiously the way he had for weeks.

"Aye."

The conversation ended there. The two of them stood silently beside each other, both watching John and Buttercup size each other up. An odd pair, to be sure. Both the two in the paddock and the two watching.

Every creature has someone who could save 'em if only they would try. Persephone glanced back at her companion. It seemed an absurdly philosophical observation for a man who, at first glance, gave the impression of poverty and the ignorance that, sadly, inevitably accompanied it.

"John is doing well with Buttercup."

Persephone spun around so quickly at the sound of Adam's voice that she felt herself topple. He reached out and righted her.

"The snow makes the ground slick," Adam said quietly, uncomfortably. His hands lingered the slightest moment on her waist.

Persephone could only nod. He wore a look she knew well but had never seen on him. She remembered it haunting her in the mirror the morning after her mother died. The midwife had handed her the baby, Artemis, and she knew in that moment that she had lost something profound. More than just a mother, she had lost her childhood.

She had pulled up her hair that day, something most girls wouldn't have done for several more years. As she had stared at her reflection, Persephone remembered being startled by the starkness in her expression, the hurt, the fear, the uncertainty.

"Are you well?" Adam whispered to her, obviously entirely confused.

Persephone could only stare back at him. She knew that look in his eyes. Had it always been there? How could she have missed something so familiar?

What happened to you? she silently asked.

"Perhaps the cold's too much for 'er," the man Persephone had all but forgotten suggested. "'Tis bitter out today."

"You may be right, Jeb." Adam nodded. He seemed to smile a little, almost encouragingly, at her. "I had come back with the intention of walking Her Grace to the castle."

"Did you really?" Persephone asked quietly, still studying those eyes she wasn't sure she'd ever truly looked into before.

"My mother taught me a few manners before she disappeared." Adam shrugged, holding out his arm to her.

A momentary intensity in his eyes spoke volumes. Persephone slipped her arm through his, her thoughts spinning dizzyingly. *Disappeared?* Persephone had seen Adam's mother at the wedding. She certainly hadn't disappeared. What had he meant by that?

"A nice hot cuppa tea'll warm 'er up," Jeb said.

Adam nodded to him.

"Good day to ye, Falstone," Jeb gave as a parting and turned back to watch John and Buttercup.

Adam led Persephone away from the paddock, toward the inner wall and the path that led back to the castle.

"Falstone?" Persephone asked, confused.

"Before my father died, I was Lord Falstone." The unease in his voice increased. "A courtesy title."

"Jeb knew you then?"

Adam answered with an infinitesimal nod. "He has been at Falstone nearly all his life. He was head gardener for many years."

"And now?"

"Rheumatism," Adam answered. "He still oversees the hedge garden. And helps his son in the stables now and then."

"John," Persephone said, understanding suddenly dawning: the familiarity of his face, his knowledge of John and the horses. Jeb was John's father.

"Have any of the other servants been at Falstone as long?" Her mind remained on Adam even as she spoke. What had happened with his mother? What was it that caused the bleakness in his eyes? It was still there, hidden behind the look of indifference she was only just beginning to see past.

"Mrs. Smithson began as a chambermaid." Adam walked stiffly, speaking in a tone of disinterest that the *ton* would have applauded. "That would have been some time ago. Barton has been here at least as long as I have."

Adam may have been disinterested—Persephone no longer trusted herself to interpret his demeanor or tone—but she certainly was not. Barton, the butler, had known Adam all his life. So had Jeb. And probably Mrs. Smithson.

If anyone understood this enigma she had married, they might. But how did someone approach her own staff with such a question?

"Pardon me, but could you please explain my husband to me?" That would never do.

Persephone looked up at Adam. His eyes were focused ahead. She walked on his left side, something she suspected he planned. She was *always* on his left side. His scars, she felt certain, were clues to his character, as was that inexplicable comment about his mother.

What she needed was someone who could help her interpret those clues. She would decipher them, she knew that much. In her heart of hearts she knew that doing so was essential.

CHAPTER TWENTY-FIVE

MOTHER HAD A WAY WITH WORDS. According to his esteemed parent, Adam's name was on the lips of every member of the *ton*. This time, the Upper Ten Thousand chose to entertain itself by speculating on his recent marriage.

Some are saying that Persephone has left you already.

"Thank you, Mother," Adam muttered, tossing her letter onto his desk. Apparently, Mother thought Adam missed the spiteful gossip of society. Unlike herself, Adam preferred being as far from London as he could possibly get for as long as he could possibly manage. Only Parliament brought him to Town.

Father had devoured the first few letters Mother had sent back to Falstone after she had moved to London. Adam had watched him read, holding his breath, hoping Father would tell him that Mother was coming back. After six months Adam had quit hoping, and Father had begun simply burning the letters unopened.

"We are fine without her," Father had told him. "We do not need her here."

They hadn't needed anyone. Adam had spent his days dogging his father's heels, learning the Falstone lands inch by inch. He had learned where the forests were being replanted, where the pack would be found in each season, where the tenant cottages were and who lived in each. He had learned the servants by name, which families had served at Falstone for generations. Father had taught him to be a duke, to do his duty.

Neither he nor his father had needed a single soul beyond each other. Then Father died.

At seven, Adam was the Duke of Kielder. Mother came to Falstone for the funeral and had seemed genuinely grieved. She'd stayed long enough to help Nurse Robbie pack Adam's personal effects and wave her handkerchief as the Falstone traveling coach took Adam to Harrow.

Adam rubbed his eyes, leaning back in the armchair he always occupied when alone in his book room. He couldn't seem to stop the memories he had no desire to relive.

Harrow had been nothing short of torture those first few weeks. Father had been dead only a month. Adam wore a black armband around the sleeve of his blue Harrow jacket and, overwhelmed by his grief, had kept himself from crying by biting the insides of his cheeks until he bled. He'd grown accustomed to the metallic taste of his blood in those early months.

What he hadn't come to accept, what he hadn't anticipated, was the staring and the whispers. He'd known his face was scarred, knew what the surgeons had done to him. But no one at Falstone had stared. No one at Falstone had cared, beyond Mother and her unceasing "my poor boy."

"Do not pity him, Harriet," Father would insist every time Mother had called Adam by her favorite moniker. "Adam will be Kielder someday. He has to learn to fight battles."

Jeb Handly and Father had taken up his education early on, teaching him to fight in the back courtyard of Falstone. Harrow had provided ample opportunity to use those skills. Between his indisputable tone and air of authority—another weapon he'd learned from his father—and his ability to back up his threats, the other boys had quickly learned to take the Duke of Kielder at his word.

The boys left him alone and, in his solitude, Adam had thought of Falstone and Father and had done his best not to think of Mother. His isolation had lasted all of two terms, ending abruptly the day a group of older boys had decided to rough up a scrawny boy far younger than they were.

Adam had seen their victim before—he'd always seemed too small, too defenseless. Despite being outnumbered and puny, the kid had been defending himself with a determination Adam couldn't help admiring. So Adam had stepped into the fray. He'd only been seven himself, but the dynamics of that brawl had changed the moment he'd joined. All of Harrow knew he didn't find it necessary to fight politely: no holds were barred, no part of the anatomy was off limits. He was unrelenting and, at times, vicious.

By the end of his first year at Harrow, Adam had no longer needed to fight. He had become legend. And he had a shadow.

The scrawny boy hadn't left him alone since the day Adam broke the noses of two of his assailants and very nearly broke the arm of the third. In fact, Harry, who was no longer scrawny, was in Adam's library at that very moment. He was the only person Adam had ever known who had stayed with him.

Some are saying that Persephone has left you already. Adam glanced uneasily at Mother's letter where it lay discarded on his desk. His plan had been to marry a lady who could leave, as she inevitably would, and her absence wouldn't have bothered him in the least—a woman he would be better off without, whom he wouldn't need. But the thought of Persephone leaving had a far from neutral effect. Adam rose abruptly to his feet, pacing to the fireplace.

Mother had stayed for years before moving to Town. Before that final departure, she had been gone often. Every time a new surgeon had arrived, Mother had left. She would tell him to be brave, say how very sorry she was, and then she would leave. New-castle had been one of her favorite destinations. About the time his new wounds had healed enough for the pain to be bearable, she would return. "My poor boy," had always been her words of greeting.

What difference would it make to him if Persephone decided to spend weeks, months, away from Falstone? Or when she eventually left altogether?

Adam pushed away from the mantel and crossed to the French doors overlooking her garden. He'd begun thinking of the hedge garden as somehow belonging to Persephone. She spent a great deal of time there, reading, sitting, walking. Twice he'd watched her as she'd sat on the stone bench in the back corner and wept.

What difference would it make if she left? More than he would ever have guessed when he'd first written his offer. For one thing, he knew he wouldn't be able to sleep. And he'd found, the day before, that he liked walking with her. They'd only gone from the stables to the castle, but he liked having her there, her arm linked in his.

She'd made him laugh. He still chuckled when he thought back on their late-night conversation. In his mind he could picture the two of them clanking about in full armor attempting to take the neighborhood by force and claim it for Kielder. Who would he laugh with if she were gone?

Adam shook his head. There was no point denying the obvious. If Persephone left, Adam would miss her. He, who never missed anyone, would miss her.

He glanced across the room at the painting hung over the mantel. It was the last portrait ever painted of his father, less than three months before he'd died. It was to have been a family sitting, but Mother hadn't returned for it. Adam knew that she and Father had exchanged heated letters over the issue. Mother insisted that the artist paint Adam without his scars. Father had insisted otherwise.

There he stood, Adam at nearly seven, scars apparent to the world, beside his father, completely oblivious to the cruel hand fate would soon deal him. His father's image drew Adam's gaze. Had he missed Mother? Looking back with an adult's perspective, Adam realized Father had.

"Adam?"

His eyes snapped to the door. Persephone stood just inside the doorway, a letter clutched in her hands. "Do you have a minute?"

Adam nodded but felt ridiculously uncomfortable. When one is thinking rather confusing thoughts about a person, it is remarkably disconcerting for that person to suddenly appear.

Persephone stepped inside, and Adam felt his pulse quicken. She'd been doing that to him lately, and he was at a loss to explain why. It was almost as if she made him nervous. No one made him nervous.

"This is a very nice room," Persephone said, looking around. "Mrs. Smithson skipped this room when she gave me my tour. I don't think I have ever been in here."

"No one ever comes in here." Adam felt inexplicably put out and decided her intrusion into his private space had unnerved him.

"Oh." She stepped back. Adam wondered if it was an involuntary instinct, for she hardly seemed aware of her retreat. "I am intruding, then?"

It was the perfect opportunity to send her away, to reclaim his last sanctuary. She'd already invaded his bedchamber. He found, however, that he didn't want her to go. He hadn't seen Persephone all day, and it was well past noon.

John had told him Atlas still wasn't rideable. What had Persephone done with her morning, having her usual ride canceled? He wondered how she spent her time, what she thought about. It was an odd feeling for him, thinking about another person as much as he did.

"Not at all," he heard himself answer her. He even motioned her inside the room.

Persephone moved to the chairs nearest the fireplace, her eyes still wandering around the room. Why was his book room so intriguing to her?

Adam studied her as intently as she studied the room. He'd selected every piece of furniture in it. He had chosen where each painting hung. Did she approve? Approval had never mattered to him before.

A sudden flash of memory took him back twenty years.

"Very good, son. Very good." Father had said that, eying the picture Adam had drawn of Falstone. He'd worked for days on it, desperate to get each detail correct. The "very good" was exactly what he'd wanted to hear, *desperately* wanted to hear. Father, Adam remembered, had always been the one person he could count on to say just that.

Adam shook off the memory only to realize Persephone was staring at the portrait above the mantel. He felt uneasy, nervous. Perhaps the artist should have painted over the scars. Persephone's childhood portraits were probably the rosy-cheeked cherubic paintings most children inspired.

"Who is this you are standing beside, Adam?" Persephone asked, tilting her head to one side as if studying the painting more closely.

"My father." He resisted the urge to move to her side.

"I thought he must be. You look very much like him."

"Do I?" No one had ever told him that before.

"Very much," she confirmed. "You have the same eyes. And there is something very similar about your mouth and the shape of your face. And, of course, you both have black hair."

"I suppose there is a resemblance." Adam moved closer, looking for the likeness.

"Your nose is your mother's." Persephone shifted her gaze from the portrait to Adam himself. "I noticed that when I first saw the two of you together."

No one had ever mentioned that resemblance, either. But then he and Mother were rarely seen together. He doubted many people even noticed his nose when presented with the rest of him.

"Are you like him in other ways?" Persephone looked once more at the painting.

"Like my father?"

She nodded.

"I hope so," Adam answered more quietly than he'd intended. When Persephone took that response as her cue to turn those scrutinizing brown eyes—why hadn't he noticed before that they were brown?—on him, Adam shifted topics. "You wanted to speak to me about something?"

He walked abruptly away. The distance, he found, didn't help. He was every bit as aware of her presence as he'd been standing next to her.

"Yes." Enthusiasm colored her voice again. "I have a letter from Athena."

Athena. She was the oldest of Persephone's sisters. Seventeen or eighteen, if Adam remembered correctly.

"They have received word that the *Triumphant* will make port the last week of November and that Linus will be granted three weeks' shore leave. Isn't that wonderful?" She smiled broadly, her eyes sparkling in a way they hadn't since she'd married him. Her face lit up when she spoke of her family. He began to truly wonder if she was at all happy at Falstone. "The *Triumphant* is docking at Newcastle. If Linus sends word when they arrive, I could be there to see him before he has to go to Shropshire."

"Be there? In Newcastle?" Adam tensed.

"It isn't so very far."

Newcastle is not far, my poor boy.

"I wouldn't be gone more than a day or two."

I will be back before you even have time to miss me.

"Of course, I would want to see him off as well, which would mean going back when the *Triumphant* set out again."

I know I was just there, but Mother has so many things to do when she is away.

"You can't go." Even as he spoke, Adam could hear his own childhood voice echoing the same words in his memory.

Then he saw Persephone pale, her smile disappearing in an instant. There was no disbelief, no shock, only disappointment. "Please, Adam," she pleaded with him. "It would only be a few days."

He felt like an ogre. He knew how devastating the past few weeks had been for Persephone, how she'd grieved the loss of one brother and feared for the loss of the other. How could he deny her the opportunity to see for herself that the lad was well?

But what if she left and never came back? Mother had found hundreds of reasons to prolong her stays in Newcastle over the years. The same had been true of London. Eventually she simply hadn't returned.

"It could be years before I see him again." Persephone's voice broke a little as she spoke.

"Bring him here," Adam blurted.

"But you don't allow visitors."

Adam shrugged off her extremely logical argument. He *didn't* allow visitors. So why had he just invited one? "It makes far more sense than your going to Newcastle. Linus can come here before going to see your family."

"Do you mean it?" Persephone sounded entirely shocked.

She obviously had not expected a simple kindness from her husband. It was a wonder she hadn't left him as society claimed.

"I don't say anything I don't mean."

"And it wouldn't be too much of an imposition?"

"I'd rather like to meet the boy myself."

"Really?" Persephone allowed the tiniest of smiles.

"Linus might make a good page." Adam shrugged, surprising himself with his own attempt at humor. "Hewitt will probably faint dead away at the first battle cry. It would be wise to have a backup."

Persephone's smile grew. For just a moment she looked as though she would reach out to him. The look passed quickly, however, as if she'd reminded herself not to. Adam wondered why that was. Why, when she had kissed him only days before—twice in twenty-four hours—was she suddenly keeping a civil distance between them?

"Thank you, Adam," she said, making her way to the book room door.

Adam waved off the gratitude. He hadn't made the offer in order to be thanked. He'd done so for entirely selfish reasons—so she wouldn't leave and so he wouldn't have to miss her.

Trouble was, there would be other opportunities, other reasons for her to leave. He couldn't prevent them all. He knew there wouldn't always be an argument to keep her at Falstone, and he wasn't about to become her prison keeper.

He needed to see to it that she wanted to stay. But how did he go about seeing that his wife was happily settled at home, was contented enough to not need to wander the country? Adam had no idea. Nothing about the home he'd grown up in had enticed his mother to remain.

"Persephone seemed in good spirits."

He didn't need to look over to see who had spoken. "Come in, Harry."

If anyone knew about not leaving, Harry did. And Adam needed some expert advice.

CHAPTER TWENTY-SIX

"You're not going to tell me to go pack my bags?" Harry dropped into his usual chair. "Are you feeling well, Adam?"

"Why don't you ever leave?" Adam jumped right into the topic.

"I knew it was too good to be true." Harry sighed and rose from his seat, a spark of laughter in his eyes.

"Sit down and answer the question, Harry."

"Is this a pointed interrogation or more of an intellectual discussion?" Harry regained his seat.

"Intellectual discussion."

"Why don't I ever leave? Honestly?"

"Yes, honestly."

Harry shrugged. "Because I like Falstone."

"Why?"

"Free food."

"I said honestly, Harry." Adam was having second thoughts.

"The food is nothing to disregard, Adam. Cook is a miracle worker. Aside from that, Falstone is, I don't know, familiar. Comfortable."

Familiar. Comfortable. Adam doubted Persephone would describe Falstone that way.

"And do you feel the same way about the house in London? You spend a lot of time there as well. And you've gone with me to Kent a few times. And on the yacht—"

"This *is* a pointed interrogation, isn't it?" Harry speared him with a look. "If you're trying to tell me to make myself scarce now that you're married, I completely understand, Adam."

"It's not that at all."

"Then what is it?"

"I just want to know why you've stayed around all these years." Adam paced back to the French doors. Why couldn't Harry ever just answer a question?

"We're friends, Adam." Harry spoke as if that ought to have been obvious. "Friends don't jump ship."

"I think your answer about the food was more honest."

"Did it ever occur to you, Adam, that I honestly consider you a friend? My best friend, in fact."

"Because of Harrow?" Adam stared out the French doors. He hated to think that Harry had spent twenty years at his side because of some overblown sense of obligation.

"It may have started that way," Harry confessed. "You saved my skin, so I sort of worshiped you for a while, like an idol who could ward off evil spirits, I suppose."

Adam smiled a little at that. Harry had come across almost as a religious zealot those first few months of their friendship. *Friendship.* Adam repeated the word to himself. It felt right describing it that way. Adam had never really thought of himself as the sort of person who had friends.

Father hadn't had many. It had felt like Mother had too many. She was always away visiting one or more of them.

"But then you landed me a facer for something stupid I did or said—"

Adam remembered that fight well, though he no longer had any idea what they'd been scuffling over. They were eight at the time. The two-boy brawl had been ferocious. It was as if something inside Adam had snapped. He couldn't have been fiercer if he'd been actually fighting to save his life.

Harry had fought back, hard. By the time the scuffle was broken up—by the headmaster, of all people—they were both bloody and exhausted. And, he remembered with some unnameable emotion, he had been crying. Sobbing, really. And had been unable to stop.

No one but Harry and the headmaster had witnessed his breakdown. Neither one had ever mentioned it to him afterward.

"—and we were sent down," Harry continued. "My parents were away on holiday so we both came here. In those two weeks of our expulsion I met Adam Boyce. The Duke of Kielder still scared the guts out of me. But Adam Boyce was just a boy like me."

That was when Harry had started calling him Adam. Until those two weeks of punishment, which had actually been the happiest days of his life since his father had died, Harry, like everyone else, had referred to Adam as Kielder or Your Grace or the Duke—he being the only duke at Harrow. But during that time he'd become Adam. He'd never before understood what had brought about the change.

"I remember Jeb Handly teaching me the finer points of fisticuffs on the back courtyard so you wouldn't beat me so thoroughly the next time."

"Finer points?" Adam replied dryly. "He taught you to fight dirty."

Harry grinned at that. "Just like you. I suppose, though, when one's lessons are given in the shadow of a well-used gibbet, dirty is the only option."

"I thought you would faint like a schoolgirl when you first caught sight of the gibbet." Adam chuckled at the memory.

"At least you didn't make me sleep in the Orange Chamber."

They'd spent the two weeks in the nursery. "Do you remember Nurse Robbie?"

"The one who used to sing that song?" A smile was obvious in his voice. "The one about the boy who was small as a dandelion or something."

"It was a thistle."

Just then a movement down below caught his attention. Persephone was walking in her garden. Why did she wear that old, brown coat? Certainly she had the pin money to buy herself a new one. She ought to be wearing something warm but fashionable, the way the ladies in London dressed. The black of her day dress peeked out beneath the long coat, a perpetual reminder of her grief.

Had she retreated to the garden for another bout of weeping? Adam watched her more closely, hoping she hadn't.

"So why this sudden interest in our colorful childhoods?" Harry asked, moving to Adam's side.

Adam shrugged, watching Persephone make her way slowly along the hedge. He could see her breath condensing in the cold, even from so far away. She had to be freezing. He ought to send word to the kitchen to have a pot of tea or chocolate ready for her when she returned.

"Looks bloody cold out there, doesn't it?" Harry said.

"It does."

"She must really like that garden to stay out there when it is so much warmer inside," Harry said.

"Why does she stay?" Adam muttered to himself, not particularly thinking of the garden.

"If there is one thing I will never understand, Adam, it's women. Why does she walk through the garden in the freezing cold? I don't know. There must be something about it she likes, something worth being out there for."

What, Adam asked himself, made the hedge garden so appealing to Persephone? She went out there every day. Adam had watched her wandering about when he ought to have been seeing to estate business. Something drew her back day after day. If Adam could just figure out what that was and implement it elsewhere around Falstone, then Persephone would never want to leave.

"What is it that women love about gardens?" Harry could have been reading Adam's thoughts.

"I have no idea."

"My mother spent hours in her garden whenever my father was away from home." Harry shook his head. "One would think if she was lonely, she would have visited the neighbors instead of the shrubbery."

"The garden kept her company?" Adam asked doubtfully.

"Like I said, there is very little about women that I even remotely understand." Harry moved away from the French doors. "Persephone looks cold, Adam," he said as he made his way across the room. "You should go keep her warm."

"Keep her—?"

"The fact that my suggestion confuses you does not bode well, my friend," was Harry's parting shot.

"Didn't confuse me," Adam muttered, turning back to watch Persephone. He simply couldn't imagine her wishing for the sort of attention Harry had suggested.

She did look cold. What kept her out there? Harry's mother had been lonely. Could that be Persephone's reason as well?

Adam thought back on the vicar's visit. She'd been so disappointed when she thought Adam would bring the call to a premature close. She made the trip to the Pointers' twice a week to visit with the local ladies. He'd seen her face light up whenever Barton delivered another letter from her family.

"She *is* lonely," Adam said with bleak resignation. He watched Persephone turn another corner of the garden, walking alone. Isolation was heaven for Adam. It seemed quite the opposite for Persephone.

I require people, Joseph, Mother had said so many times to Father, though Adam hadn't thought about those conversations in years. *There are more people in one neighborhood of London than in all of Falstone.*

So Father had hosted countless balls and dinners. Mother had been "at home" to callers every day for hours on end. Still, she'd left dozens of times, and always when Adam had needed her most. She hadn't even been at Falstone when Adam and Harry had been sent down. Jeb Handly and Nurse Robbie had looked after them.

Adam turned his head and looked up into the frozen face of his father. "The balls didn't work," he said, as if his father hadn't noticed that the endless diversion he'd provided for Mother hadn't kept her at home. "I—" The words stuck, but Adam pushed them out. He could always talk to his father. "I don't want Persephone to leave me."

Admitting it out loud somehow drove home how true the words were. The thought of Persephone disappearing the way Mother had made his stomach knot. The thought of hundreds of people prowling around Falstone Castle—be it a ball, a dinner, or a neighborhood invasion—made him feel ill.

"Blast it!" Adam crossed to the fireplace, throwing himself into a chair. Being married wasn't supposed to be this complicated.

A wolf howled outside. Howling during the day wasn't entirely unheard of. The noises of the household generally drowned out their cries. But that howl had been uncommonly close to the castle.

Persephone! She would be insane with fear. Adam jumped to his feet again and crossed back to the French doors. He didn't see her in her garden. A second howl sounded.

Adam spotted her running back toward the castle. She *was* hysterical, he realized.

He moved swiftly across the room and out into the corridor. A moment later he reached the first-floor landing and watched as Persephone flew through the front door. Barton stood in obvious confusion, but Persephone didn't seem to notice.

Adam met her halfway up the stairs. Persephone nearly knocked him over. She wrapped her arms around his middle and buried her face into his lapel. She was trembling. So was he, but probably for entirely different reasons.

"I heard them, Adam!" Her words cracked with fear. "The wolves are inside Falstone!"

"No, Persephone." Adam held her a little closer. She was cold, he told himself.

"I don't know how, but they must be inside." Her voice rose in alarm. "They were so loud."

"They aren't inside the castle walls, Persephone."

"Are you certain?" She buried her head more deeply against him.

"Positive." Adam spotted Barton near the door watching the exchange rather too closely for Adam's tastes. "Barton, will you send tea up to my book room?"

"Yes, Your Grace." That took care of the butler.

Adam kept one arm around Persephone and led her up the stairs.

"The wolves sounded so close," she whispered.

"I will have my steward check on the pack," Adam assured her. "They always give the castle a wide berth."

Adam walked her directly to the book room's most comfortable chair, grateful it sat so near the fire. She'd been out in the cold too long. "Tea should come soon."

"Thank you, Adam." Persephone smiled up at him as she sat, but she still looked worried.

"Persephone?"

"Yes, Adam?"

"I think . . . I think we should have a ball."

"A ball?" She couldn't possibly have sounded more shocked. Adam was a little surprised, too.

"Unless you don't want to." Adam shot a look at Father's portrait. He should have known the ball wasn't a good idea.

"I assumed *you* wouldn't want to," Persephone said. "It would mean a lot of people in the castle."

"Every bride should have a ball," Adam muttered.

"We are still in mourning." She spoke uncertainly.

"I think a wedding ball would be permissible." Anything he did was considered permissible by society. No one dared contradict him.

"Really?" The hint of hope in her voice tugged a smile from Adam's lips.

"Really." He allowed the smile to remain, small as it was.

Again a look crossed Persephone's face, one that seemed to hint that she held something back, a word or a gesture. In the end, she simply smiled. "I think a ball would be nice."

CHAPTER TWENTY-SEVEN

HARRY ACTUALLY HAD TO SIT DOWN. "Adam *suggested* it?" He shook his head almost convulsively. "*Adam?* The Adam I know?"

"I don't understand it, either," Persephone admitted. "I never would have thought that Adam was capable of suggesting a ball at Falstone Castle."

"He didn't mention this at dinner last night." Harry continued his head shaking. "When did he propose this scheme?"

"Yesterday afternoon. I fully expect to hear he has changed his mind."

"No doubt." Harry's expression grew ponderous. "Adam has been doing a lot of uncharacteristic things lately, come to think of it."

"Has he?" Her quest to understand Adam better had only left her more confused than before. Hopefully, Harry could provide her with some insight.

"Just yesterday, in his book room, in fact." He gave her an ironic look. "He talked for twenty minutes, at least, about our days at Harrow and his old nurse, Nurse Robbie. He kept asking me why I haven't dropped his acquaintance. Adam doesn't talk about things like that. He doesn't talk about anything remotely personal."

She'd wanted insight. That was certainly a great deal to think about. Adam didn't discuss personal things. Persephone had noticed that herself. Apparently, however, Adam had been doing just that—insisting upon it, if Harry was to be believed. It was entirely out of character, and Persephone wondered what had instigated the sudden need in Adam.

She felt certain Adam had spoken with Harry on the topics he had because he needed to for one reason or another. Artemis became that way at times. Generally, she preferred not to talk about the mother she had never known. The subject invariably left her quiet and unusually distant. Persephone suspected that Artemis silently blamed herself for their mother's death, passing as she had in childbirth. But there were times when Artemis simply had to speak of her, to hear of her. Those times nearly always came when Artemis felt most needy, when she was ill or upset or frightened.

Persephone wondered what it was that Adam needed.

"Barton says Cook is in tears." It was an uncharacteristic entrance for Adam, who, generally, chose the more formal and impersonal approach. He raised his eyebrow the way he always did when he found something humorous. Adam never actually laughed. Except, Persephone remembered with a secret smile, for the time they'd spent a few nights ago planning a fictitious attack on the neighborhood.

"What did you do to her?" Harry asked.

"I didn't do anything." Adam walked to the windows of the sitting room, his back now turned to its other occupants. "She was informed about the upcoming ball."

"She is that upset about it?" Persephone's heart sunk.

"She is that *pleased* about it," Adam corrected. "She's been reduced to weeping at the kitchen table."

"How has the rest of the staff reacted?" Persephone kept her amusement at Cook's response to herself.

"Mrs. Smithson is acting as urgent as though the ball is this evening instead of three weeks from now. Barton has simply begun grinning when he thinks I am not looking."

"Three weeks from now?" Persephone rose to her feet as she spoke. "But, Adam, Linus is supposed to be coming in three weeks' time. Please tell me you haven't changed your mind about his visit." She stood watching him, knowing her face had probably gone unflatteringly pale.

Adam looked almost hurt at her words. Hurt? She'd never imagined that Adam could be injured by anything any person said. "Of course not, Persephone." His eyes connected with hers, and she felt a twinge of shame for doubting him, so obvious was his frustration at her assumption. "I thought Linus would like to be part of the celebration." Adam looked away from her. "He is a little young to dance at a ball, but he might make an appearance, at least."

"I think Linus would appreciate being included," Persephone answered as Adam walked away.

She wanted to be Adam's friend and, thus far, had managed only to isolate him further. The silence in the room grew heavy. Harry, Persephone noticed, watched Adam with a degree of perplexity that did not bode well. If Adam's closest friend found his behavior confusing, then Persephone did not stand a chance.

She searched her mind for the right thing to say, the right topic to pursue. Harry had said Adam seemed determined lately to discuss his childhood.

"Would you have enjoyed a ball when you were thirteen?" Persephone asked him.

"He does not enjoy a ball *now,*" Harry said.

Persephone gave Harry a frustrated look.

"So why the sudden urge to entertain, Adam?" Harry pushed the subject.

Adam paced to the window but didn't answer.

"You've invited Persephone's little brother. And, now, with the ball, I imagine every family of consequence in the northern half of England will be at Falstone at the same time." Harry's comments were not having a positive effect on Adam's mood. "That is precisely the sort of thing that makes you miserable."

Miserable? "I don't want you to be miserable, Adam," Persephone said, her attention entirely focused on him.

"I will not be miserable," he grumbled.

He seemed miserable already.

"You will simply make the rest of us miserable," Harry said. "Perhaps you should call the entire thing off and save us the suffering."

Call it off? Not extend the invitations? Including Linus's? Persephone's eyes were glued to Adam. He wouldn't actually do it, would he?

"I, for one, am in favor of keeping Falstone as quiet and undisturbed as possible. For then, you will be as quiet and undisturbed as possible, and that is best for all concerned," Harry continued.

Persephone could feel her alarm growing. Suppose he managed to convince Adam to take back his invitation?

"And I don't believe any of the invitations have actually been sent yet," Harry added. "So there should be little difficulty preventing any visitors from actually arriving—"

"Shut up, Harry." Persephone barely recognized her own voice, choked as it was by a sudden influx of emotion.

Both gentlemen's eyes fixed on her, shock apparent in Harry's, surprise mingled with something nearing amusement in Adam's.

"So help me, Harry, if you talk him into turning my brother away," she said, her voice unnaturally high, "I'll . . . I'll have you put in the gibbet cage!"

"Do not forget my crossbow, Persephone." Adam moved to stand directly beside her. "It would be an efficient means of silencing him."

"But the gibbet is crueler," she mumbled, lowering her eyes to hide the sudden sheen of moisture that entered them.

Persephone realized in that moment that despite her determination otherwise, she had her heart firmly set on seeing her brother. Should Adam back out of his offer, she would be devastated.

"I had no idea I deserved such a fate."

Persephone glared at Harry but couldn't prevent the slightest tremor in her chin.

"Harry is not nearly persuasive enough to convince me to cancel Linus's visit, Persephone." Adam sounded frustrated anew. Persephone listened without looking up. "I have told you before that I do not say things that I do not mean. I told you Linus was coming to Falstone. There is no need for you to worry over that."

"But there is." She turned to face him, her own frustration nearly boiling over. "You tell me to trust you, but I don't know that I can. I don't know anything about you, Adam. I have no idea what kind of man you are. And that . . . that frightens me."

"I frighten you?" His voice was low, a troubled look in his eyes.

"That isn't what I said."

"It really isn't," Harry confirmed.

"Shut up, Harry," Persephone and Adam snapped in unison.

He smiled as if entirely amused by the situation. "I am happy to see I am a unifying force."

It was too much. Feeling her resolve crumble, Persephone spun away from them both and began a flight for the door. After one step, a hand caught hold of her wrist.

She glanced back, surprised, confused, and a little concerned. Adam held her there, forehead creased in apparent frustration. "Don't go," he said, his voice full of command and authority.

Persephone attempted to pull free, but he held her fast. "Let me—"

"Please don't go," he amended.

Persephone ceased struggling the moment she looked into his face. There was that look again, the one she would have sworn came from pain or fear or both. It was subtle, almost lost in the detachment and sense of superiority he exuded.

Sometime along the way, Adam had been hurt, and the pain still clung to him. And in those rare moments when a gentler Adam emerged from beneath the hardened surface, Persephone thought she was seeing who he truly was.

"Now would be a perfect opportunity, Harry, for a timely exit." Adam didn't look at his friend. He still held Persephone by the wrist, though not at all painfully.

"Hint taken." Harry swept an overdone bow before gliding from the room.

"Now listen to me, Persephone Iphigenia." Adam gave her a very determined, almost fierce look, his tone one that brooked no arguments. "I have faults, like any other man, but I am not a liar. I have promised that your brother will visit you here and no one, not Harry, not anyone else, will browbeat me into going back on that promise. Is that clear?"

She felt her chin quiver even as she nodded her understanding. And in an instant the duke seemed to melt away, and she felt almost as though she were looking at an ordinary man.

"Don't start crying," he said, sounding confused and concerned.

With her free hand, Persephone brushed at an escaping tear. "I guess I didn't realize how much I want to see my brother until I was afraid I wouldn't be able to."

Adam seemed to study her for a moment, indecision flashing through his eyes.

"Forgive me," Adam muttered uncomfortably as he released her wrist.

Persephone shook off the apology. Neither of them moved, but they stood not more than an arm's length apart, eyes darting around the room, settling occasionally on one another, though never remaining there for more than the length of a breath. It was not a comfortable silence. The air around them seemed jumpy and anxious.

"Have you walked through your garden today?" His voice was almost unrecognizably soft.

"My garden?"

"The hedge garden," he awkwardly corrected. Adam even looked a little embarrassed.

He thought of it as *her* garden just as she did, Persephone thought with awe. Did he understand why it had become so important to her? Why she treasured it the way she did? "It has been snowing," she answered his question.

Adam actually smiled. "This is Northumberland."

Heavens, he looked so much more pleasant when he smiled. The smile reached his eyes that time. His blue eyes. Divinely blue.

"It will snow for months."

"In other words, I need to grow accustomed to snow." She smiled back.

He nodded mutely, studying her the way she studied him. How she wished mourning attire allowed for blue. She felt prettier with blue eyes, and Persephone couldn't remember a time when she wanted to look pretty more than she did at that moment.

That thought hit her hard. She had to close her eyes against the realization. If Adam continued being kind and gentle, and if she wasn't very careful, Persephone was in very real danger of developing feelings for him, feelings that went far beyond friendship. A one-sided love was not at all what she wanted.

CHAPTER TWENTY-EIGHT

ADAM WAS SPEECHLESS. HE WAS never speechless. He had entered the drawing room in anticipation of dinner only to find his mother sharing a sofa with Persephone.

"Good evening." Mother smiled that pitying smile she always used. "You look a bit unwell, poor boy."

"I am fine." Adam paced away from her. He hadn't actually expected Mother to come to Northumberland for the ill-conceived wedding ball. He ought to have known better. Balls had never kept her at Northumberland, but they had always brought her back: back from Newcastle, back from Leeds, back from London.

"I was just telling Persephone of the wonderful balls we used to have here at the castle." Mother's tone turned wistful and reminiscent. "Even the London papers were full of every detail of the evening; who attended, the decorations, the menu. Falstone balls were positively legendary."

"And completely pointless," Adam added under his breath. He knew his father had staged the monumental entertainments solely for Mother. She'd left anyway.

"I am certain our ball will be far less elaborate." No apology hung in Persephone's tone, no disappointment, merely a statement of fact. Adam was grateful for that. Somehow he couldn't bear the thought of her being disappointed by her wedding ball, or anything else for that matter—especially by him. If she asked, he would give her the most extravagant evening she could imagine.

"Oh, but it could be," Mother said to Persephone. "A few changes to the menu, perhaps a more involved decorating scheme—"

"No," Persephone interrupted. "My tastes are far more simple, I assure you. Mrs. Smithson and I have discussed the menu and the preparations, and I am quite satisfied."

"Satisfied and pleased are not the same thing," Mother pointed out.

Was she displeased, then? Adam looked over at Persephone from the corner of his eye. She did appear a little flustered.

Adam moved to the window. The informal drawing room overlooked the north garden and tower. It was the only area of Falstone permitted to run wild. He'd always liked it, the one part of his home that never felt contrived.

"I am both satisfied and pleased," Persephone insisted.

Adam wondered if she meant it. She was precisely the sort of person who would accept less than what she wanted in order to please another, in order to have peace and harmony. He didn't want her settling. He didn't want her merely contented. Adam wanted her to be happy. He wanted Falstone to be her home. He wanted her to have everything she wished for.

Rubbing his forehead with his hand, Adam let out a long, silent breath. "I sound just like my father," he said to himself. For the first time in his life, Adam wasn't at all certain he liked the idea of having inherited one of his father's traits. Father had spent Adam's early years catering to Mother, trying to give her everything she wanted. In the end he'd been left lonely, and, Adam realized with some pain, Father had been broken, undone by her defection and his own inability to please his wife.

Now Adam was attempting to do the same thing. He meant to keep Persephone at Falstone through bribes, entertainments, visitors, whatever he thought she wanted. "It will never work," he told himself. "It didn't before, it won't now."

"You really must let me help with the next entertainment," Mother was saying when Adam's ears returned to the ladies' conversation. "I could recommend a few individuals whom you should consider including." Her enthusiasm grew with each word. Adam felt himself stiffen with tension. "Friends of mine who are simply delightful."

Mother's friends walking the corridors of the very home they'd pulled her from? After all Father had done, after all the time Adam himself had spent praying, begging her to stay, Mother was suddenly so willing to be at Falstone? And she wanted to bring with her the sort of people who had pulled his family apart when Adam was only a child.

"Excuse me," he said, his voice stern enough to cut through their conversation.

Both ladies looked up at him. It was the perfect opportunity to end all of Mother's schemes. He could tell her that there would be no other entertainments once the blasted ball was over.

But something in him felt five years old again, running to the front doors because Mother had returned, promising to be a good boy if only she would stay for a while. He would cling to her skirts and beg her to tell him about her excursions and to come to the nursery to read to him. Father would smile at her and greet her with a fond kiss on the cheek and tell Mother how happy he was that she had returned.

Sending her away would feel like letting Father down, which made no sense. Father was no longer there. Neither was that tiny boy, yet Adam could clearly see the pain in his face as his mother had slipped away again.

"Excuse me." His voice emerged softer than before. He walked back to the door of the drawing room.

"But dinner," Mother protested.

At least she'd left off the "my poor boy."

"I am not particularly hungry, Mother." Anger gripped him, but he could not explain exactly why.

"You are ill, you poor—"

"I am not ill," he snapped. "I am simply not hungry."

"But skipping a meal is not good for you." Mother used the tone she had employed when he was still in the nursery.

"Adam is perfectly capable of deciding what is good for him," Persephone said, a gentle scold in her voice.

"Thank you, Persephone." His tension only grew as he stood in the doorway. "Excuse me, ladies." He offered an abbreviated but strictly appropriate bow and left the room.

Only two weeks remained until the ball. In the week since Adam had proposed the mad scheme, he had more than once regretted it. But as he'd told Persephone, he was a man of his word. There was no question of calling it off.

Every invitation extended had been accepted—except for the Jonquil family, they being still in deepest mourning over the passing of the earl—so the ball would be precisely the sort of crush London idolized and Adam despised.

He stood in the middle of his book room, having arrived there without even noticing the path his feet had taken. Just as automatically, Adam's eyes turned to the portrait of his father and himself. What had happened to "Dukes do not depend on people" or "We are better off without her?"

If they had been so much better without Mother around, why had Father tried so hard to keep her there? Adam stared at the portrait as if it would answer. She'd left anyway. And Father had died a frustrated and lonely man, despite Adam's attempts to be something of a balm. It hadn't been enough. *He* hadn't been enough for either of them.

Mother had left him. Then Father had, too. And Persephone, he felt certain, would be next. How often he had told himself that he didn't care, that he needed no one? He was no longer a child begging for his mother's affection or his father's approval. He didn't need it anymore.

Adam muttered a curse and stormed across the room to the French doors. It was too dark to see Persephone's garden, so standing there was pointless, and yet he didn't move away.

What was happening to him? He'd been calm and level-headed and undisturbed by anything for decades. He kept his head in every situation. He dealt with problems swiftly and decisively. And suddenly, Adam was wandering his own home, confused and frustrated. And he, who never bothered with emotions of any kind, was angry, tense, and boiling.

With a sound filled with anguished frustration, Adam pounded his fist against the wall, feeling the pain of flesh connecting with thick, solid stone. Another curse slipped from his lips, not at the pain but at his own inability to keep himself in check.

Adam felt a soft, gentle hand slip over his fist where it still lay against the wall. Persephone.

"You will hurt your hand if you keep doing that." She tenderly pulled his throbbing hand from its punishing block.

He did not want Persephone saving him from himself. It would simply be one more thing he depended on her for. "Go eat your dinner, Persephone," Adam muttered, pulling his hand free and returning his gaze to the darkness outside.

"I plan to," she said. "Right there will be fine." She spoke the last to someone apparently behind them.

Adam glanced over his shoulder to see a footman, accompanied by an upper maid, setting a heavily laden dinner tray on Adam's desk. Both appeared anxious and uncertain. Why shouldn't they? Neither was among the few on the staff permitted in his book room. After a bobbed curtsy and a bow, the servants quit the room with all the speed of a fox during hunting season.

"I told you I wasn't hungry," Adam grumbled.

"I know." Persephone appeared entirely unperturbed. "But I am."

"Mother—"

"Is taking her meal with Harry," Persephone cut across him. "And I am eating here."

"No one eats in this room." Adam called forth his authoritative duke's voice.

"You would rather I starve?" He heard not the slightest catch in her voice or quiver of apprehension.

Adam turned to look at her. Persephone stood with her chin raised, voice determined, but eyes betraying a nervousness that cut him to the quick—the same look he'd seen in her eyes these past two weeks when the wolf pack made their presence known. She was trying to be brave again.

Adam's steward had confirmed that the pack had drawn closer to the castle than usual, something their sheer volume had already made obvious. The two of them had taken turns reassuring Persephone that there was no danger, and she had made a valiant effort to appear reassured. But there had always been that look in the back of her eyes, the one that lingered there now.

"If you truly are on the verge of expiring, by all means, take some nourishment," Adam answered impatiently as he crossed to the fireplace and deposited himself in his usual chair.

The sounds of a plate and cutlery being set out clanged around the room. She was invading every aspect of his life, changing his rules, his routine. He ought to be growing angrier, more frustrated. Instead he found the noises and the aroma of her dinner and her very presence soothing.

"Blast it," he muttered.

"It does smell good, doesn't it? It really is too bad you aren't hungry."

Adam turned his head enough to watch her fill her plate with a selection of the courses laid out there. Suddenly Adam, who had, in fact, earlier lost his appetite, was extremely hungry. "Is that a hint, Persephone?"

"A hint?" she asked, far too innocently.

"You are trying to convince me to join you." Adam suspected she knew that. Was she teasing him? No one teased the Duke of Kielder.

"Join me?" she repeated. "I told you this meal was provided for me. If you want something, you will simply have to send to the kitchens for it yourself."

Adam eyed the extensive spread of victuals doubtfully. There was more than enough food there for two people. She couldn't possibly have expected to eat it all on her own.

"You plan to eat an entire chicken?"

"It is not an entire chicken." She continued filling her plate. "And not such a very large one, at that. In fact, it is a very good thing the kitchen sent along a great deal more to go with it. Otherwise I would be in very real danger of wasting away."

Adam shook his head and muscled back a laugh. He had the strangest conversations with Persephone. And yet he enjoyed them. Just last night she'd told him rather dryly of her latest difficulty with

Atlas. The horse had decided several minutes into her daily ride that he would much rather stand still than move about the paddock. Her retelling had him chuckling despite his determination otherwise.

He'd told her several weeks earlier that her presence in his room helped him sleep. That was becoming less true all the time. When she wasn't entertaining him with stories from her day, he was watching her sleep or thinking about her or wondering what else he needed to do to make her happy at Falstone.

Obsessions cannot possibly be good for a man, Adam had been telling himself for days.

A plate of food was placed on the end table beside his chair. Adam shifted his gaze from the low burning fire to Persephone, where she stood next to him. How could she possibly be happy at Falstone with him?

But she offered a friendly smile. "You didn't expect me to eat the entire chicken, did you?"

She *was* teasing him. Even the novelty of that did not break through his pensive mood. Persephone continued to stand there, but Adam kept his gaze diverted from her face. He did not want to see any revulsion now that she stood in such close proximity or, worse yet, pity.

He found himself, quite without intending to, focusing on her hand hanging at her side so near his own. Women always seemed to have such tiny hands. Adam lifted his fingers from the arm of his chair just enough to brush her fingertips with his own.

Persephone stood perfectly still. Adam looked up at her from his position in the chair. There was something almost painful in her expression. He dropped his fingers immediately.

"Thank you for dinner, Persephone."

"You're welcome." With that, she returned to the table.

He was as foolish as his father had been, reaching out to a woman who wanted nothing to do with him. But Adam would not make the same mistakes. He wanted her to stay—that much he couldn't help—but he swore to himself that he wouldn't allow himself to care about her.

CHAPTER TWENTY-NINE

"It is one o'clock in the morning, Persephone."

She turned toward the door of the nursery. She truly hadn't expected Adam to come looking for her. He'd been quiet and distant during their dinner in his book room. She'd hoped to reach out to him, as a friend would. But her attempt to be supportive and comforting hadn't seemed to work.

Persephone closed her eyes as the memory of his feather-light touch on her fingertips flashed painfully through her mind. If he were fond of her—if theirs were the type of marriage Persephone had always wanted—that touch might have felt affectionate. Instead, it had been excruciating, almost torturous. She'd wanted, in that moment, to hold his hand, but she knew that doing so would only open her up further to feelings that would hurt her in the end.

"I cannot help but think that Linus would not be happy in here." Persephone kept her warring emotions out of her voice. "I have been trying to determine what I ought to do about it."

"You would place a midshipman of the Royal Navy in the nursery?" Adam asked.

"He is only a child." She crossed the room toward the door, running her fingers over a tabletop as she passed.

"A thirteen-year-old is not precisely a child," Adam said. "Especially after two years in the navy."

She didn't want to hear that. In her mind Linus was still her little boy, the affectionate child whom she'd taught to read and write, the brother who had retaught her to play spillikins. She wasn't ready to accept that he had changed so much. She felt unaccountably nervous at the thought of seeing her little Linus again. How much had he changed?

"I should select a different room for him, then?" Persephone tried to sound less affected than she was.

Adam stepped aside to allow Persephone to pass through the doorway. "There are plenty of rooms in the family wing," he said.

"Within Harry's sphere of influence?" Persephone smiled, walking down the corridor.

"Perhaps a room on our end of the wing would be best," Adam said.

Persephone wondered if he was smiling, even a little. He walked behind her, so she couldn't say for sure. She pulled her dressing gown more firmly around herself as the chill of the corridor began to penetrate her nightdress. "It is hard to imagine Linus grown up."

"How long has it been since you last saw him?" Adam followed her down the stairs to the family wing.

"Fifteen months." She did not even have to think or calculate. She knew precisely how long she'd gone without seeing her brothers.

"You've missed him."

"I have missed all of them," she replied.

A sudden lump formed in her throat. Good heavens, she missed her family. She had once been a central part of all their lives, but now she no longer felt part of anything.

"Mr. Pointer has volunteered to bring Linus back from Newcastle," Adam said as they stepped inside her sitting room. "He will be there on personal business on that day, as it is."

Persephone turned swiftly toward him. "I wanted to meet the *Triumphant* myself."

"There is a ball to plan, Persephone," Adam argued. He stepped past her.

"Mrs. Smithson can certainly do without me for a day or so," Persephone insisted. "And your mother would be more than happy to take over while I am gone."

Watching Adam cross the room into her bedchamber, Persephone could see him tense. "You will not be going. So there is no need for either of them to take charge of the preparations."

She followed him in. "But he is my brother."

"And he will be arriving with Mr. Pointer."

"A stranger." Persephone did not like it at all.

"After more than two years in the navy, I doubt Linus will be reduced to childish tears by a sixty-year-old vicar." He employed that dry, sarcastic tone that always seemed to cut at her.

"Now you are making fun of me," she muttered, crossing away from Adam to sit on her window seat.

Disappointment and frustration surged within her. She'd had her heart set on going to Newcastle and not just to retrieve Linus. Persephone had never been to Newcastle and was curious to see the town.

"You really wish to leave, then?" Tension sat thick in Adam's voice.

"I do, yes." She watched his reflection in the window.

His face hardened in the next moment, something flashing in his eyes that made her instantly nervous. "Go, then," he snapped. Suddenly he was the Adam she'd met on her wedding day: distant, intimidating, unfriendly. "Go wherever you bloody well want to. I don't care."

The connecting door slammed behind him, rattling the windows and Persephone's nerves.

What had just happened? The Adam she'd been so afraid of losing her heart to had disappeared in an instant. She'd gone from feeling content, if not happy, to feeling very much alone.

* * *

Perhaps Harry had been right. He had flatly refused to accompany Adam on his morning ride. "In all this fog?" Harry had asked incredulously. "A man's likely to run directly into a tree and not even realize it."

But Adam had needed to get out, to escape the castle. Mostly, he admitted with frustration, to avoid Persephone.

She wanted to leave Falstone—she'd said so the night before. A brief journey, to be sure, but that was how it always began. A day away here and there, then a week, then a month. Eventually she simply wouldn't come back.

He told himself he didn't care, which was, of course, a blatant lie. He'd told *her* he didn't care, which meant he'd lied to Persephone—something he'd promised never to do.

It was no wonder she was ready to "jump ship," as Harry would have said.

He could learn to live without Persephone. Father had gone on without Mother. He'd been miserable, but he'd gone on. And Adam had long ago reached the point where he no longer needed anyone. Only since Persephone's arrival had that begun to change. Well, he'd changed once; he would simply change back.

The Duke of Kielder was an island, beholden to no one, dependent on no one. He simply had to convince himself of that.

The air swiftly grew almost too cold to breathe. The fog turned thicker with each passing moment. It was time to return to Falstone. Adam turned Zeus toward home.

"I can be indifferent," he told himself. He had been for twenty years. It wouldn't be impossible. Then Persephone could make whatever journeys and trips she chose, and he would do what he'd done in Mother's absence all those years ago. He would ride the estate, manage his finances.

It would be fine.

"Fiends, it's getting cold," Adam muttered.

As if to prove his assertion, Zeus shuddered. Beneath his hooves a frozen layer of snow crackled and broke. Yes, maybe Harry had been right.

Somewhere in the distance a howl sounded, only slightly muffled by the thickening fog. It was an eerie sound, almost like a warning.

"Go on, Zeus." But the horse didn't appear to be listening.

Smaller footsteps, like a fox or dog, broke the silence. Zeus skittered nervously. The sounds, the feelings of the moment were horrifyingly familiar, though Adam knew he'd never before taken a ride through fog so thick.

A chorus of growls echoed around him.

It was the pack. Hayworth had said they were hunting nearer the castle than usual. Adam's hand went automatically to the pistol in his greatcoat pocket. He had no plans to use it, but if worse came to worst, he would be prepared.

A series of long, bone-chilling howls had Zeus dancing beneath him. "Steady, boy." Adam urged him on.

He heard other hooves nearby, perhaps approaching. The fog made sounds bounce unnaturally and made seeing further than a few yards almost impossible. He kept his hand at his pocket, waiting, anticipating.

"Yer Grace!" a voice bellowed, as if calling out in search of someone.

Had someone come looking for him?

"Yer Grace?" the same person repeated.

"John Handly?" Adam thought he recognized the voice. The hoofbeats grew louder.

The howling grew more chaotic. Zeus seemed ready to bolt. In the next instant, Adam spotted John. One look at his face told Adam something was wrong.

"Have you found her?" was the first thing out of John's mouth.

"Her?"

"Then you haven't . . . ?" John looked more frantic.

"I don't know what you are talking about." Adam held Zeus steady but barely. The pack sounded closer.

"Her Grace," John breathed out quickly. "We was riding to Pointer's, and Atlas bolted. No reason to, just bolted. She ain't that good a rider yet, and I'm afeared she might've been unseated."

"Persephone?" Adam could manage no other words.

"And with the pack soundin' so close and angry—"

"Persephone!" Adam shouted, his panicked call dancing in the thick emptiness around him.

"She ain't been answering, and I'm afeared something must've happened."

"Don't say that," Adam snapped. "Persephone!"

The howls had dissolved into aggressive barking. Adam had a horrible feeling, one he refused to even put into words. "I think we need to find the pack."

"I've been thinking that myself." John sounded as worried as Adam felt.

He wanted to bolt, to charge, but the fog made it impossible. He could only guess which direction the barks and howls came from. The fog rendered his senses unreliable. Then he heard a sound that chilled his very blood: a horse, obviously in pain.

It was his dream come to life.

"I heared it, too, Yer Grace." John must have seen Adam tense. "We're getting closer."

Adam's heart pounded. The growling and snarling and the sounds of paws on crisp snow were now echoing at them from all sides. They were surrounded.

"Persephone!" Adam called out.

The pack answered with a fearsome chorus of howls.

"There, Yer Grace!"

Adam snapped his head around, first toward John to see which direction he pointed then in the direction of his finger.

Atlas, bloodied and breathing hard, stood not far from them. Persephone was not in the saddle.

Adam looked frantically around, inching closer, not wanting to push the pack into an attack. As he approached, Atlas snapped at him. Zeus shied back but continued his approach at Adam's command. Atlas assumed an aggressive stance, something Adam had never seen him do—his docile nature was one of the reasons Adam had approved of him as a mount for Persephone.

In a flash of fur, a wolf darted across Zeus's path. Atlas immediately switched his aggression to the snarling newcomer. A second wolf came from behind, and Atlas kicked out at it. The horse shifted, and Adam understood the reason for the horse's behavior.

Kneeling on the ground just behind Atlas was Persephone. She held a large tree limb in her hand the way a warrior of old might have hefted a club. She swung it at a shadow that instantly became a wolf. Adam drew Zeus up just as the wolf lunged.

He reacted automatically. His pistol smoked before he even registered that he'd drawn it. The wolf lay unmoving at Persephone's feet. The rest of the pack seemed momentarily startled into a retreat.

"Hand her up, John," Adam instructed swiftly, John having dismounted already.

John helped Persephone to her feet. Adam saw in an instant that she was injured. Limping and sagging, she barely managed the few steps to Zeus. John helped Adam pull her into the saddle in front of him.

"Take Atlas's reins," Adam said.

John nodded.

"Be quick about it. The pack won't stay spooked for long."

John remounted and led Atlas away as fast as the fog and the horse's injuries would allow. Adam turned Zeus about and pulled Persephone close to him.

"John?" Adam asked as they passed him.

"Yes, Yer Grace?"

"If the pack gets aggressive again, you leave Atlas behind and get to safety. Understood?"

John nodded, but Adam couldn't say with any certainty if the man would actually abandon a horse to save his own skin. He returned the nod and urged Zeus to a faster pace.

"Persephone?" he asked as he negotiated the trees and fog.

She didn't answer.

"Persephone?" he repeated more urgently. "Are you well?"

"No," came the sob, tiny and quiet and filled with fear.

Adam tightened his hold on her. Behind him another howl sounded.

CHAPTER THIRTY

"Blast this fog," Adam muttered, turning Zeus around once more. He'd never been lost in Falstone Forest in his entire life until that moment. He could hardly make out the trees around him, let alone any landmarks that might have told him where he was.

Somewhere in the impenetrable fog, the pack continued to make their presence known. They sounded closer. Zeus all but jerked the reins out of Adam's hand. He needed a firmer grip on his horse.

"Persephone?" When she didn't respond, Adam simply continued. "Zeus is going to run off with us if I don't have a firmer hold on him." Still no response. If he hadn't felt her shift now and then, Adam might have wondered if she was even conscious. "I cannot hold on to both of you at the same time."

"You're going to leave me here?" Her voice filled with panic.

"Of course not." How could she even think that? What kind of a monster did she think he was? "You are going to have to hold on to me instead of the other way around." His frustration and sudden anger entered his tone.

"Don't yell at me, Adam."

"I'm not—" He stopped, quieted his tone with some effort, and spoke again. "I am not yelling at you."

He guided Zeus around a thick tree trunk that suddenly appeared out of the fog in front of them. He pulled Zeus to a stop. Holding the reins with the arm that ran behind Persephone's back, he awkwardly undid the front buttons of his greatcoat.

"Arms around me, Persephone," he instructed sharply.

She obeyed immediately. Ignoring the sudden pounding of his heart, Adam buttoned the coat around her. Only one button would fasten and not in the hole it was intended to occupy, but it might help Persephone stay mounted.

"Hold fast," he said. "If I find the road, we are going to run."

Adam felt what he thought was a nod buried deep inside his coat. Her arms closed more firmly around him. The position must have been deucedly uncomfortable: sitting sideways, sharing a saddle, and twisting enough to get her arms around his middle. And she was shivering.

"Blast it," Adam grumbled. Both hands now on the reins, he nudged Zeus into a slow trot.

A grumbling growl stopped their progress in the next moment. Zeus nearly bucked Adam off, though he managed to subdue him. Persephone seemed to be slipping.

"Hold tight." Adam pulled Zeus around.

A wolf appeared directly in their path, his growls aggressive. Adam hoped it was the only one.

Another member of the pack darted out of the fog and ran alongside Zeus. The shadow of yet another lingered just out of sight. And Persephone still seemed to be losing her grip.

Where the deuce was the road? Adam veered Zeus to the right, catching one of their pursuers off guard and into a retreat. The others weren't so easily distracted.

"Stay with me, boy," he muttered to Zeus, feeling the horse grow more jumpy.

His heart raced. He'd never seen the pack so aggressive, but then, he'd never ventured very deep into the forest in the dead of winter. Adam knew precisely what they were doing. Hunting was their natural instinct. Adam, Persephone, and Zeus were the prey.

"I am dizzy, Adam." Persephone's voice sounded odd, like she struggled to form the words.

A lightning-split tree appeared to Adam's left, the charred trunk thick and gnarled. He knew that tree, knew the thinner side pointed toward the front gates of Falstone Castle. Could they really be that close without seeing the walls?

He forced Zeus to a faster canter, easily negotiating his way to where he knew the road would be. They were a quarter mile from home. On the open road they would arrive in minutes.

Around and through trees they wove. "A little further," he encouraged Zeus.

The instant they reached the road, Zeus went into flight. He obviously knew the way home just as Adam did. He heard snarls at his ankles. He had never seen the pack on the road. What the deuce was going on in Falstone Forest?

Teeth bared, a wolf stood in the middle of the road, not backing down as Zeus approached. Adam couldn't go for his pistol—Persephone leaned increasingly heavier against his arm. If he took his arm away to aim, she'd likely slip off the saddle entirely.

"Over top, Zeus," Adam instructed, giving Zeus his head entirely.

He had never been more grateful for a mount he knew could clear any fence put before him. Even with two riders, Zeus flew over his would-be assailant and continued at a full gallop.

Falstone seemed to appear out of nowhere. The fog must have been unprecedentedly thick for something as imposing as Falstone to be undetectable for so long.

They passed through the gate as if running the final leg of the Epsom Derby. Adam reined Zeus in as they reached the inner wall. He looked back. The pack hadn't followed him inside. At least that barrier hadn't yet been breached.

"Yer Grace." One of the undergrooms reached them, confusion written on his face and in his tone.

"Arm the stable staff." Adam barked out the instruction. "The pack is within a few yards of the castle."

"Wolves," the undergroom muttered, face paling.

For a fraction of a moment, Adam considered reminding the man that they were not technically wolves. That might ease his worries. But if the animals were behaving precisely as wolves, the distinction didn't matter. Adam thought of them that way—he likely always would after his encounter with them.

"Watch for John Handly," Adam said. "He is on his way—"

John came through the gates at that moment, his own mount and Atlas both running. The horses came to a stop beside Zeus, all three panting and obviously spent.

"Pack was at my heels." John struggled to catch his breath.

"Ours as well," Adam said. Both men shifted their eyes to the gate. "I've instructed the stable staff to arm themselves, in case the pack enters the walls."

John pulled his forelock and swiftly dismounted. Three other grooms led the horses away.

Adam handed Persephone down. She could hardly keep her feet. Adam was at her side the next moment and slipped an arm around her waist. John Handly had run to the stables, no doubt to carry out Adam's instructions.

"I'm so dizzy," Persephone muttered, leaning heavily against him.

"Can you walk?"

"I think so."

She managed the rest of the journey. Barton held the door open for them, his face betraying his confusion and concern. Harry arrived in the next moment.

"What the—" Harry stopped what would obviously have been a curse when his eyes settled on Persephone. He need not have censored his words, as Persephone had heard plenty of profanities from Adam during their ride back to Falstone.

"She was unseated," Adam explained, reaching the bottom of the staircase. "The pack, apparently, has taken to hunting bigger prey."

"She was mauled by the wolves?" Harry's eyes grew large.

"Does she look mauled?" Adam snapped. With the danger no longer imminent, his anger and frustration reached the boiling point.

"You really aren't going to make her climb those stairs, are you?" Harry asked.

His jaw set, shoulders tense, Adam lifted Persephone into his arms and marched her up the stairs. She made not even a squeak of protest.

"Should we send for the apothecary?" Harry asked.

"And have him eaten alive at the castle gates?"

That seemed to drive home the precariousness of the situation. "The pack hasn't backed off, then?"

Adam shook his head. "I've armed the stable staff."

"'Pon rep!"

"Cut the cant, Harry." They reached the stairwell leading up to the family wing. "Where's Mother?"

"Sitting room, I think."

"Send her to Persephone's room."

Harry went directly to comply. Adam felt his arms and legs beginning to give out. He couldn't remember ever being more completely spent. With an inward sigh of relief, he laid Persephone on her bed. She kept her eyes closed.

Adam sat on the bed beside her, ready to collapse.

"Adam?" he heard Persephone whisper.

He shifted to look down at her. In the brighter light of her room, Adam could see an enormous purple bruise already forming just above her left eye, which had begun to swell shut, and a trickle of blood cut a track across her forehead.

"Are we safe now?" Persephone asked as quietly as before.

"Yes." As if to contradict him, a howl, closer than any he'd heard within the walls of the castle, sounded at that moment.

Persephone didn't shudder as Adam expected her to. "I am never going to ride again as long as I live," she declared feebly.

"I doubt that." Adam felt himself sag.

"I was afraid no one would find me."

Adam's heart skipped a beat. Throughout their ordeal he'd refused to even consider what could have happened to her out there. What if he hadn't been out, if Persephone hadn't been found? She would be dead.

Suddenly, he had no more strength. Adam dropped onto the bed, stretched out beside her, greatcoat still hanging around him, damp from the fog. He closed his eyes and drifted into a dreamless, restless sleep.

* * *

"Merciful heavens!"

Adam stirred at the sound, recognizing Mother's voice.

"They're not dead, Mother Harriet." That was Harry.

Adam opened his eyes and looked across the room at them.

"I think Adam hoped you could help see to Persephone. We cannot send for an apothecary or surgeon with the pack still prowling at the gates."

"Heavens." Mother swayed a little.

"Help her to a seat, Harry." Adam pulled himself to a seated position, still a little groggy.

Persephone was holding his hand, tightening her grip every time he moved. Adam's eyes drifted to her. She was awake, definitely a good sign. Her face had swollen more, the bruise deepening. She looked up at him. No words, just stark need in her eyes.

Adam squeezed her hand and kept it securely in his own. He shifted to sit on the edge of her bed, facing the chair near the door where Harry had deposited Mother. She looked decidedly unwell, pale and fidgeting.

His eyes burned and his head remained cloudy. He'd never had so much difficulty awakening before and after only drifting off for a moment or two. "Harry, will you ring for Persephone's abigail, please?"

Harry turned to Adam with a look of complete shock, which he quickly shook off, and crossed the room to comply. A few drawn-out blinks and a roll of his shoulders awakened Adam a little further.

"Adam?"

He turned back toward Persephone, shifting so he could face her.

"Can you take my boot off? It feels too tight."

She'd been limping. How had he forgotten that? A person could break an ankle being thrown from a horse, and, of course, it would swell.

"Which foot?"

"The right foot," Harry answered.

Adam looked over at him, standing on the right side of Persephone's bed. He followed Harry's wide-eyed stare to the bloody, torn mess of her riding habit. Adam jumped to his feet, crossing to where Harry stood.

"A compound break?" Alarm filled Harry's voice.

Adam shook his head. "She couldn't have walked on a compound fracture." Then why all the blood?

He pulled back the tattered hem of Persephone's riding habit. Blood soaked every layer she wore: boots, stockings, petticoat, riding habit. Bits of rock and wood were embedded in long, deep gouges.

"She needs a surgeon," Harry said.

"I know," Adam whispered in reply, feeling entirely inadequate. All she had was him.

CHAPTER THIRTY-ONE

Persephone's abigail arrived in the next moment.

"Boiling water," Adam commanded. "Several cans of it."

Staring openmouthed at the bloodied mess that was Persephone's right leg, the abigail managed a nod.

Long, deep cuts ran down her leg, bleeding and swelling. None ran parallel to one another, however, and Adam felt immediate relief. If she had been bitten, there would have been a pattern.

"And the strongest brandy Barton can find," Adam added, taking another look at the mud and dirt and rocks.

Adam took off his greatcoat, laying it over the back of a nearby chair, and set to unlacing Persephone's boot. Her leg continued to swell, further tightening the boot. It wouldn't tug loose.

"Help me, Harry."

Persephone moaned in pain as both Adam and Harry attempted to pull the boot free.

"You'll have to cut it," Harry said.

"Scissors, Persephone," Adam said. "Do you have scissors in here?"

"Sewing room." She kept her eyes shut, tears streaming down her face.

"Mother—" But she was sobbing in the corner.

"I'll get them," Harry said.

"You don't even know where the sewing room is. Adam touched Persephone's face, leaving a streak of blood there as he did. "I'll be right back."

She nodded mutely.

"Help Mother to the settee in Persephone's sitting room, will you, Harry?"

Adam ran to the sewing room next door. Several needleworks in various stages of completion were laid neatly on a table. Adam wiped his bloodstained hands on the sides of his breeches as he looked around the room. The tiny scissors on the table would be no match for leather.

He muttered an oath. The longer this took, the more swollen Persephone's foot would become, increasing the chances that he would cut her in his attempt to free her foot.

"Ah!" he exclaimed, catching sight of a pair of sheers at the top of a box of fabric scraps.

Adam grabbed them. Harry stood beside Persephone's bed, holding her hand when Adam returned.

"Mother?

"Lying down," Harry answered. "Just kept saying she was sorry."

Adam undressed to his shirtsleeves, needing the freedom of movement.

"Hold her still." Adam motioned to Persephone's leg. "I don't want to accidentally cut her."

Harry nodded and pinned Persephone's leg to the mattress with his hands. She cried out at the pain.

"Sorry," Harry said.

Adam slipped the tip of the silver scissors beneath the taut edge of her boot and cut. An inch at a time he carefully peeled back the leather. Blood had seeped inside, but the wounds did not continue. Her boots had proven something of a shield.

Adam breathed a sigh of relief when her foot finally came free. He hadn't cut her or hurt her further. A great deal of the pain in her foot and leg would subside just from being freed of the confines of the boot.

"Will you bring over the washbasin, Harry?" Adam heard the weariness return to his voice.

"You do realize that's the third time you've asked me to do something in the past few minutes." Harry crossed the room to Persephone's washstand.

"Forgive me, Harry." Sarcasm dripped from his words as he pulled a washcloth from the table. "Seeing as there is no one else to help, I assumed—"

"I wasn't complaining about the workload." Harry set the basin down on the bedside table and poured water from the pitcher. "You just don't usually ask. You command."

"You would rather I commanded?" Adam dipped the cloth in the ice-cold water.

"No, actually."

Was he usually so dictatorial? He was. The realization bothered him. Adam couldn't say why, but it did. He put the thought out of his mind and set about cleaning as much blood from Persephone's foot as he could. She winced at the first swipe.

"I am sorry. I know the water is cold. It will be some time before the kitchen can send up hot water."

Persephone didn't reply but kept quite still, eyes closed against the pain. Adam continued cleaning. Her ankle was swollen, a sprain at the least, perhaps a slight break. Still she'd walked on it, without complaint, without a single tear. To think he'd once thought her a coward.

"Harry—" Adam stopped the instructions that came immediately to mind. For reasons he had no desire to evaluate, he shifted his words into a request. "Will you see if Mother is in need of anything?"

"Absolutely." Harry produced something of a smile and left the bedchamber, just as the abigail entered.

"First can of hot water, Your Grace." She set the can on the table beside the washbasin.

"Empty the cold water, if you will."

He'd cleaned nearly all the blood off Persephone's foot, and set himself to doing the same for her ankle. Persephone whimpered almost inaudibly.

"I will try to be gentle," he said.

Adam sat on the bed, holding her foot in one hand and washing it with the other. The ministrations were oddly calming, reassuring. He hated feeling useless and knew, in that moment, that he was helping. Not just helping in a general sense. Helping *her.* Somehow that distinction was important to him.

"I can do that, Your Grace." The abigail apparently expected him to relinquish his duties.

Adam silently shook his head, softly rubbing more blood from her ankle.

"It is not seemly for a duke to be acting as a lady's maid or a physician, Your Grace."

"Perhaps not." Adam didn't take his eyes from his task. "But a husband is charged with keeping his wife in sickness, is he not?"

"Yes, Your Grace." The maid sounded more confused than anything else.

"Then I would venture that tending to my wife is perfectly seemly."

Lud, her ankle was terribly swollen, and tender, if her continued grimace were any indication.

"It is highly unusual."

"And when has the Duke of Kielder cared what was usual?"

The bones didn't feel out of place. If anything, there might be a small crack. Persephone was fortunate in that, at least.

"Yes, Your Grace."

The abigail quit her lecture after that, contenting herself with retrieving needles and tweezers to help Adam clean the debris from Persephone's wound and providing fresh cloths until a second maid arrived with the next can of water from the kitchen. In silence the two of them worked, Adam cleaning gashes and washing Persephone's leg and foot, the abigail tending to her bleeding head and swollen eye.

Persephone didn't say a word.

Adam personally cleaned every drop of blood off Persephone's leg, from knee to toe. He counted four deep gashes, each measuring several inches in length, some two dozen more superficial wounds. Her ankle worried him most, especially as he knew he could do nothing about it.

Two footmen were enlisted to hold Persephone still while Adam poured nearly an entire bottle of brandy over the cuts in her leg. She broke her silence for the first time in over thirty minutes. No words escaped her tongue, only a heart-wrenching cry of agony.

By the time he'd finished cleaning her wounds, Adam was spent. Hearing her obvious suffering and knowing he'd caused it—no matter how necessary the infliction—proved nearly too much for him. He placed his hands, shoulder length apart on the bed, hunched over, and hung his head. He could not continue. He hadn't the willpower.

"I will stitch up her leg, Your Grace." For the first time in the months since she had been employed, Persephone's abigail spoke to Adam with entirely unfeigned kindness and respect. Before, she'd seemed more awed and impressed by his title and, perhaps, his reputation. In that moment, she seemed most impressed with Adam himself. It was an unprecedented experience for him.

Adam turned his head enough to look at her. She offered a small smile, something he might once have disapproved of from a servant. But Adam only nodded and moved away enough to allow her to finish tending to Persephone.

An upstairs maid, the same who'd assisted their ministrations, cleared away a large pile of wet, bloodied linens. She, too, smiled empathetically at him. Adam couldn't remember ever being the recipient of so many smiles. It was unnerving.

"She's lookin' better, a'ready," the maid said. "Not quite so pale."

Adam glanced at Persephone and knew in an instant it wasn't true. She had grown paler than before the brandy, more still and quiet. Lies, however white or well-meaning, had never been permissible in his mind. Until that moment. He needed the lies.

The little maid, one he'd seen around the castle dozens of times, was offering him comfort. She generally bobbed a nervous curtsy then scurried away. All the staff did. But there she stood, unafraid, unquaking, offering him what reassurance she could.

"Thank you," Adam muttered.

She held a clean cloth out to him. "'Tis fresh water." She nodded toward the basin. "So you can wash your hands clean."

Adam looked at his hands then. Every inch was stained, the shade varying from pink to nearly black. He could do nothing but stare at them.

"You'll feel better cleanin' it off, Your Grace," the maid told him gently. "'Twould ache any man's heart to have to see his wife's blood that way."

He nodded, mutely crossing to the washbasin. Adam thrust his hands into the warm, still water. Wisps of red began to swirl and cloud the clearness. The water alone wouldn't be enough. Adam took the cloth—the only clean one left in the entire house, he'd guess—and began to scrub.

'Twould ache any man's heart. Adam couldn't imagine the sensation being described in any other way. He had escaped their ordeal physically unscathed, and yet he was in pain—an internal, aching pain.

Adam glanced at Persephone. She wore a look of utter anguish on her face. Tiny moans of pain escaped her throat as her abigail painstakingly sewed closed her wounds. Adam remembered that pain, the feeling of being sewn together. It was pain added onto pain. He hadn't allowed himself to think of those times in years, of the brutal surgeries and long, difficult recoveries.

Adam rinsed and scrubbed, again and again, until his hands were no longer red from blood but from scrubbing. Still, every crease, every wrinkle remained unnaturally darkened and residue remained under his fingernails. It would take time to clear the remainder away entirely, although Adam didn't believe he would ever get the images of the last few hours out of his mind.

"Adam" reached him as a choked whimper.

He quickly dried his hands and abandoned the basin of salmon-colored water. He sat beside Persephone and wrapped his fingers around hers. A tear trickled down the length of Persephone's nose. Adam gently brushed it away.

"Is she almost done?" Persephone struggled to get the words out.

"Very nearly," Adam whispered.

She looked relieved, if only a little. Adam didn't imagine she could see very much through her badly swollen eye. Her pain must have been nearly unbearable.

"Adam?"

"Yes, dear?" *Dear?* Adam sat stunned for a moment that such a word had come so naturally to his lips.

"Please stay with me," Persephone whispered.

He didn't know what brought on the impulse, but he leaned over and kissed her lightly on the forehead, lingering a moment longer than necessary. "If you will stay with me," he answered silently.

He remained at her side until the abigail tied off the last stitch and Persephone's leg was wrapped in clean strips of linen.

A few minutes later, he sat on the bench at the foot of her bed, Persephone curled up beside him, leaning against the side of his chest, his arm wrapped around her. The maids were changing the linens on her bed, those that had been there having been destroyed by blood, water, and brandy. She could just as easily have lain on the settee in her sitting room, but Adam had insisted. In the short few minutes he'd held her, Persephone had fallen asleep

Watching her sleep had become a hobby of his over the past two months. But never had he watched her with the level of intensity he did just then.

She was pale and bruised and in such obvious pain. Until the surgeon in Hawick or the apothecary in Sifton arrived, they could not know if her ankle was broken. Only time would bring down the swelling in her face.

Suppose her leg became infected? Wounds could turn septic quickly.

No, Adam shook his head. He'd used enough brandy to cleanse the wounds of an entire army regiment.

But would it be enough? He was not a medical man.

"Your Grace?"

He looked up at the abigail.

"Her Grace really ought to be changed into a fresh nightdress."

"Of course." Adam leaned toward his wife. "Persephone." A slight nudge and she roused. "Persephone?"

She looked up at him, exhaustion and confusion clouding her eyes.

"Your ladies' maid is going to change you now. It would help if you were awake."

She nodded but still seemed distant, half asleep.

Adam glanced at his blood- and mud-splattered clothing. "I should change as well."

Persephone sat up a little more and offered a shaky smile. Obviously her pain lingered. Adam touched her gently on the cheek.

"We'll take care of her, Your Grace," the abigail said. Adam caught the other maids nodding out of the corner of his eye.

"You'll send for me if she needs anything?"

"Of course," was the reply.

The maids were all looking at him with that look one gives a calfling who is quite unmistakably enamored: overly emotive eyes and sentimental smiles. Adam grew suddenly terribly uncomfortable.

"Try to rest," he said to Persephone, watching the other women with a wary eye, then he left as quickly as his dignity would allow.

CHAPTER THIRTY-TWO

THE FALSTONE STEWARD, MR. HAYWORTH, was in Adam's book room when he arrived there minutes after changing his bloody clothing. Barton had told him the steward wished to speak to him.

"I hope you have some information for me regarding the pack." Adam didn't bother with a greeting but crossed directly to his desk.

Hayworth nodded, hat clutched in his hands. He took a seat when Adam indicated he should. "My boy and I have been riding through Falstone Forest the past few days. There are signs of poaching, Your Grace. A lot of poaching."

"Then the pack is having trouble finding game?"

"Expanding their hunting grounds," Hayworth confirmed.

"Even in the worst of winters, they haven't attacked riders nor approached the castle gates," Adam said. "They did both today."

Hayworth repeated his signature nod. It didn't always mean "yes"; generally he meant simply to acknowledge a statement. "Bein' more aggressive, 'specially toward people, ain't a good sign in wild animals."

"Believe me, Hayworth, I am acutely aware of that."

"I have a suggestion, Your Grace, for pushing the pack back into the forest."

"Make your suggestion."

"First we have to cut back the poaching. Guards along the road would help and might keep the pack from the gates."

"Unless the pack simply devours the guards," Adam said.

"A few lures would pull 'em back into the forest. There's more game on the north end. Once the pack realizes that, they'll stay there."

"How do we make the pack discover as much?"

"Smell," Hayworth answered. "Wolves have keen noses."

The idea had merit. Hound dogs were trained using scent.

"It is worth an attempt, at least," Adam said. "There are, of course, two tenant cottages as well as your own in Falstone Forest. Find a path that bypasses those."

"Of course, Your Grace."

"John Handly, Your Grace," Barton announced from the door.

Adam looked up. John looked deucedly uncomfortable. He'd outrun a pack of attacking wolves while leading a lame horse without so much as paling, but place him inside one of the family rooms of the castle, and he looked ready to faint.

"Come in, John." Adam used a tone that required obedience.

He entered a step or two but stood, head lowered, as near the door as possible.

"What is it?" Adam asked.

John would not have come to the castle nor allowed himself to be shown inside—neither would Barton have led him to the book room—if his message were not urgent.

"Atlas, Yer Grace," John muttered.

"What about Atlas?" Had the horse's injuries proven fatal already? Persephone would be heartbroken. Adam felt something of an ache in his own chest. He'd seen Atlas defend Persephone in that forest. He no doubt had saved her life.

"I think I know . . . I have an idea why the pack attacked him."

"Other than his being in the forest in the dead of winter?"

John nodded.

"What have you discovered?"

"We was cleaning his wounds and couldn't help noticing a strange smell, Yer Grace."

"Smell?" That was odd.

"Rather like, well, like a cut of bacon."

"Bacon?" Hayworth echoed Adam's response.

"Yes, Yer Grace. And I'm wondering if that might be why the wolves attacked Atlas. They didn't bother with me and my horse, neither you and Zeus. Not really, considering how intent they was on Atlas. Her Grace might have picked up some of that smell, and that'd be why the pack seemed interested in her, but not as much as Atlas."

"You spoke of smells, Hayworth." Adam looked at his steward. "Would bacon be a luring smell?"

Hayworth nodded in confirmation.

"How does a horse come to smell like a cut of meat?" Adam asked John.

"All I can think is one of the stable boys didn't wash up good after breakfast or was holdin' on to a piece of bacon in his pocket or sommat, wantin' to eat it later and got the smell on the horse or saddle or sommat like 'at." John's accent always grew cruder when he was upset. Slovenliness among his staff would be upsetting to the man who prided himself on his stable.

"That might account for a slight smell. You seemed to indicate it was stronger than that."

John raised his hands in a gesture of frustrated confusion. He was obviously at a loss to fully explain it.

"Did the pack ever enter the walls?" Adam asked.

"No, Yer Grace," John said. "They stayed just outside the gate for a while but then went back into the forest."

"That is a good sign, Your Grace," Hayworth said. "They haven't grown more aggressive, it would seem. They were just too tempted to resist."

"Talk with your staff," Adam instructed John. "Find out how this happened. If it had anything to do with the attack, I do not want the same mistake to occur again."

"Yes, Yer Grace." John bowed and quit the room in an enormous hurry.

Hayworth took his leave next, promising to report to Adam in a day's time with a specific plan for dealing with the pack.

Adam propped his elbows on the desk and rubbed his forehead with his fingertips. Could something as simple as poor washing after breakfast have led to such a grueling ordeal? It hardly seemed possible. How many times had Adam gone for a ride after having kidneys or ham at breakfast? There was no guarantee he had been thorough enough in his ablutions to completely eradicate any lingering aroma. Yet the pack had never attacked him.

He interlaced his fingers and rested his chin on his clasped hands, thinking. John had been right on one count: the pack had been decidedly more interested in Atlas than any of the others. Even Persephone, who had been in the midst of the fray, had sustained more injuries from her fall than from the pack, though that had been an instant from changing when Adam arrived.

The pack had returned to the forest. Adam remembered this information quite suddenly. He got instantly to his feet and crossed to the book room doors. He made his way to the first-floor landing. Either Barton or a footman would be positioned at the front door.

A footman.

Adam thought a moment before recalling the man's name. "Joseph."

He looked up.

"Inform Barton that I wish him to send for Mr. Johns in Sifton." If the pack no longer posed a threat, the apothecary ought to be brought in.

Joseph, the footman, offered a bow and left to deliver the message.

"Adam?" That was Mother's voice, oddly choked and broken.

He turned around to see her standing just outside the doors of the informal drawing room, balled-up handkerchief in her hands and actual tears on her face. Tears? Adam had never seen his mother cry. Not once in all his life.

"What is it?" Anxiety touched his tone.

"Could I speak with you? Please?" Where was the pitying tone? She addressed him almost as if he were a grown man.

Adam was decidedly uneasy. He moved warily into the drawing room, keeping one eye trained on Mother. She was acting strange: fidgety, nervous.

"Perhaps you should sit down," Adam suggested.

"I am so sorry, Adam. I know you wished me to help with Persephone." She seemed to pale a little further. "I am sure I let you down. You must be so disappointed . . ." Her voice broke. Mother took several gulps of air.

"Sit down, Mother." Adam cupped her elbow with his hand and guided her to a seat.

She smiled shakily at him. "Sometimes you are so like your father," she said, her eyes misted, "the dear man."

Adam's eyes must have grown to twice their size. Mother had never compared him to his father. He would not have been able, until that moment, to guess whether she would consider a likeness a positive or a negative trait.

"Are you quite well, Mother?" Adam watched her with increasing alarm.

"Oh." She waved a hand, though her face was a study in overset emotions. "I had hoped you would never discover my most mortifying flaw."

"Flaw?"

"I have always been . . . been *horrible* in the sickroom. Horrible, Adam!" She wiped at her eyes. "Even as a child, one of my siblings would come down with a cold, and I would fret our poor nurse into a fit of nerves. My mother always told me it would be different when I was a mother—that some maternal instinct would take over."

Adam was completely lost. Mother quite obviously needed soothing. "There was a great deal of blood, earlier, with Persephone. I do not blame you for not being up to the task."

"But I am certain I only made the situation worse." Mother rose to her feet once more and began pacing as she wiped and dabbed with a shaking hand. "I always did."

"Did?" Adam could hardly believe what he was seeing. Mother was ever calm and collected, undisturbed by anything. The poor woman looked on the verge of collapse.

Poor woman. Adam shook his head.

"The second surgeon actually sent me to the vicarage for two days," Mother said, a sob making the last few words difficult to discern. "Banished from my own home. From my poor boy."

"Wait." Adam froze. "Banished? The second surgeon?"

"I am certain I made it worse. I was so nervous, so concerned through the first one—"

"The first *surgery?*" Adam pressed.

She nodded and continued. "And I didn't get better. Worse, in fact. The second surgeon sent me away. The next few insisted I be gone before they even arrived. And . . . and . . ." She very nearly wailed. "I was grateful to go. Happy to. What kind of an unnatural mother wishes to leave her child at such a time?"

Mother dropped onto a sofa, crying loudly.

Adam sat, too. All the times she'd left before Adam's surgeries, she'd done so at the surgeon's request—no, *requirement,* if her retelling wasn't exaggerated. Could her eagerness to go really have been an indisposition toward the sickroom?

She always had come back once he was well into his recovery, after all difficulties and dangers had passed. But there had been other times when she had left Falstone, times unconnected to illness or surgeries or injuries. At least that was how he remembered it. Perhaps he'd had a stomach illness or a head cold and simply didn't remember it. Adam couldn't recall Father being ill during that time.

"Your Grace?" a voice politely inquired from the doorway.

Didn't anyone in this house realize he had a great deal on his mind? Every few minutes, it seemed, someone was vying for his time.

"What?" he snapped.

The young maid at the door shrunk back a little. Adam recognized her—the maid who'd provided him with fresh water to clean his hands and words of encouragement during the ordeal caring for Persephone.

"Her Grace is asking for you," the maid said. "She seems anxious."

Adam was on his feet before she'd finished the first sentence. "Excuse me, Mother," he said as he crossed the room.

The little maid stood at the door as Adam passed through it, eyes cast down and expression hurt.

"I am sorry for snapping at you," Adam said, hardly believing he was apologizing to anyone, let alone a chambermaid. "I have had a very trying day."

"Thank you, Your Grace," she answered quietly.

"Thank you?" Adam asked as he walked toward the stairs that lead to the second story, the maid following.

"For apologizing," she said. "I know you don't have to, probably aren't supposed to, even."

Adam shrugged. "Probably not."

"You know, you're not much like people think you are."

"How is that?" Adam asked, beginning to regret his slip in rigidity.

"You're supposed to be fearsome and unkind, but I ain't never seen a man care for his wife the way you did for Her Grace. And you apologize to someone who really ought to be beneath your notice. It's not what people would expect from the Duke of Kielder."

"Then perhaps you would be so kind as to keep that a secret from the masses." His tone had lightened a bit, his mood actually improving after such a short conversation.

"Yes, Your Grace." The maid curtsied as they reached the door to Persephone's sitting room. "If you don't tell Mrs. Smithson I been talking to you instead of disappearing like I'm supposed to."

"What is your name?" Adam asked.

"Fanny Handly, Your Grace."

"Handly? Jeb Handly—?"

"My pa's uncle."

"I will keep your secret, Fanny Handly, if you will keep mine."

She smiled, the same uneven smile all the Handlys seemed to have.

Adam found Persephone awake when he entered the room. She was sitting up, something that surprised him to no end. She would have been more than justified in remaining prostrate in bed for days. Adam discovered with each passing day just how many ways he'd underestimated her.

The look in her eyes stopped him in his tracks. She looked worried, afraid, even.

Adam sat on the edge of her bed. When had that become a favorite place of his to perch? "What is it, Persephone?"

"I have been thinking back on my ride." She spoke quietly.

"Surely that can wait until you are more fully recovered." He allowed his fingers to inch closer to hers. He wanted to hold her hand but didn't dare reach out, knowing she'd pulled back the last time.

"There were some strange things, Adam."

He brushed his fingertips along hers. She didn't seem to notice.

"Things I thought at first were just oddities, but . . ." She shifted, wincing at what must have been a sharp stab of pain, no doubt in her leg. "But there are too many to be coincidences."

"What do you mean?" Something in her tone told Adam that Persephone was in deadly earnest.

"What happened today," she said, "I don't believe was an accident."

CHAPTER THIRTY-THREE

THE FACT THAT ADAM SEEMED to believe her so instantly worried Persephone even more. She'd hoped that her suspicions were the result of a rather telling blow to the head or perhaps the piercing pain in her leg.

"Tell me these coincidences." Adam looked her full in the face without a hint of discomfort.

"John didn't help me mount," she said. "Usually the stable hand waits for him, but this time he didn't. John seemed surprised but didn't say anything. And—I know this will sound strange—the groom who helped me smelled like . . . well, like—"

"Bacon?" Adam finished for her. He looked alarmed.

"How did you know?"

Adam rose from the bed. Persephone wished he hadn't. He'd been touching her fingers, the gesture immensely comforting and pleasing in a way she needed at that moment. He'd told her only the night before that he didn't care where she went or what she did. When he touched her so gently and tenderly, she couldn't help thinking he wasn't entirely indifferent.

"Was it a faint aroma?" Adam's face was set in a look of concentration.

"No." She remembered with a wave of nausea the almost repugnant smell that had met her when she'd stepped onto the mounting block. "At first I thought perhaps he'd been helping in the curing house or had slipped in a lard spill in the kitchen. The scent was so strong I could still smell it—"

"—while you were riding."

"Exactly."

"Anything else unusual?" Adam paced the room.

Persephone took a difficult swallow. Her suspicions mounted. Something had happened, something deliberate. She didn't like the idea of someone setting out to hurt her. "Atlas never spooks," she said. "We were riding along fine. I shifted in the saddle a little, and suddenly he bolted. It was so unlike him. I can't help thinking something must have been wrong."

"Most likely," Adam muttered.

Persephone watched him pace. His was not the look of a man at ease.

His expression grew suddenly very contemplative. "The groom who helped you mount, does he assist you often?"

"Occasionally."

"Do you know his name?"

Persephone shook her head. It had never seemed odd before, but it did then. She knew the names of everyone else in the stables who regularly assisted her. "He wears a green handkerchief around his neck," she remembered out loud. "None of the others do."

"John Handly will know who it is." Adam sat on the edge of Persephone's bed, facing her.

"You are going to talk to him? That groom, I mean?"

"If he had any hand in this, I intend to do far more than talk."

The thought of Adam brangling with a potential murderer sent a chill through her. "But what if he's dangerous?"

"No one is as dangerous as the Duke of Kielder."

"Would *I* have to talk to him?" She shrunk at the idea of confronting someone who might have deliberately sabotaged her ride.

"Of course not. I'll not allow him within several counties of you again."

Persephone had always dreamed of marrying a man who would take some of her burdens away. Papa had never been good in difficult situations, often too preoccupied with the distant past to deal with the here and now. Adam couldn't have been more different from Papa in that respect.

"Thank you, Adam." She smiled up at him.

He actually smiled back. Her heart flipped over inside her chest.

"How is your leg?" he asked.

"It hurts terribly." The throbbing grew just at the mention of it.

"And your head?" His eyes traveled to the wound of which he spoke.

She grimaced. Her head pounded, though the pain was not as bad as in her leg.

"Your eye is still swollen. Can you see out of it?"

"A little," she said.

He brushed his fingers along her hand again. She held as still as possible. If Adam realized he was touching her, he would probably pull away, and she did not want him to stop.

"You do not appear to be feverish." Adam examined her so intently that Persephone felt almost as though he'd touched her face. She'd never before *felt* a person look at her.

He was closer to her than he'd been a minute before.

"Mr. Johns has been sent for," Adam said. "He'll no doubt administer some laudanum for the pain."

"That would be helpful."

He drew closer, leaning toward her as he spoke.

"And he'll check your wounds—see that they're healing properly."

She couldn't vocalize a response.

"He'll let us know when you can expect to be on your feet again." Adam's voice dropped so low it was barely audible. A mere inch or two separated them. She saw his eyes drift to her mouth. Could he possibly be longing for what she was? Did he too ache for even the smallest of kisses?

Her heart raced frantically, pounding a chaotic rhythm in her ears. He didn't pull back, didn't look away. Why didn't he simply kiss her instead of torturing her this way?

"Perhaps in time for the ball," she muttered when nothing else came to mind.

Adam seemed to snap back to attention. "The ball." He pushed out a breath. "Perhaps. Perhaps." Adam rose to his feet, shaking his head as if to clear it.

He walked distractedly to the doorway. "I will go speak to that groom now."

"You will be careful, Adam?"

He looked back at her. For a moment, he just stood there, still and watching her. Then he nodded and silently left the room.

* * *

Adam had far too much to think about. Mother's inexplicable, teary-eyed confession. Continuing flashes of memory from that frantic ride through the forest with Persephone. Thoughts of the pack. Of bacon. He'd never once spent more than a moment thinking of bacon, and now he pondered it in tremendous detail.

His mind raced as he made his way to the stables. Jeb Handly walked alongside him.

"How fares Her Grace?" Jeb asked, real concern in his voice.

"Considering what she's been through, she is doing well."

Jeb nodding sagely. "The sickroom always was a trial to Her Grace."

Adam stopped and looked at him. "You're speaking of Mother?"

"Aye." He said it as if it ought to have been obvious. "And how fares your wife?" Jeb continued undeterred.

"She is in some pain but doing well. You say my mother had difficulties in the sickroom?"

"Aye. Even a bloodied nose'd set her to swaying. The Old Duke never could convince her it weren't a horrible failing in her."

Why had no one told him any of this?

"You seem set on gettin' somewhere," Jeb said, as they began walking again.

"Stables," Adam muttered the answer, still thinking over what he'd learned that day. "I need to speak to one of the grooms."

"Which'en?"

"I don't know his name. He wears a green—"

"Calls 'imself Jimmy," Jeb answered before Adam had even finished his description. "New one. Quiet like. Keeps to himself."

"Any idea where I might find this Jimmy?"

Jeb motioned with his prickly chin. "Here comes me John. He'd know."

They walked toward John Handly, going about his duties despite the horrors of the day. He could always be relied on.

"What can I do for you, Your Grace?" John asked.

"I'm looking for a member of your staff. Jimmy."

"With the green—?" John motioned at his neck.

Adam nodded.

"He'll be around somewhere." John glanced around the paddock. "He in some kind of trouble, Your Grace?"

"He helped Her Grace mount this morning, and she tells me he reeked of bacon, more than could have been accidental." Tension coursed through Adam at the thought of someone intentionally harming his wife.

"On purpose, then?" John's search grew noticeably keener.

"That is what I mean to find out." If it proved true, the man would pay dearly.

John moved swiftly in the direction of the stables, searching the faces of his staff as he went. Adam kept pace with him, his jaw clenching more with each step.

"We're looking for Jimmy," John called out to a group of stable hands nearby.

"Ain't seen him in a while," one of them answered.

"I 'ave," said another. "A minute ago, at the back of the stable. Putting some things in a bag, he were."

John's eyes shifted to Adam, and he could see the man had the same thought he did. Jimmy meant to slip away unnoticed. No one ran from the Dangerous Duke and got away.

"'At's him, Faltsone." Jeb pointed a knobby finger across the paddock.

Sure enough, a man with a green handkerchief tied messily around his neck moved swiftly along the far end of the stables. He walked with his head down.

"Jimmy!" John called out.

The man looked up. In an instant, Adam knew him—the groom was none other than the innkeeper at the Boar and Dagger.

His temper snapped. "Smith!"

The man took flight instantly. Adam didn't hesitate.

"Stop him!" he bellowed to the stable hands.

The entire staff sprang into action, chasing the man down. He headed toward the front entry of Falstone Castle, his destination, no doubt, the forest beyond. He'd be harder to find once he passed outside.

Adam ran hard, pushed on by his anger. He would have the man's neck!

"What if the wolves come back?" John managed to ask as they both sprinted after their prey.

"He tried to kill my wife," Adam threw back. "If the wolves don't tear him to pieces, I will."

None of the stable staff were closer to the gate than Smith. He'd reach it without any of them stopping him.

A few of the undergardeners watched in obvious confusion. They were smaller than Smith, but they were armed in their own way. Shovels and picks and axes make effective weapons.

"Stop him!" Adam shouted.

They needed no further instructions. Brandishing their tools, they ran at full speed to the entrance, blocking Smith's path out.

Smith veered away, changing directions. He wouldn't make it outside the castle walls. He was trapped. Smith skirted the outer gardens, running along the stone walls. He'd reach the dairy next. Who knew what he'd do to the maids working there if given the chance. Desperation made a man unpredictable and, thus, extremely dangerous.

He waved the stable hands, following close on his heels, to the left. "Half of you cut him off before he reaches the dairy. The rest, head straight for him," Adam instructed. He motioned to the gardeners still guarding the exit. "Some of you take his path, don't let him backtrack."

All obeyed orders without hesitation.

Adam, with John at his side, cut through the gardens, over hedges and low walls. Smith stopped when he saw the small army from the stables closing in on him, but he couldn't retrace his steps for the gardeners blocking that path.

Adam reached him. A single blow produced enough blood to prove the man's nose was broken. He grabbed him by the shoulders and pinned him to the thick, stone outer wall.

"How long has this vermin been working at the stables?" he asked John.

"A month or so."

"His real name—" Adam shoved him harder against the unforgiving stone wall "—is Mr. Smith. He is the former owner of the Boar and Dagger, which was forced to close because—"

"Because the High an' Mighty Duke of Kielder got his skirts in a bunch," Smith replied with a sneer.

Adam shifted his grip to the man's throat, holding tight enough to give the man pause but not to cause any actual harm. "Because he is a cheat and crook."

"The Quality thinks they can take whatever they want from an honest working man."

"Which you are certainly not," Adam growled. "And you had bloody well better have a good reason for being here."

A crowd of grounds staff and stable hands pressed in around them.

"Earnin' a livin', Yur Grace." It was, apparently, possible to address a Peer by the proper title and still sound condescending.

Adam squeezed a little harder. "Explain to me—" He barely refrained from strangling the man on the spot "—how it was that my wife's mount reeked of bacon."

Smith just grinned, the same slick, oily grin he'd offered when Adam had arrived at the Boar and Dagger looking for Harry and had asked why no one had sent for a physician.

A fist to the gut wiped that smile from his face.

"You expected the wolves to attack," Adam growled in the man's ear.

"You took away the only thing that mattered to me." Smith wheezed out the words. "Jus' returning the favor, guv'nuh."

"You'll hang for that!" John Handly shouted at the man.

"I have a better idea." Adam shoved Smith upright and flat against the wall once more.

"Ye let us 'ave 'im, Yer Grace!" a stable hand shouted behind him.

"No one hurts our duchess!" another called out.

Adam looked at Smith, stared him down until he saw fear creep into his defiant eyes. He heard him force a difficult swallow.

"Put him in the gibbet."

"What!" Smith roared.

"Right-o!" someone in the crowd called.

"Ye can't do that!" Smith shouted, panic-stricken. "Ye have to consult the law!"

Adam grasped him by the throat once more and, his face an inch from Smith's, growled out, "I am the Duke of Kielder. I am the law."

CHAPTER THIRTY-FOUR

AFTER LESS THAN TWO HOURS in the gibbet, Mr. Smith was taken from the grounds, his final destination a cell in Sifton. Smith lost a great deal of his cockiness during his confinement in the swinging cage. A charge of attempted murder does that to even a hardened criminal.

Mr. Johns, the apothecary, arrived at Falstone shortly before Smith's departure and declared himself so impressed with Adam's work that he suggested he forsake his role as duke and go into medicine. Persephone, he predicted, would be fine. She needed several days in bed to recover and would require several weeks off her feet to prevent the wounds from reopening. A cane, Mr. Johns said, would suffice after a week had passed.

Mother expressed her relief at the diagnosis, though Adam noticed she avoided Persephone's room almost religiously. She was not unconcerned nor uncaring, simply unable to maintain her countenance when faced with the prospect of another's pain and suffering.

Deep in a laudanum-induced sleep, Persephone did not even stir when Adam stole into her bedchamber late that night. The roles, he thought ironically to himself, had reversed. He was now the interloper turning to her for reassurance—not because of the pack, nor its noises, but because he could not free himself from the sight of Persephone kneeling on the ground, face twisted in terror, her very life on the line.

He sat for a while on the edge of her bed before lying down beside her. She made not one of the noises he had grown accustomed to hearing while she slept. The laudanum pulled her too deeply into oblivion.

Adam let out a difficult breath. After weeks of worrying that she would leave him, he'd nearly lost Persephone that day. She had almost been taken away from him because a scoundrel decided to hurt her in order to get revenge. No doubt Smith thought it a fair trade.

Are you a great deal different? a voice in Adam's head inquired. He'd used trickery to lure Persephone away from her family, to convince her to accept him based on as little information as he could possibly provide. He intentionally made his offer in a way he knew she could hardly refuse. He'd heartlessly presented an exorbitant amount of money to a family that had always been a breath away from financial ruin, knowing their desperation almost guaranteed their agreement.

And why? To upset a cousin he didn't care for. There'd been no thought of her feelings nor the feelings of her family. He'd felt no concern over what she was sacrificing, what the decision would cost her.

Her family missed her. One need only watch the constant barrage of letters she received from them to realize as much. She herself had admitted that she missed her family. Adam had even heard her, in the midst of her tears, declare that she wished to go home.

Adam turned on his side and looked at her. She was battered and bruised and, if not for the laudanum, would have been in too much pain to even sleep. That is what living with him had done for his Persephone.

She would be better off away from Falstone. She would, no doubt, be happier. He couldn't bear the thought. Despite his determination otherwise, Persephone had become essential to him.

He shifted closer to her and gently laid his arm across her middle, careful not to disturb her blankets. He leaned in to her ear. "I am sorry, Persephone," he whispered to her as she slept. "But I cannot let you go."

CHAPTER THIRTY-FIVE

"I like Falstone, Persephone."

She smiled at her brother. "So do I."

Linus studied her quite thoroughly as they sat on her bench in her garden. Linus had developed a very penetrating stare whilst at sea. He hadn't had the ability to disconcert her with a look before. "Then why don't you look happy?" he asked her.

"Probably because I am in pain." She tried to laugh off the question. "I had no idea how long a few simple cuts could take to heal."

"I understand they weren't simple at all." It was very much like speaking with a fully grown man instead of a thirteen-year-old boy. Life at sea had forced him to grow up.

"Considering what might have befallen me, I think of my injuries as comparatively simple."

Linus seemed to appreciate the straightforward approach. He nodded his agreement, golden hair shimmering as he did.

Persephone had always envied him his curly, golden locks. Linus, Athena, and Artemis all inherited their mother's coloring: green eyes, fair hair. Daphne and Evander favored Papa with their dark hair and dark eyes. Persephone was the odd one out, her looks a muddied mixture of countless relatives, both distant and near.

"It is so good to have you here, Linus." She resisted the urge to embrace him the way she once had when he was small child and contented herself with grasping his hand as they sat beside one another.

"I am happy to see you again." He squeezed her hand. "But I am discovering that every time I am on shore, I quickly find myself missing the sea."

A wistfulness entered his tone that added emphasis to his words.

"You are more suited to the navy than we originally believed." Persephone felt infinitely grateful to know he did not feel unhappy in the occupation fate had dictated he take up.

"I am." Linus smiled at her, his green eyes twinkling in the dim winter light. In the next moment his countenance seemed to fall. He looked away from her, straight ahead into the unseen distance. "Evander was not, however. He sorely missed home."

She took a slow, unsteady breath. "I believe he is home, now."

"And he is with Mama," Linus added, sounding his age for the first time in the two hours since he'd arrived at Falstone.

Persephone held his hand more tightly and bit down on her lip to stop its quivering. She would not spend a single minute of Linus's short visit in melancholy reflections.

"If I had known, Midshipman Lancaster, that your intention in visiting here was to make your sister cry, I would not have invited you." Adam's stern reprimand cut the air.

Persephone glanced nervously at Linus. Would he be upset? Offended? But Linus was smiling at Adam, looking as though he were very near to chuckling.

"You have guessed my devious plot with alarming precision, Your Grace. Every young navy man wishes to bring his female relatives into varying states of hysteria on every possible occasion."

Adam raised an eyebrow, but his lip twitched with suppressed mirth. How odd that these two, so different in many respects, had already reached an accord with one another. Linus, after two hours at Falstone and one brief conversation with the Duke of Kielder, had learned to not fear his new brother-in-law but return his own dry humor.

Persephone couldn't have been more pleased.

"And apparently," Adam went on, "you are also intent on bringing Persephone down to her deathbed."

"Alas, it is true." Linus shook his head, those envy-inducing curls shaking with him. "Though I have momentarily forgotten how I intend to do that."

Adam didn't miss his cue. "By keeping her out of doors on a cold late afternoon when she ought to be inside where it is warm and staying off her feet so she will have the stamina to endure the ball being thrown here tomorrow night in her honor."

"Ah, yes. I remember now," Linus said. "Though I suppose since you have discovered my plot, I shall have to give up my ill-fated scheme."

"I am afraid it was inevitable." Adam gave Linus a look of condolence before turning to face Persephone.

She smiled—he no longer averted his face. That was decidedly a good sign. "Persephone." He held his hand out to her.

She laid her hand in his. Linus placed his hand under her elbow and helped her to her feet. Then her brother retrieved the walking stick Jeb Handly had carved for her, allowing it to take his place at her side.

Linus walked back toward the garden entrance. He had, indeed, grown, and in more ways than the physical difference between eleven years and thirteen. He wore an aura of maturity that went beyond his age. The naval uniform, of course, only added to the effect.

"You seem pleased," Adam said.

She looked up at him. He still stood directly in front of her, closer than he used to stand. He'd taken to shorter distances in the week since their desperate ride through the forest. Every time she found him in such close proximity, Persephone forced herself not to simply throw her arms around him, to tell him how much she treasured his caring, to tell him how brave he'd been, how much she longed to close the distance between them. But in the past he'd always pulled away at the first sign of intimacy. She wouldn't for the world undo the progress they'd made.

"I have missed my brother," she said.

"He is not at all what I expected." Adam walked with her in the direction of the castle.

Persephone looked at him out of the corner of her eye. Adam did seem pleased with Linus.

"From your description, I expected an infant." Persephone had the distinct impression that Adam was barely preventing himself from smiling. "Imagine my shock when he walked out of the carriage unassisted. No leading strings or nursemaids in sight."

"Adam Boyce, are you teasing me?" She hoped her shock sounded feigned enough to not offend him. She'd more than once seen Adam close up after what he perceived as a criticism.

"I never tease."

"You also, apparently, never host balls. Yet you are doing exactly that tomorrow."

"I am beginning to suspect I have begun a descent into senility."

"You are in the oddest mood this evening." Persephone shook her head in awe.

Adam glanced over at her, obviously seriously pondering something. The moment stretched before he abruptly pulled his gaze away. "You have no idea," he muttered.

The walk back to the castle was necessarily slow. Persephone's sore leg hampered her progress, though she didn't regret taking Linus to her garden, the part of Falstone that felt most like her own. She wanted Linus to see her happy. Perhaps he would convey that impression to the rest of her family—their letters of late had hinted at concern for her.

Their slow progress gave Persephone time to ponder Adam's sudden shift. She had no complaints. She loved this unforeseen playful side of him, but it confused her. If she understood what had brought the change, she would be easier.

They reached the front steps of Falstone, and Persephone realized she'd pushed her battered body more than she ought to have. With the assistance of both her husband and brother, she climbed to the front door.

"Perhaps I ought to retire." She eyed the grand staircase with a sinking heart. "Else I'll never survive the ball tomorrow."

"Then I will bid you good night, sister." Linus kissed her on the cheek, his signature gesture—the one Persephone had received every night before bedtime for the six years between their mother's death and Linus's departure for the sea. It momentarily undid her.

"How I have missed you, Linus," she whispered, her voice choked with tears.

"Now, no crying, Persephone." Linus chuckled. "Your husband already suspects me of having sinister motives."

She smiled. "I'd hate for Adam to put you in the gibbet."

"I would hate that, also."

"If the two of you are done with your sentimental good nights, I believe Persephone is in need of some rest," Adam said.

Linus offered them both a bow from the waist and made his way up the stairs, no doubt toward his own chambers.

A maid slipped out the doors leading to the great hall, careful to close the door behind her without offering the slightest glimpse inside.

Persephone had noticed similar behavior in all the servants. "The entire staff has been very secretive today."

"They are under orders to be secretive," Adam said. "Your ballroom is to be a surprise."

"*My* ballroom?"

"It is certainly not mine. If this were left to me, there would be no decorations of any kind and only horribly watered-down tea served from chipped china in the corner."

Persephone laughed lightly. "No one would ever come back."

"Precisely."

She felt instantly uneasy. Adam couldn't possibly be looking forward to the ball nor the visitors it would bring. "If you really would rather we not—"

"Do not start putting words into my mouth," Adam gently scolded.

"I do not want you to be unhappy, Adam." She had seldom been so sincere in a wish.

"If you are too unwell to attend tomorrow, and I am left to deal with all of this on my own, I will, indeed, be unhappy."

Persephone nodded but didn't reply. She looked quickly at the towering staircase in front of her. She'd been standing far longer than she ought to have been, and her leg was loudly protesting.

"I think," Adam said as he lifted her quite easily off her feet and held her in his arms, "that Jeb should have carved you a set of crutches. The walking stick seems entirely inadequate."

"Don't you dare tell him that." She put her arm about Adam's neck, knowing it was one of the few times he would allow such close contact. "I treasure this stick—it is positively gorgeous."

Adam carried her up the stairs, not seeming at all annoyed at the task. "The man has a great deal of time on his hands now that he is no longer in charge of the gardens."

"He employs himself wisely, then, I would say."

The next moment, it seemed, they reached her dressing room, and Adam slowly lowered her into the chair at her dressing table.

"I will ring for your maid," Adam told her then disappeared into her bedchamber.

She stole a glance at herself in the mirror while he was gone. How she wished there were more there for a gentleman to admire. She hadn't the fair looks of her mother, and the perpetual black of mourning kept her eyes a dismal brown. If only she'd been able to dance at the ball the next day, then Adam might have found reason to be proud of his wife. Persephone had her shortcomings, but she had always been lauded as an excellent dancer.

"I will see that the kitchen sends up a tray," Adam told her from the doorway.

Persephone nodded, still scrutinizing her reflection. Her frequent visits to the garden had multiplied the number of freckles marring her complexion. Those, however, were hardly noticeable next to the slightly green-tinted bruise still evident on the left side of her face. What a time to be sporting grotesque injuries. Adam was going to be unhappy enough with the next night as it was.

His reflection joined hers in the oval-shaped mirror, and Persephone locked eyes with him that way.

"I am sorry your family could not come," Adam said and looked as though he meant it.

"It is fine, really."

But it wasn't. She'd been devastated when Athena's letter had arrived the day after the disaster in the forest. Artemis and Daphne had contracted chicken pox, and though both were progressing without complication to recovery, the family would not be able to make the journey to Northumberland. Linus would travel to Shropshire with a manservant from Falstone in one of the Kielder carriages.

"Do you miss them?" Adam asked quietly.

Persephone felt her chin quiver. No amount of willpower could prevent her emotions from showing, though she managed to hold back the tears. She more than missed her family. She mourned them, in a way. They felt so distant, so far. If she had some future date to which she might look forward—the knowledge that a reunion was only a short while away—the separation might not sting so acutely.

She dropped her eyes. Far too much had happened recently. The wolves, the pain of her injuries, the shock and joy of seeing Linus again. But far and above all of that was the immense change in Adam. He'd been attentive and kind and tender in a way she could not possibly have dreamed possible. He had become in his own way very much the sort of gentleman she had always dreamed of falling in love with. She could no longer deny that he touched a vulnerable place in her heart.

She was irrevocably and inexplicably in love with her husband. It was, perhaps, not the all-consuming passion of which most schoolgirls dream nor the earth-shattering emotion one often equates with love. It was a sensation of safety, contentment, and the feeling that she was, in an unexpected way, cherished.

Adam had made her feel that way, and she couldn't say precisely how. It was looks, words, a hint of a smile, a suppressed laugh. It was his arm supporting her when she attempted to walk, his eyes studying her in those first days of her recovery, his immediate acceptance of her brother. So many little things.

She ought to have been happy, satisfied with the turn in her marriage, and yet she felt as though something was still missing. She felt isolated and, at times, painfully alone. He had shown that, to a degree, he cared for her. But Adam never gave any indication that his feelings ran deeper than caring regard. She needed more than that from him.

"Cook has sent up some liniment," her abigail said as she entered the dressing room.

Persephone looked up, wondering what she would see in Adam's face. She saw nothing, for he was no longer there.

CHAPTER THIRTY-SIX

PERSEPHONE WAS FAR MORE AT ease in society than Adam, despite his prestigious position and her years spent confined to the wilds of Shropshire. He watched her from the moment the first guests arrived.

Mother had ever been an anxious and energetic hostess. She held a great many events in Town, and Adam always felt obliged to at least put in an appearance. Her intensity penetrated her gatherings, giving them a feeling of barely leashed energy.

Persephone was completely different. She exuded calm and reassurance. The guests, almost without exception, arrived at Falstone noticeably worried and concerned. Persephone set them immediately at ease, not with soothing words but by her own tranquil demeanor.

She looked beautiful, despite her bruises. In honor of the evening, Mother had convinced her that half-mourning would be appropriate. Her lavender gown lent her eyes a hint of blue. Vitality lit in her face once more. She smiled as she introduced her brother to the guests. Her eyes twinkled as she greeted each arrival. Persephone never wanted for company—the entire assembly seemed drawn to her.

Adam appeared to be the only one not enjoying himself. For once, it was not the looks and whispers that bothered him, though he certainly endured a great deal of both. The memory of Persephone's expression the night before still unsettled him. He'd asked about her family, and she had all but dissolved in front of him. She was unhappy at Falstone. She missed her family, and nothing he did seemed to relieve that longing.

She had seemed genuinely pleased by the decorations in the great hall. Sheer white fabric draped the ceiling and dropped like waterfalls down the walls. The floor had been chalked in elaborate white flowers and pale green leaves. Bundles of flowers from the succession house filled the corners and niches of the expansive room. It looked just like winter brought indoors.

"Beautiful," Persephone had whispered as she looked over the preparations in the moments before their guests arrived. "Simply beautiful."

Still a look of longing hovered in the back of her eyes.

Adam stood on a deserted end of the terrace leading off the great hall. He had hoped the ball would bring a change to Persephone, that she would show by a look, a word, a gesture that she could be happy at Falstone. She seemed to be enjoying the evening, but her happiness was noticeably incomplete.

"The evening seems a success." In the twenty-four hours Linus had been at Falstone, Adam had learned to recognize his voice as quickly as that of his closest associates.

"Indeed," he answered noncommittally.

Linus, quite impressive in his deep-blue naval uniform, leaned against the terrace railing, his gaze focused somewhere between straight ahead and Adam's face. "Persephone seems to be wondering where you are."

"Has she asked after me?" Why had that question come out sounding desperate?

Linus shook his head. "Just a look in her face. We could always tell growing up when she was worrying about one of us."

"Your family?" Adam knew the answer already.

"Persephone was always the glue in our family," Linus said. The seasoned seaman seemed to melt away, and Adam found himself faced with the thirteen-year-old boy, a look in his eyes so like Persephone's: concerned, reminiscent, and yet hopeful. "After Mama died, Persephone became the mother, the nursemaid, the governess. She took over the accounts—Papa never had the attention span for things like ledgers and bills. Persephone took it all on."

"How old was she?"

"Twelve." Linus sounded as though he truly felt the disproportionate nature of that burden compared with her age. "She lost her chance to be a schoolgirl, to be a child for a few years more."

"You did not have that opportunity, yourself," Adam said.

"I think that is why Persephone tried to prevent our leaving as long as she possibly could." Linus's brow creased with the difficult memories.

Adam had experienced more than his own share of difficult times he did not like to relive.

"She kept the family afloat for years by ingenuity and sacrifice," Linus continued. "By reducing the staff, she extended our finances, but it meant she, personally, did more work."

Adam had the sudden image of Persephone as a young girl scrubbing a floor, tired and worn. He closed his eyes. She ought to have been spared that.

"Eventually there simply wasn't enough. Papa couldn't be counted on to devise a solution, so Persephone wrote to our grandfather, who was able to call in enough favors to find Evander and me positions aboard the *Triumphant*."

Linus seemed to need to talk about these things, so Adam let him.

"It was necessary—the only way for the family to survive—but Persephone hated it. I think if she could have, she would have gone to sea in our place. Her life these past eight years has been one unending sacrifice for the sake of the family."

"Including her marriage?"

Linus didn't answer.

They stood on the terrace in the cold air, neither breaking the silence between them. In the background, music floated from the great-hall-turned-ballroom, voices mingling among the notes. They were sounds of happiness and lighthearted frivolity. None penetrated the tension on the terrace.

"Do you know why my papa named Persephone as he did?" Linus asked unexpectedly.

"Obsession with all things Greek?" he ventured dryly, still smarting from the sting of Linus's failure to contradict Adam's earlier insinuation.

"Other than that," Linus answered with a hint of a laugh.

Adam offered no reply.

"The story of Persephone is his favorite," Linus said.

"Persephone seems likewise fond of it." Adam remembered her speaking of the myth. "A testament to the love of family, I believe she described it. *Ironic,* I suppose."

"That is not why Papa likes the legend." Linus paused. "Persephone was abducted by Hades, who wished for a wife to rule the underworld at his side, but because of the general fear connected with him, he could not obtain a bride by any means other than trickery."

Adam shifted uncomfortably. Did Linus have any idea how close to home his retelling hit?

"So Hades stole Persephone and carried her off to his kingdom." Linus, the sailor, had returned once more, almost as though he were a man of twenty, rather than a child of thirteen. "Her mother, as the legend goes, was so distraught at the loss of her daughter that she, the goddess of the earth, cursed the world with famine. The suffering was so great that Zeus found himself forced to intervene. All the gods knew Persephone was with Hades, but Hades refused to allow her to leave. He was known, you see, for never permitting anyone to leave his kingdom."

"And Persephone was no doubt miserable in her marriage," Adam said, trying to shrug off the pain Linus's words inflicted. The message came through clear. He, Adam Boyce, was Hades—Falstone, the underworld. He was destroying Persephone just as Hades had in the myth. "Married to the devil as she was," Adam added.

"Do not let Papa hear you refer to Hades as the devil." Linus seemed to chuckle. "He is quite adamant that the two are very different. Hades ruled the land of the dead but was not evil. He was only feared because of his association with death and because he was known to be unyielding and tempestuous. But he was also just and fair."

This conversation was proving uncomfortable in the extreme. "So how did it end?" Adam asked, wishing to speed up the retelling. He knew perfectly well how the story concluded, and it did not speak highly of Hades, Adam's apparent role in their current situation.

"Hades was forced to relinquish his bride, for the sake of her family and mankind," Linus said.

"And Persephone's happiness, no doubt," Adam added.

"Her family could not come to the underworld, and Persephone could not leave. I imagine she was anxious to see her loved ones again. But Hades was not willing to give her up entirely."

"So he tricked her again with the pomegranate seeds." Adam repeated what he'd learned during those long days of mythology at Harrow. Adam found he had a great deal in common with Hades and did not like the implications of that observation. How many methods had he employed in his attempt to keep Persephone at Falstone?

"Papa belongs to a different school of thought on that," Linus said. "There are those among scholars of the classics who believe that Hades did not trick Persephone at all, but that they, together, devised the scheme by which she would be assured the right to return to him. The gods forced her release, and, for the good of her family, Persephone cooperated. But by eating the seeds Hades provided for her, Persephone could not be prevented from returning to him. Not even by Zeus."

"Why would she wish to return?" Adam felt his frustration bubbling. He couldn't imagine any woman desiring to return to a veritable prison and a husband known for his temper and isolationism. "She was free."

"To comfort her family, Persephone was willing to leave," Linus repeated. "But it was the reason for her return that endeared the goddess to my father."

"The seeds?" That made little sense.

"The seeds were symbolic, Your Grace," Linus answered, a chuckle in the back of his words.

"Symbolic of what?"

Linus smiled at him, popped his tricorn on his head once more, and made his way back into the ballroom. Adam felt absolutely certain that he had just been bested philosophically by a thirteen-year-old. That, he supposed, was what he deserved for marrying into a family of scholars.

Harry joined Adam only moments after Linus disappeared inside. He could not seem to find a moment's peace at his own home. This was the very reason he avoided hosting social events.

Harry slapped him on the back in an overly familiar gesture Adam had come to expect from the man who had never been one for keeping an emotional distance. "I know disappearing at balls is one of your particular talents, but it does not reflect well on your wife. You really ought to go sit beside her."

Harry had a point, but Adam didn't appreciate having his social shortcomings pointed out to him. "What I really ought to do is hang you out your bedchamber windows by a bedsheet tied around your ankles until you agree to take yourself off permanently."

"Welcome back, old friend." Harry laughed. "You've gone soft lately."

"Shut up, Harry." Adam walked away from him toward the doors that led to the people and noise he disliked so much.

The fact that Persephone's face lit up when he arrived at her side proved something of a comfort. A simpering pup of a gentleman occupied the seat next to her, a situation resolved by a single look from Adam.

"Taking a breath of fresh air?" she asked with a smile as he sat in the quickly vacated seat.

"Several breaths, in fact." Adam attempted to make himself comfortable in the most uncomfortable of situations: a place of scrutiny in a crowded ballroom.

"You haven't been too miserable, have you?" Persephone looked rather closely at him.

Adam averted his eyes, her scrutiny making him uncomfortable. Did she see Hades when she looked at him? "The evening has gone well, I think," he said, hoping to divert her attention.

"It has." A smile of satisfaction crept across her face. Why did she never look like that when just the two of them were together?

A country dance began, and every couple within shouting distance of them, it seemed, eagerly joined the sets forming. Persephone watched as the guests worked out their starting positions and negotiated partners and places. She really did seem happy.

"What do the pomegranate seeds symbolize?" Adam asked quite suddenly, quite without forethought.

"What?" Persephone asked, obviously taken aback.

"In the Persephone myth." Adam was unexpectedly determined to have the answer. He would understand at least one mystery. "Linus said the seeds are symbols."

"Has he been waxing philosophical?" Persephone smiled. "That is the one trait he inherited from Papa."

"What do they symbolize?" Adam persisted.

Persephone looked at him, confused, intrigued. She finally relented, though her expression didn't clear, "According to Papa, the seeds are symbolic of love."

"Love?" Adam hadn't been expecting that.

"Hades's love for Persephone and her love for him."

"How could she love someone who kept her prisoner?"

"Papa always believed that she came to know him beyond his fearsome demeanor and came to love him." She still looked entirely bewildered. "Hades fell in love with Persephone as well. She was his match. Eating some of the seeds allowed her to return."

"Then why not eat all of the seeds?" Adam watched her closely. "If they were so in love, why did she leave at all? If she had eaten all he offered her, she would have stayed forever."

"Papa always believed that Hades did not force her to remain always because of her family's grief."

That didn't sound right. "Linus said Hades never allowed anyone to leave his realm."

"But Hades *loved* Persephone," she said.

"He let her go because he loved her?"

Persephone nodded. "And she returned because she loved him."

* * *

Adam had sat beside her for hours. Persephone smiled at the memory. She couldn't have been more content had she danced with a hundred gentlemen. Her husband had been attentive and kind and had endured what must have been a very miserable evening for her sake. At one point he'd even held her hand. She would cherish that memory for all her life.

He'd mentally been far away—she'd seen it in his face. Their unexpected conversation about mythology had been quite odd. Perhaps he had simply been bored out of his mind, seeking entertainment where he could find it.

Still, it had been progress. They had spent the evening much as two longtime friends would, sitting in companionable silence, sharing observations of their fellow man, talking of the little nothings that filled the conversations of the well-acquainted. She decided weeks ago that she wished for his friendship.

Now she wanted more.

She felt certain she merely needed time to come to know him better, to understand his moods and thoughts. On more than one occasion in the past week, Persephone thought Adam had been moments from kissing her, from reaching out to her. In time, he would stop fighting those instincts, she assured herself. She held out hope that he would, that she might even be able to resurrect a few of her now-dead dreams of love and happy ever after.

Persephone stepped out of her dressing room, grateful for her warm wool dressing gown now that winter had begun to make itself known. She stopped not a single step inside, surprised by what she saw.

Adam was pacing in her bedchamber.

"Adam?"

His expression concerned her. Something was on his mind, something that did not seem pleasant.

"Linus leaves for Shropshire in the morning," he said, continuing to pace, not looking at her.

"Yes, I know." The visit had been far too short, but Linus had only three weeks of shore leave.

"You will be going with him," Adam said decisively.

Going with him? "I don't understand."

"Your maid can pack your bags, and you can leave with Linus after you break your fast." Adam stopped his pacing abruptly. He seemed to be struggling for a moment, as if a word lodged itself in his throat. "I am certain your family will be pleased to see you again."

"Adam—"

"I will let you rest before your journey." With that he left.

Persephone stood alone in her room, heart pounding even as it dropped to the pit of her stomach.

After all that had happened between them, Adam was sending her away.

CHAPTER THIRTY-SEVEN

"I DO WISH YOU WOULD consider coming to London for Christmas," Mother said once more as she climbed into her traveling carriage.

Adam had no intention of going anywhere. He would spend the rest of the winter seeing to Falstone as he always had. "I am certain your holiday will be perfectly fine."

"But will yours be?" Far too much empathy filled her voice. "How you must miss her." She looked at him like a little boy who'd lost a playmate.

"I never miss anyone." He turned and took the steps back up to the castle.

Persephone had been gone for a week. He'd told her to go, released her, as it were. He'd never done anything so difficult in his life. But part of him had believed she wouldn't actually go or that, at the very least, she would promise to return on a given day.

She hadn't. Persephone had eaten her breakfast in heavy silence and offered little more than an awkward, stuttered farewell before climbing into her carriage.

"Adam?" Mother called behind him.

Adam stopped just inside the Falstone doors and waited.

"Adam," she repeated, now directly behind him. "Please may I say something before I go?"

He nodded. Mother eyed the footmen on either side of the doors with wariness.

"In the drawing room?" she requested.

Adam crossed the entrance hall and stepped inside the drawing room, preparing himself for an outpouring of pity over his lonely state and promises to reassure society that her "poor boy" was fine despite the disastrous outcome of his marriage.

"You'd best not keep the horses standing, Mother."

"This will only take a moment." She took a fortifying breath. "Your father and I had an arranged marriage."

Adam turned away. He did not want to hear about his father, not from the woman who had, through her continued absence, caused him as much pain as Persephone was causing him.

"No accounting was made for the differences in our dispositions," Mother continued. "I was raised in Town, among society. London, the *ton,* was what I knew and needed. Your father was raised here, in quiet and solitude. We wanted very different things in life."

He paced to the window.

"Your father was a good man, and we cared for each other." The conversation seemed as awkward for her as it was for Adam. "We did try to compromise, to blend our preferences. There were lavish balls at Falstone. Your father allowed them, even took part in planning, then spent the entirety of each event in the book room. He never made calls with me nor accepted invitations to gatherings away from Falstone."

Adam shook his head. "He wouldn't—"

"I was away during your convalescences and found in the company of my childhood friends and family the companionship your father seemed unable to provide. They went about in society the way I wished to. For a time the occasional trips from Falstone were enough."

"I do not wish to hear this—"

"Resentment grows quickly, Adam. He did not wish me to leave, and I found myself staying away longer."

Was Mother predicting Adam's future? Did she think Persephone was gone for good?

"Do you know why I stayed away?" she asked.

"Because you didn't love—" Adam bit back the *us* "—him."

"Oh, Adam." Mother spoke with such sadness that Adam turned to look at her despite himself. The slightest sheen of moisture clouded her eyes. For the second time in two weeks, and the second time in all of Adam's life, Mother was crying. "Of course I loved your father. He was a good man, despite his implacableness."

"Then why did you go? Why did you stay away?"

She produced an utterly sad smile. "I was waiting, in my foolishly romantic heart, for him to come for me." A tear streaked down her face. "He never did."

"Did you ever tell him—?"

"Of course not. I was certain that if he truly cared, he would miss me enough to meet me partway. I should have—*we* should have spoken of this, but neither of us was willing to.

"I saw you at your wedding ball, Adam. You are more willing to compromise than your father ever was. And Persephone is more suited to quiet and solitude than I will ever be. She is your match, Adam." Mother stepped to where he stood at the window and laid her hand on his arm. "Do not throw away this chance by making her guess at your feelings."

Mother kissed Adam on the cheek, an affectionate, maternal kiss. She had never kissed him before. If she had offered such a heartfelt gesture during his childhood, Adam might have grown up feeling quite differently about his mother.

"Good-bye, Adam." For the first time in more than twenty years, she made her farewells without a single "poor boy."

"Have a safe journey, Mother."

"And you as well," she replied mysteriously before sweeping from the room.

Adam stood at the front windows, watching as her carriage pulled away. *You as well.* What had she meant by that? He would not be wandering from Falstone grounds for months yet. Not until Parliament required he return to London. He didn't want to be anywhere else. It was his home. Where he belonged.

"She has a point, you know."

Harry. Adam spun from the window to find his friend sitting quite at his leisure not far away, feet crossed at the ankles and propped up on a footstool.

"You've taken to listening to private conversations? Haven't you any other forms of entertainment?"

Harry shook his head and smiled mischievously.

"Every other guest has left the castle, Harry. Why haven't you?"

"I am here to be your conscience, Adam. To save you from yourself."

"No, thank you." Adam made to leave the room.

"She'll come back, you know," Harry said behind him.

Adam stopped at the threshold.

Harry continued. "I know Persephone well enough to be certain that, when Linus returns to his ship, she will return to Falstone. And I know you well enough to predict that you will act as though you couldn't care less whether she came back or not. Do you really want her to wonder about that?"

"This is none of your concern, Harry."

"You miss her, Adam." Harry did not seem at all concerned about Adam's reprimand. "Persephone deserves to know that."

"She is happy with her family. I would only interfere."

"So go be part of her family," Harry replied as though the answer ought to have been obvious. "Go to Shropshire."

"That isn't how it works, Harry," Adam muttered and stepped out of the drawing room.

Harry followed him. "How what works, Adam?"

"Persephone receives her reprieve, and Hades stays in the underworld waiting for her to return," Adam grumbled. "Waits to see if the seeds worked."

"Obviously you were sleeping during *that* lecture at Harrow." Harry shook his head as he stepped past Adam and made his way up the stairs.

"What do you mean, sleeping?" Adam called after him.

"Adam." Harry turned back to face him, an unmistakable scold in his tone. "Hades did not sit back and wait for Persephone. When the time came for her to return, he went after her."

Adam stared back. He did not remember that.

Harry chuckled. "Hades was not the sort to sit around and fret, Adam. When the time came, he slipped past the hellhounds—"

A howl outside sounded as if on cue. Harry raised an eyebrow in mock salute to the irony of that noise. "—and ventured into the realm of the living to reclaim his bride."

"I do not remember that."

"Look it up. Hades was no pambsy fribble, Adam. And I'd bet a pony *his* Persephone knew exactly how her husband felt about her." Harry gave him a very pointed look.

By the next morning, Harry was gone, off to make holiday visits to relatives before returning to Falstone for Christmas. Adam remained behind, alone.

* * *

"Are you sure you are warm enough?" Athena asked for the hundredth time that afternoon.

"Athena." Persephone spoke as patiently as possible. "I am dressed as warmly as I am at home, and it is far colder there. I assure you, I am perfectly comfortable."

"Well, *I* am cold," Athena said.

"Why don't you go in and warm up."

"I wouldn't want to leave you out here alone," Athena said. "Your leg is not fully healed yet."

Persephone smiled. "I doubt I will be accosted in a walled garden behind my childhood home."

Athena returned the smile. "I suppose not."

"And I am perfectly able to get about. I am simply not as fast as I will be in another week or two."

Athena nodded her agreement. "Very well." She rose from the seat she had shared with Persephone. "But do not be too long. The Uptons are coming for dinner tonight."

At last she was alone. There had been precious little time for reflection since leaving Falstone. She and Linus had spent most of the journey recalling events from their childhoods and catching up on their lives since they'd been apart.

Once arriving at the family home, life had included a constant influx of people. Persephone had forgotten how a large family in a small house could create chaos on a constant basis. She loved being at home with her family but found herself longing for the tranquility of her new home.

Thoughts of Falstone inevitably brought Adam to mind. She'd had such hopes for the two of them and still clung to a few. If only he'd given her some indication that he would miss her while she was away or some reason for his sudden insistence that she go.

Instead he'd been stubbornly quiet the entire morning of her departure. He'd not appeared the least bit upset at their separation, merely impatient for her to go. She, on the other hand, had almost brought herself to beg him to go along. But Adam did not like society or mingling with strangers. He never left Falstone if he could help it. Adam had told her that more than once. Asking him to accompany her would have been a pointless endeavor.

Brooding in the garden was not precisely productive, either. Persephone rose to her feet with the help of her walking stick. Her leg was still a bit sore but improving every day. Papa insisted the Shropshire air had speeded her recovery.

She walked through the back door to the house and moved slowly up the corridor. The house sat oddly quiet. Artemis was far too recovered from her bout with chicken pox to be as quiet as she was being. Daphne was perpetually quiet, illness or no. Had the girls gone out? It was too late in the day for a picnic.

Persephone made her way closer to the front of the house. The door to the sitting room stood ajar. She stepped closer. She could hear footsteps inside but nothing else, heavy footsteps, like boots instead of slippers.

A gentleman caller? Athena was of age, Persephone reminded herself. Was Papa making the prospective suitor wait? More likely he had completely forgotten about the unfortunate young man's existence.

Determined to see this beau herself, Persephone stepped inside. She had every intention of making her own assessment, knowing Papa's could not always be counted on.

Persephone stopped just past the threshold, her breath suddenly impossible to catch.

"Adam," she whispered.

He opened his mouth to speak, but closed it again without saying a word. There was an awkwardness to him that was entirely foreign. Vulnerability touched every inch of his face.

"Have you come to take me home?" Persephone hoped he had and yet also hoped he hadn't. She'd missed him terribly but was enjoying visiting her family as well.

"When you're ready," he answered after a moment. "But I . . ." He let out a breath. "I wanted to see Shropshire," he said. "To see where you grew up."

"You did?" His explanation proved somewhat disappointing.

"And get to know your family."

That was a little better.

"And, I . . ." He shook his head, letting the thought dangle. Adam moved closer to her, a sudden intensity in his look. "Hades always went after Persephone."

"Yes, he did." She stepped closer to him.

"He waited as long as he had to," Adam said, "then he left his kingdom and didn't come back until he found her." He stood close enough she could have reached out and touched him.

Persephone's lungs tightened inside her. "I think Hades must have missed his wife," she said, her heart suddenly pounding.

Adam didn't look away, didn't step back. "I think he knew to the very minute how long she had been gone. But was Persephone as anxious to return as he was to have her with him again?"

"I think she was."

Adam reached out his hand and softly touched her cheek. Persephone closed her eyes, determined not to be distracted from the sensation of his touch. She could hear him, feel him close the distance between them.

Her heart soared with newfound hope, and she clung to it desperately.

Adam pressed a kiss to her forehead. "Why did Hades go after her?" he asked in a low voice, his lips still brushing her face.

She barely managed to keep breathing. "He must have loved her," she whispered.

Adam's response emerged breathless. "He must have."

His other hand joined the first, and he cupped her face in his hands. Persephone opened her eyes to look at him.

Adam met her gaze. "But did his Persephone love him in spite of his flaws, in spite of all he'd done to her?"

"Oh, Adam." Tears fought for release, her voice quivering with emotion.

Adam pulled her to him, his arms wrapped firmly and protectively around her. "Am I too late?" he whispered against her hair. "Is there nothing I can . . . nothing to . . ."

Persephone cut across his stumbling attempts at expression. Any speech even slightly tinged with emotion would be difficult for Adam. Persephone understood that. And she didn't need flowery speeches. The fact that he had come for her, that he was holding her so tenderly and trying so desperately to express himself, was enough. "I have been falling in love with you for weeks, Adam. I was certain you would never return those feelings."

"What can I do, Persephone?" He tightened his hold on her. "How can I prove . . . show . . ."

She gazed up at him. "You are here."

It was, apparently, all he needed to hear. "I have missed you," Adam whispered in the moment before he kissed her.

Their only other kiss, discounting the one he'd not returned, had been breathtaking, leaving Persephone in awe for some time afterward. This kiss proved quite different. Where the last had been intense, this was endearing and tender. Adam held her to him as if he meant to never let her go.

Persephone touched his face softly with her fingertips, hardly daring to believe this turn. The ruts of his scars were there beneath her fingers. Adam did not pull away, did not flinch under her touch. She slipped her arms around his neck and returned his attentions kiss for kiss, embrace for embrace.

"You do that very well," Adam breathed when they finally broke apart.

Persephone smiled.

"Mother has invited us to Town for Christmas," Adam said.

Persephone recognized the sacrifice that suggestion entailed. She shook her head. "I want to spend Christmas at home."

A look of disappointment flashed through Adam's eyes, and Persephone knew on the instant he had misunderstood.

"At Falstone," she said. "With you."

"The *ton* would not believe that even if they heard you say it." Adam took one of her hands in his and raised it to his lips.

"Then we shall have to convince them."

He kissed her fingers. "I may enjoy London yet."

"Your mother would be pleased to hear that." She nearly sighed out loud at the comfort of leaning her head once more against his shoulder.

"I need to spend some time with my mother." A hint of emotion touched his voice.

"So do you still think marrying me was a mistake?"

"It was never a mistake. I simply didn't see it for the miracle that it was."

"A miracle," Persephone repeated with quiet awe.

"Does this mean I can come to your castle?" a voice asked from the doorway.

"Artemis," Persephone quietly warned, stepping away.

Adam pulled her immediately back to him and addressed Artemis himself. "Our castle is in need of a good exploration," he said. "I believe we should schedule one. Perhaps if you have no other plans for Christmas, you might do so then."

Artemis grinned and ran to where they stood, throwing her arms around Adam's legs. "You're the best duke that ever lived!" she declared.

"Yes, he is." Persephone smiled up at Adam.

"Yes, I am." Adam didn't force down his grin. "The luckiest, at least."

Artemis continued circling them, even spinning as she did so. Again and again she thanked him.

"You realize she will bring the rest of the family, and Falstone will be overrun with people."

Adam nodded. "Which means I will probably be in a foul mood from time to time." His expression turned more serious. "You will, once again, have to save me from myself. You have done that, you know."

"Saved you?"

"My Persephone," he whispered in her ear. "Do you know I would have come for you no matter how far you'd gone?"

"Hades always came for Persephone," she echoed his earlier explanation.

He lightly kissed her again. "And she always returned home."

"Always," Persephone repeated. "Always."

ABOUT THE AUTHOR

Sarah M. Eden is a USA Today best-selling author of witty and charming award-winning historical romances. Combining her obsession with history and her affinity for tender love stories, Sarah loves crafting deep characters and heartfelt romances set against rich historical backdrops. She holds a bachelor's degree in research and happily spends hours perusing the reference shelves of her local library. She lives with her husband, kids, and mischievous dog in the shadow of a snow-capped mountain she has never attempted to ski.